The rubine beam changed in an instant,

grew stronger, and its light changed from the dim red to which they had been accustomed. It now blazed forth in a white violet that made their eyes smart and water. The effect had far more impact on their foe. The charging monstrosity hauled up short, crouching and snarling not more than a half-dozen paces distant. What a thing it was, there revealed in the harsh glare of the reversed-spectrum witchlight.

If in nightmare the fevered mind of the sleeper combined the forms of such terrors as a mad mastiff and an attacking adder, the monstrosity before them might begin to be explained. It was as heavy as a black bear, but its six legs were stumpy and its bristled body long and low. Waving wetly in their direction was the thing's proboscis, a trunk-like snout as long as a man's arm and thicker through than Ferret's own waist. That snout ended in a sphincter-like orifice filled with a double ring of shearing teeth, and that disgusting mouth dripped thick saliva as the trunk that bore it waved this way and that, questing for prey. Behind the proboscis was a huge head displaying four putrid yellow eyes in a line above its snout, those organs now weeping matter as the light struck them. It had fan-like ears that stood out and up, unfolded so as to catch the slightest sound. Set all round its neck and shoulders were a bristling growth of spikes like those of a hedgehog, and the ugly body showed a mangy coat of corpse gray which sported patches of these same short quills. A maroon streak of the thing's weird blood indicated that one of Ferret's knives had inflicted a negligible wound on its flank. The second point could be seen caught harmlessly in the bristled protection of its mane..

Praise for Gary Gygax

"A pioneer of the imagination."
—*The New York Times*

"One of America's most talented writers."
—*The Guardian*

"His impact was enormous.... Today's world is a nerd's world, and Mr. Gygax did much to change it."
—*The Economist*

"As much as Gene Roddenberry and George Lucas, Gygax helped muscle fantasy into the mainstream."
—*SFGate.com*

"Through Gygax's creativity and inspired descendents, the realm of nerddom has found eternal life."
—*Slate*

"An icon of a time of wonder and imagination."
—*Tracy Hickman, author of the Dragonlance Chronicles and the Death Gate Cycle*

"Gary Gygax is a giant."
—*Ed Greenwood, creator of the Forgotten Realms Campaign Setting*

"We live in Gary Gygax's world... on that foundation of role-playing and polyhedral dice he constructed the social and intellectual structure of our world."
—*Adam Rogers, Senior Editor of Wired magazine*

THE PLANET STORIES LIBRARY

The Secret of Sinharat by Leigh Brackett
The Ginger Star by Leigh Brackett
Infernal Sorceress by Gary Gygax
The Anubis Murders by Gary Gygax
The Samarkand Solution by Gary Gygax
Almuric by Robert E. Howard
The Swordsman of Mars by Otis Adelbert Kline
Elak of Atlantis by Henry Kuttner
Worlds of Their Own edited by James Lowder
City of the Beast by Michael Moorcock
Lord of the Spiders by Michael Moorcock
Masters of the Pit by Michael Moorcock
Black God's Kiss by C. L. Moore
Northwest of Earth by C. L. Moore

STRANGE ADVENTURES ON OTHER WORLDS

AVAILABLE MONTHLY EXCLUSIVELY FROM PLANET STORIES!

FOR AUTHOR BIOS AND SYNOPSES,
VISIT PAIZO.COM/PLANETSTORIES

Planet Stories is a division of Paizo Publishing, LLC
2700 Richards Road, Suite 201
Bellevue, WA 98005

Visit us online at paizo.com/planetstories

Printed in China

Planet Stories #13, *Infernal Sorceress*, by Gary Gygax
First Printing July, 2008

10 9 8 7 6 5 4 3 2 1 2008

Infernal Sorceress

by Gary Gygax

Introduction by Erik Mona

Cover by Andrew Hou

PLANET STORIES
Seattle
Erik Mona, Publisher

The Last Adventure

BY ERIK MONA

Gary Gygax died in March of this year, leaving behind a legacy that will live forever. As the co-creator and "voice" of the Dungeons & Dragons roleplaying game, Gygax engaged a generation in the trappings of sword and sorcery, inspiring them to create imaginary worlds and characters of their own design. Writers from Raymond E. Feist to China Miéville felt the pull, incorporating elements of the game's fantastic creatures and themes into their own distinctly original fantasy work, and thus the cycle continues and will continue so long as kids of all ages keep throwing funny-shaped dice in their tabletop pursuit of glory, honor, and treasure.

Gygax's creation was more than just a collection of numbers and charts, more than a simple game. Because the action in a D&D session takes place in the minds of its players, the game is a framework for imagination built upon the common tropes of the fantastic fiction that fired Gygax's own potent sense of wonder since childhood. Because the first rules set hit the shelves in the early 1970s, Gygax's vision also synthesized the popular fantasy renaissance going on in the paperbacks thanks to efforts like Ballantine's Adult Fantasy imprint and Edgar Rice Burroughs reprints, Ace's Conan line, and of course the hugely popular Lord of the Rings epic. To give D&D its animating spirit, Gary Gygax took all of these influences and mixed them into a single milieu, a dangerous world where Tolkien's noble elves and curious hobbits lived alongside Howardesque barbarians and thieves in cities inspired by Fritz Leiber's Lankhmar in a world governed by the magical laws of Jack Vance's Dying Earth.

This synthesis of sword and sorcery influences wove disparate elements into a single set of expectations for the game, so that the fantasy world of one D&D campaign shared common elements with the world of another. So potent was Gygax's fantastic mixture that today it has become the default assumption of fantasy fiction. Take a look at the submission guidelines for *Black Gate*, the premiere sword and sorcery fiction magazine in today's market: "If your story opens with an elf, dwarf, thief, and ranger about to enter a dungeon, odds of acceptance are not in your favor. Quick rule of thumb: the less your fiction reads like a gaming session, the more we're likely to be interested."

As the literary pillars of Dungeons & Dragons fell increasingly out of print in the 1980s (when the game became more and more popular, especially with kids), D&D became the primary cultural access point to much of what had once been mainline fantasy material. Millions of D&D gamers have faced off against the feline monstrosity of the displacer beast, for example, but relatively few of them know the creature is a direct lift from A. E. Van Vogt's "Black Destroyer." Thus has the mythic background of D&D become a signifier without a signified. The pastiche has grown much more powerful than the sum of its original parts.

I launched Planet Stories in part to return to print some of the great fantasy classics that inspired Gygax's D&D. Today, D&D's publishers churn out scores of their own fantasy novels every year, each set in one of the company's shared worlds and each based on the Gygaxian cocktail that has kept the game popular for all these years. With a massive book publishing outfit of their own (and one that brings in more revenue than the D&D game itself, at that), D&D's publishers have little reason to point out the game's literary origins these days. But such was not always the case. Gygax himself presented a thoughtful appendix in the back of his magnum opus, the Advanced Dungeons & Dragons *Dungeon Master's Guide*, which outlined the game's thematic foundation with a run-down of the authors and books that had inspired it: Tolkien, Leiber, Howard, Vance, Merritt, Burroughs, Brackett, Dunsany, Lovecraft, Moorcock, Zelazny, and more.

Gygax himself published an early line of fiction novels set in one of his D&D universes, the enduring World of Greyhawk. The series followed the exploits of a cat burglar named Gord the Rogue who, in the course of seven books, became embroiled in a cosmic struggle as an agent of Balance. The treacherous alleyways of Gord's city of Greyhawk owe a great deal to Leiber's Lankhmar, and the politics of the later novels clearly follow in Michael Moorcock's multiversal tradition. But the Gord books work for the same reason D&D works: Gary Gygax understood sword and sorcery, and he understood how to blend his influences into something new and powerful.

When I launched Planet Stories, I knew I wanted to lead off with a novel from Gary Gygax, the man personally responsible for my own lifelong love of fantasy and the guiding spirit who pointed me in the direction of my favorite authors and books. With the Gord the Rogue books already at another publisher, we instead turned our attention to a trilogy of novels published in the mid-1990s, several years after D&D's original publisher TSR had ousted Gary and he had moved on to a new RPG called Dangerous Journeys. Like D&D, Dangerous Journeys synthesized pulp fantasy, this time mixing it with mythological and historical influences into the world of Ærth, a place where the pharaohs of ancient Egypt lived alongside Arthurian knights before a backdrop right out of the Middle Ages.

Gygax's Magister Setne Inhetep trilogy features the exploits of a powerful Ægyptian wizard-priest with a nose for solving mysteries involving death by magic. The first novel, *The Anubis Murders*, led off the Planet Stories line, with the second volume, *The Samarkand Solution*, following shortly thereafter. *Death in Delhi*, the third and final Magister Setne Inhetep book, is set to release in December. And that, as I thought, was that. The first few months of Planet Stories found Gary in ill health after suffering a stroke in 2004, and it seemed no new fiction would come from his pen. Sure, he sent encouraging emails about the line, always egging me on to publish the works of A. Merritt, his favorite, but his declining health and piles and piles of new gaming projects kept him busy and away from the business of fiction. *Death in Delhi*, last published in 1993, was destined to be the last Gary Gygax novel. Or so I thought.

About a year ago, on a whim, I asked Gary if he could summarize for me the unpublished or seldom-published fiction he had sitting around, with an eye toward perhaps one day assembling an anthology of his short fiction. He dutifully provided me with a list of shorts, but his reply carried an unexpected shock. Digging around his files, he had recently discovered an unpublished novel manuscript, set in the world of Ærth, but featuring entirely new characters. Might Paizo be interested in taking a look, he wondered?

The book, *Infernal Sorceress* (subtitled "Tales of the Ferret, Volume 1"), was to be the first in a new series of Dangerous Journeys books for TSR, who had acquired the rights to Gygax's second RPG in an attempt to prevent it from competing directly with D&D. Despite their rocky past, TSR's management assured Gygax that they would gladly review any manuscripts he submitted for publication to their book department.

"Gullible chap that I was," Gary wrote me, "I sent *Infernal Sorceress* to TSR, and the jerk that she had hired as editor berated me for ripping off Fritz Leiber. I wrote to Justin Leiber in a fury, and he assured me that he saw no such thing. I sent a copy of his response to TSR ... all to no avail, of course. That soured me sufficiently to bury the book."

Timestamps on the *Infernal Sorceress* files, rescued from near-forgotten floppy disks, suggest the book was written in 1993, shortly after the publication of *Death in Delhi* and shortly before TSR mothballed the entire Dangerous Journeys line. Thus has Gary Gygax's final novel languished in obscurity for the last 15 years.

I call it his final novel with a sad certainty, as Gary Gygax died in his sleep about three months ago, just as we began work in earnest on this edition of *Infernal Sorceress*. The novel you hold in your hands is a rare treasure indeed, the last great adventure from one of the 20th century's greatest adventurers.

I last saw Gary Gygax in August, for the official release of *The Anubis Murders* at Gen Con, an annual convention Gary himself founded that now draws more than 30,000 attendees. As the show's Guest of Honor, Gygax had more than a full schedule, but he was able to carve out a couple of hours a day to sit at the Planet Stories booth and sign autographs of his book while sharing thoughts and memories with his fans.

And the stories those fans told were just incredible. For a full hour I listened as gamer after gamer approached Gary and told a variation of the exact same story: "Thank you for a game that has brought me so much joy. Thank you for a game that has brought me so many friends. Thank you for making such a positive impact on my life."

Sitting next to Gary at last year's Gen Con made me realize what a huge cultural impact Gary Gygax had made on all of us, gamer and fantasy reader alike. Never before have I seen such honest appreciation. Never before had I been so moved and so proud to be working with a man who had made such an impact on my life. On all of our lives.

When a friend passes away, it is easy to be sad, to think about what might have been had he lived another year, another ten years. But my friends, I am here to tell you that Gary Gygax knew what a difference he had made in all of our lives, and he was proud to have made it.

Not bad for a life's work.

Erik Mona
May, 2008

Erik Mona is the publisher of Paizo Publishing and the guiding spirit of the Planet Stories fiction line. He formerly served as editor-in-chief of Dragon *and* Dungeon *magazines. His numerous RPG writing credits include the* Pathfinder Chronicles Gazetteer, Expedition to the Ruins of Greyhawk, Fiendish Codex: Hordes of the Abyss, *and* Forgotten Realms: Faiths & Pantheons. *In addition to his work for Paizo, Mona's writing been published by Wizards of the Coast, Green Ronin, and The MIT Press.*

Infernal Sorceress

Chapter One

"STOP THEM, YOU fools!"

The desperate though distant shout from the gaudily uniformed officer approaching at a run brought the soldiers at the gate to instant activity. There were three guardsmen there, but one crashed into another in his eagerness to obey, so only the third soldier was there with leveled partizan. Two mounted desperadoes thundered between the gate and the officer, coming straight on so as to ride down that lone figure. He aimed his spear-tipped weapon at the broad chest of the nearer of the two horses, braced the butt of the partizan's shaft on the cobbles to absorb the impact, and braced himself as well.

It was no contest. The horse was being urged from a canter toward a full gallop, and it had no chance to slow, even swerve. The point took it squarely. Its untouched neighbor shot past it, but the animal struck by the steel was brought to a sudden halt. It voiced its agony then, the scream ear-shattering. The wooden shaft of the polearm had splintered upon impact. The guardsman and his victim both recoiled, one frantically attempting to draw his sword in replacement of the now-useless partizan, the horse instinctively rearing back and striking out with its hooves.

Again it was no contest. One of the iron-shod hooves of its flailing forelegs struck the soldier, and there was a sound like a splitting melon. Then the mortally wounded animal collapsed upon the pavement, as if to complete its phyrric retaliation. Gore oozed from beneath its corpse.

The officer, cape streaming out behind him, ran full-tilt toward the melee. "UP! UP! DON'T LET THEM THROUGH!" he screamed as he saw the two remaining soldiers disentangling themselves, for the second fugitive had reined his steed, spun it around, and was returning to the fight.

As one guardsman scrabbled for an arbalest, his fellow managed to pick up his partizan. Fear motivated them to Herculean effort, for if they failed to obey, both men knew that execution was in store for them. Cursing, the first jerked the crossbow upward, but before he could shoulder it, a sword's steel tongue was where the arbalest's butt was to sit. The guardsman gasped in agony and reeled back, the crossbow clattering to the stones. The second soldier was likewise attempting to bring his weapon to bear upon the foolhardy desperado daring to return. That was a mistake. The dismounted fugitive had survived the slaughter of his steed intact. When the horse reared, its rider had leaped clear, fallen, tumbled, then stood upright, unharmed if somewhat worse for wear. Unnoticed for the space of the few heartbeats the tableau took to play out, that desperado now acted. He leaped toward the guardsman, a long dagger sunk in the soldier's exposed neck, and then his comrade was there, pulling him up behind him on the prancing horse's back.

The officer in his finery came panting up to the carnage seconds later. His face was a mask of rage as scarlet as his silk doublet, the flush growing more lurid still as the fleeing man riding double turned and saluted the captain of the city guards with a rude gesture indeed.

"DEMONS TAKE THE PAIR OF YOU!" the officer screamed. Then he spun on his heel, determined to rouse the cavalry and chase the two criminals down. "Ferret. Raker!" he muttered ominously between clenched teeth. "Names I won't forget...."

In fact, a few days later those names were inscribed in the duchy's records of the most wanted outlaws, and reward posters depicting the pair circulated throughout the islands. Alas for the outraged captain and other officials, and no few wealthy citizens as well, it was all to no avail.

"So much for Puertal Mago."

"And Palamabel."

"The whole of the Balearics!" As he said that, the longish, thin face of the speaker lost its gloomy expression. Dark eyes sparkled, and white teeth gleamed against tanned skin as the man grinned at his companion in the little fishing boat. "At least we now have a *fine* boat...."

"Don't show those fangs to me," his friend chided in response. The thin man opposite him did have rather prominent canines, although that was not the reason he was called Ferret. "What about my horse?"

"Enjoy the fresh sea breeze," his comrade countered. The remark failed to relieve the hard stare, so the man at the tiller said, "You stole it anyway, just as I got mine, Raker. Stop complaining. When we get to the mainland we'll sell this tub and get new mounts."

Raker wasn't mollified. "I had to leave a fortune in jewelry back there," he grumbled, adjusting the single sail as he spoke, for it was flapping and the little boat began to luff.

"'*I* had to leave a fortune'? Half of that was mine, I remind you. It was *your* trying to pay for our bill at the tavern with that medallion that brought the law down on us."

"And the wench, Tarla, I had to abandon—"

"Sooner than usual, who likewise was half mine!" Ferret interjected.

Raker swore and flung a dried fish toward his comrade, then laughed. Ferret grinned, then chuckled as Raker began to really guffaw as the whole of what had just passed came to his mind. "That *was* one hell of a time we had there in Puertal Mago, wasn't it," he finally managed to gasp as he wiped tears of mirth from his eyes. "And you capped it off perfectly by whipping a screw-you salute to the good captain as we galloped away!"

That made the thin man sober. "You know, Raker, I suspect I shouldn't have done that. When Captain Gorlanca and the Puertal Mago horse came thundering after us I thought we'd had it."

"Bah! Give me credit for some skill at evasion. Shit, even riding double I'm a better horseman than all those islanders combined."

Ferret allowed there was a mite of truth in that, even though it had been nip and tuck until they had made it to the port city of Palamabel. "Good thing for you I was there to handle our escape thereafter, my friend. Everybody certainly recalled us coming through the gate in a hurry, but nobody paid any attention as we skulked separately out of that place by the dockyard portals. Captain Gorlanca and his dolts were turning Palamabel inside out for us, even when we 'liberated' this stinking collection of planks and fish orts to sail free."

"Humph. Nothing I wouldn't have thought of myself, Ferret. Say, now that you mention it, where in Neptune's name are we sailing anyway?"

With a gesture toward the bow, his comrade told him, "Due west. Iberia lies just there—the dark line on the horizon. I'm aiming toward Aragon, not the Coata Brava of Catalonia, but just below it... I hope. There's a nice place, a sort of a port, only up-river from the shore, so it's kind of out of the way."

"You sure seem to know your way around these parts," Raker said in a tone halfway between doubt and admiration. "I didn't think you'd ever been to Iberia. How can you be so sure? We sure don't have a map!"

"No need for a map, old chum. I have a memory," Ferret reminded him with a hint of braggadocio. No question that there was a continuing rivalry and plenty of needling about past triumphs and tragedies between the two. It was another mark of their close association over the last decade. "You weren't around when I was in these parts—that's when I was a mere stripling and sailed with a crew of freebooters. Sailed all through the western Mare Librum, even raided into Phonecian waters! We made port a half-dozen times hereabouts in those days."

"Didn't the Genoese sink that ship?"

Ferret's face grew longer, and he stared toward the growing rise of land ahead. "Trim the sail properly there, you lubber, and we might make land before nightfall."

Chapter Two

IT WAS A dreary evening in Dertosal. The city was small, generally dull even on low summer market days. It was dun colored and old. Its tall, narrow buildings of heavy granite bulking over its narrow, twisting streets and alleys seemed to be trying to shoulder aside neighbors to gain breathing room. To say the place wasn't exciting would be an understatement, just as it would be wrong to say that the free city thrived. It existed. Dertosal crouched on the left bank of the Ebro River twenty or so miles upstream from where the waterway ran eastward into the sea. City and river were busy, the populace industrious, and there was modest wealth there, even if gained by unglamorous drudgery—fishing, rope-making, soap, pottery—no matter. Dertosal was a backwater, even if its liquorice was sought after by many. Iberia might boast of cosmopolitan cities, even a metropolis or two. Hardly anyone outside of the County Tarragona, of which it was the largest community by perhaps a couple of thousand souls, even thought of Dertosal—save to curse its name.

With it being a Free City of Catalonia, the count of Tarragona could not interfere with Dertosal for fear of incurring the enmity of the Prince of the Catalans. The masters of the city were careful to play one lord against the other, of course, for they were rapacious. Truly profitable commerce of a sort could be encouraged, its rewards reaped. Dreary, dull, cramped, crowded, unexciting. All true. But Dertosal was also thickly walled, well-fortified, strongly garrisoned, and a hotbed of thievery. Thus its leaders were wealthy and growing richer.

Why? Because bandits could find haven there—for a price. So, too, all manner of pirates and other outlaws. Thus local industry was augmented by great sums of illicit coin, from bribes to shares of loot as well as trade in stolen goods. Many times in the past outraged sovereigns and nobles had gathered armed forces and attacked the city. Now and again Dertosal had succumbed to such attacks, but she always arose again thereafter, just as rapacious and ready to accept the outlaws into her precincts. The city was now careful not to directly attack their king's subjects or property. With the Aragonese strength at sea to contend with, her neighbors to the east—Mago, Corsica, Sardinia, Francia, Arles, even Genoa and the other Italic states—hesitated to do more than send forth warships to hunt pirates at sea. The small, fast ships of the wise corsairs found protection anchored in the Ebro River before the walls of Dertosal. So city and environs all were drab but prosperous, a backwater haven for outlaws, the place for disposing of loot, roisterous fun, refitting before returning to whatever illegal trade was the forte of the band in question. Smugglers, brigands, pirates, and thieves abounded in this place.

The fading twilight made the narrow streets night-dark. It was also warm, humid, and thus doubly oppressive therein. Across the river, lanterns and witchlights could be seen gleaming in Roqueta, the suburban village where most of the outlaws lodged when they came to the free city. The two residential districts of Dertosal were busy as folk there returned to their homes. This was a rustic community, in truth, and while sophisticated Iberian cities were coming alive at this time, Dertosal's solid citizens were settling down. Up on the ridge where the mayor's palace, city administration buildings, and citadel loomed, all was virtually still. The waterfront was always active, of course, even though factories and warehouses were dark and empty of workers, for near there were the quarters of the thieves and their ilk, low dives for watermen, laborers, off-duty soldiers, some few select pirates, and beggars.

Above, along the lanes and what passed for avenues of commerce in Dertosal, some few folk went listlessly about their affairs. The Street of the Leatherworkers was fairly crowded, although many of the people there were now slowly leaving. Vendors and sellers of wine and beer in the plaza at the end of that street were becoming busy. In most other areas things were near their end for the day. Passersby ignored the pleadings of shopkeepers, the cries and shouts of straggling peddlers, oblivious to such cajoling and demand, intent on either homes or less wholesome houses of entertainment. Shopfronts were closing, lights being snuffed, thin old cloaks were pulled off pegs and donned by equally worn proprietors of tiny establishments. Gray light, gray people. Night was come, and all there faded into its ebon.

In the small but desperately poor slums, dark-clad denizens were slipping forth. The young and bold to seek a place with pirate crew or bandit company, others to try yet another round of begging or stealing in hopes of gaining enough to never have to return to this place again. Forlorn hope. The bourgeoisie either dreaded and feared such folk or else disdained and maltreated them. The aristocrats ignored all lesser sorts, naturally, although an offending beggar or thief was fair game for a rapier's point.

High walls, barred windows, locked doors, bright lights, and city watch served Dertosal's better citizenry quite well. The workers were content enough, the middle class prosperous or even vastly wealthy and anxious to buy their way into the elite circles. Everyone paid relatively low taxes, enjoyed considerable trade, made plenty of profits, and had little to fear, even from the worst of the foreign outlaws to whom Dertosal played host. Most of such a roisterous lot was kept safely out of the city across the Ebro in Roqueta. Crime was quite low inside the massive walls, considering.

Just a little to the right of the citadel and lower down the ridge lay the most important shops in the city. Two doors around the point of the corner delta formed by Plata Lane and the Row d'Oro a glow as bright as the afternoon sun and as warmly hued as the gold sold nearby bathed a patch of the way. This light spilling out into the otherwise gloomy street proclaimed that one purveyor of the precious metals remained ready for business despite the rows of dark and triply locked establishments to either hand. The establishment—rather pretentiously, perhaps—proclaimed itself as the "Casa Chasal Mer-al, Goldsmith and Gemner to the Great".

There was indeed a Chasal Mer-al, an artisan able to create great, even unsurpassed beauty in precious metals and jewels.

His reputation in Dertosal was the highest, albeit that fame did not stretch much beyond the confines of the city and earned him but scant profits. Chasal's creations of gold were exquisite, but he was bitter. The jeweler was of mixed heritage—Phonecian and Iberian most strongly, but certainly some Atlantlan, Italic, and Berber, too—not unusual in Dertosal. Acceptable in all levels of society save the aristocratic. The patrons of his shop paid him as a mongrel. Chasal, never married, had always been reclusive, and now in middle-age he was even more bitter. Not because of his racial extraction or the scorn of the nobility for such mixture. Not because of his loneliness.

"Garlands for goats!" This was his typical pejorative. "It is no wonder my name is not breathed reverently in Paris and Venice. These brutes who bedeck themselves with my creations never see such places, so my artistry in turn remains obscure, and I languish financially too." And always thereafter he would ask himself, "How will I change this?" For a year now such muttered musings had come more frequently to the ageing man's lips. His fellows knew all of this, thought Mer-al overweening and growing even crazier, so they avoided him almost totally now. How glad he was they shunned him! Of course, they were jealous. The goldsmith recognized that. "Surrounded by no-talent brass-beaters, patrons not worthy of what I sell them, why do I remain here?!" But of course he had complained to nobody save himself. Then came the special order...

Tonight Chasal Mer-al was not complaining. No indeed. That he was there past afternoon was unusual. No custom was done after sundown in this quarter. Mer-al, though, was not hoping for a chance buyer. He was soon to receive more than sufficient money to meet his needs; ten times over his needs for life, life in a *real* city, too. That knowledge would surely have made the others in his craft envious, but Chasal had kept his own counsel. Thinking of that envy the master goldsmith laughed. "Genius and artistry shine in the dark as do night's stars. The clouds part, and soon my jewels will radiate light—not mere starshine, sun and moon!"

Smug in his secret knowledge, Chasal Mer-al hummed to himself as he worked. His alternation between themes from a Parisian operetta and a popular aria from a Venetian opera reflected his thinking. In truth the master gemner was still undecided as to which of those two great cities he would travel, go to instantly upon the consummation of this night's work. Night? He looked up, swore, and hastened to the front of his shop. Barred windows or no, he wanted no skulking thief spying into his establishment. Chasal banged closed the heavy interior shutters, locked them fast. Outside the narrow street was darkened considerably, only a few flaring lanterns and the odd witchlights left to enable vision for passerby or patrol of watchmen.

"So! Now I am safe. You fools won't know of my fortune," he said quite loudly as he turned and stumped back into the rear workroom. Again, he pulled the drapery there separating it from the shop's front sales room so as to be doubly obscured. The special patron he had acquired he would keep. Nobody at all would know any of it, and tomorrow Mer-al would be gone. A fitting end. Let the petty craftsmen left provide their turds of jewelry for the swine who were masters of Dertosal. "Paris. It will be Paris," he concluded in a mutter as he smiled mirthlessly. The night was hot and sticky, especially in the closed workshop, but Chasal shrugged that off. He had promised the work no later than tomorrow morning, and he would complete it this night. Despite the dullness of the city, its oppressive air, he felt exhilarated. With clear eye and steady hand the great artisan picked up his tools and returned to his work. It might take four hours, maybe twice as long. No matter. This is my lifetime's opportunity, Meral-al thought. I will go beyond even my usual brilliance to assure that there is no rejection. Then he considered that and affirmed it was no mere mental boasting to reassure himself. I can do this work, for I am a genius, he preened. It was no effort, it was a symphony of beauty and splendor he wrought. Masterpieces of the jeweler's art. More! Then he cleared his mind and went back to his labors.

Chapter Three

"HEY, THERE, TITS!"

"Whar, har, har! . . ."

". . . ome on over and s—"

"I told this bastar—"

". . . on the face of a refined—"

"More wine!"

Midnight in the Quatro Rio. Music and ribaldry abounded. As the two men left the tavern the catcalls assailed their ears above the cacophony of background noise. Both ignored what they but half-heard, for it was no business of theirs, and on the street outside the voices disappeared into oblivion. Although neither of these strangers was big, burly seamen and mercenaries moved out of their way, some by instinct alone, others after a glance at the eyes of the two.

"Where now, Ferret?"

The taller man glanced left and right, then nodded toward an alley. "Let's try down there, Raker. It's been a long time." He was looking for a place he vaguely recalled. An especially interesting place from what he remembered, one where there were all sorts of folk, including men who knew where enterprising fellows could make money. As he thought of that he patted his tunic. Only a few coins therein. The best they could manage selling the fishing boat for was a few hundred.

"We're near broke," Raker drawled, noting his friend's unconscious gesture.

"Look for a sign with a big cat."

They found Ferret's goal down the alley. Above the door swung a weathered plank of faded yellow upon which a black lion rampant was crudely painted. Letters beneath in Iberian proclaimed this to be the Taverna Leon Negro. The thin man led the way, and soon the two were deep in the dim tavern's confines, drinks before them, eyeing the others there. The place was quite full; most of the customers were Iberians, although the two were by no means the only non-natives in the crowd. Pale northerners, coppery Atlantlans, blacks, swarthy easterners who were probably Phonecians—a quarter of those in the big room were foreign by heritage.

Soft strumming of chords from the rear of the tavern gave way to a tempestuous outburst. The two guitars were joined by a cornet and drums. At that the crowd of revelers in the Black Lion quieted, making the music seem louder yet. A trio of dancers appeared in the cleared space there, two women and a man. They began performing a complex series of movements, steps, and sounds which both followed and was contrapuntal to the melody and rhythm of the instruments. Song, slap, castanets, cry, bang, and clack of heels served to interweave with the quartet's music to create a living tapestry of color and motion, an interplay which evoked emotions far beyond the song and story so told. When the performance ceased, the place was rocked by cheers and applause.

When the noise of accolade finally abated the muscular man spoke. "You said this was a dive frequented by the worst outlaws in Dertosal," Raker said under his breath. He was still shaking his head at the power of what they had just seen.

"So it is," Ferret affirmed. "Look around. Those two are desperadoes for sure. He's a sell-sword—she a harlot most certainly. And over there, the greasy fellow with the fine cap and silver chain. A swindler, probably, or a criminal boss. The shifty man is a petty thief, his partner a gambling cheat from the look of his eyes and hands. Mark, too, the merry crowd at the big table—actors and performers, certainly. Pirate officer and his lieutenant over there, a quartet of brigands in the rear, and by the door various roughnecks who most probably supplement their daytime labor by nighttime muggings and strong-arm robbery." He smiled at Raker. "A sampling of the underworld of Dertosal, from the cream to the dregs, more or less. Being outlaw doesn't mean inability to appreciate artistry of that sort, does it?"

"No." Raker looked around, then took a swallow of his beer. The Black Lion did indeed cater to a most questionable clientele, but it was a place to remember. "Now I understand why you sought the tavern out."

"It hasn't changed a bit. We came on a good night, too. Sometimes when there's a new group of entertainers, the place is packed with rich merchants and slumming aristocrats come to see the show. Of course on such occasions the usual patrons melt away to drink, gamble, and ply their trades elsewhere."

Raker nodded, saying, "We've been eyeballed pretty well a half-dozen times."

"Koval...? No, Galvo! He's the big fellow behind the bar. Owns this place. I think he recognized me from years back, although he wasn't sure and doesn't know my name. I saw him nod an okay to his bully-boys, so at least our host finds us passable."

When that exchange ended both men drank slowly, glanced around slowly now and then with seeming uninterest. They had time to bide. Raker saw the bulky Galvo personally serve a dozen different patrons. Raker made a mental note of each, for such ones were the elite. The two-score others he spoke to in passing or nodded at, but allowed the wenches to serve, were ordinary regulars of the Black Lion. Now and again one or another of the revelers there would glance their way. Both men could feel the stares, looks which slid away easily but were penetrating nonetheless. One ugly fellow allowed his eyes to stay fixed. Raker shifted his own gaze to return the stare, and the other man looked away after a moment. Raker had pale gray eyes which could be as hard and cold as stone.

Ferret signaled for another round. To both men's surprise, Galvo himself appeared at their little table a minute later. "You are an old customer," he said to the thin man as he set a fresh tankard before Raker and then splashed wine into the cup before Ferret. "I never forget a face, but I don't recall your name...."

"You are right, Galvo. I was here back in the days when the *Arachne's Gift* sailed the seas between Valencia and Sicily.

"And you were with Captain Malley!"

"So I was. He, though, is dead. Sent to the bottom with his ship by a Genoese fragata a long time ago."

"I hadn't heard. Pity. He was a good man." The tavern-keeper looked at the two, decided he wasn't going to learn anything more, and shrugged. "This one is on me then, in memory of Red Malley." He was about to leave when a sudden light sprang into his eyes. "Say, how do you like that pair over there?" he said suggestively, inclining his head in the direction of a couple of voluptuous women at a nearby table. They were sisters, twins. "A matched pair is always better than a singlet, no?"

Raker smiled. "They *are* pretty...." he allowed noncommittally.

"Ho, hah! Pretty? They are like nymphs," Galvo enthused. "Say the word, and I'll send them over to you."

At that Raker looked expectantly at his comrade. Ferret tilted his lean frame back in the chair, drank the bluish-red wine slowly, and only when he had set the vessel back down upon the stained table did he reply. "Don't bother. Those two are with the dancer, his name is Migueal. He'd certainly take exception to our attentions and try to knife us both—and he is a feared fellow hereabouts."

"What makes you say all that?" Raker demanded.

Ferret seemed puzzled by the question. "When the dancing started those two paid especial attention to the man in the trio, and several times they called out to him by name, Migueal, encouraging or lauding his performance. Now they wait expectantly, and nobody else here is... approaching them, shall we say?"

"Ho-hah! I thought so, and now I'm sure!" Big Galvo clapped his hands and laughed. "You are the one they called the Ferret, for nothing could get past your keen senses."

"Just say 'Ferret,' then, Galvo. I am flattered that my old comrades spoke of me thus—and you remembered."

"Not so much your friends as your foes," the barman said with a grin. "I am glad you took no offense at my little test."

The thin man shook his head. "How can I be offended; didn't you just buy us a round? When you come back this way, bring me and my comrade, Raker, here, another too," and as he said that he flipped Galvo a plata, an Aragonese coin sufficient to pay for five rounds. "Keep the change."

As the proprietor went away grinning more broadly still, Raker leaned closer to Ferret. "You spend what little we have too freely... or have you hit upon something to replenish our coffers? It wouldn't be bad to have a nice doxy or two to help pass this night."

"No."

"No to which, or what?"

Ferret made a wry face. "I don't know. I suppose that I could have meant that in this place one hardly needs to pay for company...."

"Right. I can see that. Any enterprising girl would want to get out of Dertosal. We should be heading for Madrid or even Barcelona ourselves, if you ask me. But I think something troubles you."

"It is as if I had had a dream, Raker. You know, the sort which seems somehow important, only you can't recall what it was."

"Did you dream?"

"I don't know."

"What nags at you then?"

Black eyes fixed on gray. "I believe that we are in peril. There is an itch somewhere in my brain, Raker! It started just after we came in here. That's why I've been so careful to scrutinize this lot, but... nothing."

"This is odd, for you know I have a feeling too, and it does stem from a dream. I saw piles of gems, Ferret. Not that I believe that dreams are good measures of the future, mind you, but what a score if it were true. So I keep thinking that there is something awaiting which concerns more money than even we have dreamed of. If—" Just then a woman came with the drinks Ferret had ordered from Galvo, so Raker cut himself short.

When the wench left Ferret raised a finger, indicating his friend should remain silent. One eyebrow raised, so without seeming to, Raker scanned the crowd over Ferret's right shoulder. There were three newcomers just inside the Black Lion's entrance. It was plain to the gray-eyed swordsman that the pair flanking the central figure were strong-arm guards. The one in the middle was short, cloaked, and cowled so that he couldn't tell who or what he—or she—was. The dark opening of the cowl, though, was pointed in their direction. No more than a few seconds did the three remain, then the short one turned and left, followed by the guards.

When Raker related what he had observed, his comrade seemed to grow more uneasy. "The peril I have anticipated? Let's leave."

Raker was not going to argue, but before either could get up, Migueal, the dancer, his two girlfriends, and the pair of women who accompanied him in the performance suddenly clustered round their table. Migueal spoke. "Your pardon, sirs. I am called Migueal, and I believe you are the Ferret and the Raker, no? Master Galvo suggested we join you." He smiled formally, without humor, as he said that. "You see, I have a sideline, and good Galvo was kind enough to mention that you two were likewise connoisseurs of precious stones."

"Do tell.... Please, sit down, all of you." Chairs were moved into place, and as Migueal assisted each woman to her seat he introduced her. Here was the payoff for their three weeks in Dertosal, Ferret and Raker knew, for the dancer was about to enlist them in some plan for stealing jewels.

The lanky man smiled when he was introduced to Clarinda, the prettiest, for she had made a point of sitting beside him and now her eyes burned into his own. For once, he thought, I will fare better with the ladies than does Raker. His companion might be younger and handsomer, but sometimes character and wit prevailed when there was discernment involved. Her hair was very long, and its ebony cascade glinted with an indigo sheen. "I am honored to make your acquaintance, señorita Clarinda...."

Chapter Four

In oricalcum and gold Chasal Mer-al wrought. It was nearly midnight, but he felt elated, as fresh as if he had just arisen after a long and peaceful sleep. With those lustrous metals he had enmeshed gems so perfect as to have brought a gasp from any beholding their colors, polished facets, and shining clarity. But of course the goldsmith worked alone, zealous in his warding of his work from any foreign gaze. Blue-white was the glitter of the score of great diamonds he had used to emphasize the other jewels he had so set. Even larger sapphires of cornflower blue alternated with flawless emeralds. Oricalcum clasped the diamonds between the gold-embraced stones of clear corundum, matched its loops with the golden to form the chains and filigrees. In some cases there were rosettes of brilliant gems set round the larger jewels, so that diamond was complimented by a bloom of green or blue, or emerald or sapphire enforced by dazzling diamonds. In truth, several of Æropa's petty states would have gladly traded their treasuries for the gems alone, so precious were those big stones.

Even Pharaoh hasn't such wealth—or at least such jewels, Chasal thought to himself as he admired his work. If I could have afforded such expense personally, I would be the court jeweler to Pharaoh or any king anywhere in the world. The goldsmith was not far from mistaken. The stones he had set were extraordinary, near-priceless ones. His settings were minor masterpieces. There was a diadem which was the most outstanding of the four major pieces in the ensemble. Mer-al wiped it with a velvet cloth, used that square to place the little crown beside the heavy neck chain, the rather dainty scepter, and the orb of state. Here were the most beautiful symbols of royal rulership indeed. Before them were the four lesser portions of the suite—massive ring, bracelet, brooch, buckle—which were lost before the larger pieces. It was deception, the goldsmith knew.

He picked up the ring, slipped it onto his little finger. Marvelous! Two trillion-cut thirteen-carat stones, a perfect match in all respects, one emerald, one blue, pointed up and down the hand. Four like-cut diamonds of six carat-weight radiated to the corners, as it were, so the whole effect was that of a starburst. Any pawnbroker would offer a hundred gold doubloons for it. It was worth three times that at least simply for its component parts. The goldsmith would receive fifty thousand reals for his work in fashioning it. It was the least of the lot, and the one he would receive the lowest payment for creating. Fifty doubloons! He had had an advance of twice that amount, along with most of the gems to be set. Mer-al had spent his entire savings, borrowed too, to get the metal and the rest of the stones he desired. When he received his payment this very day Chasal would have no less than two million reals left after repaying his debt. With stock and shop disposed of, he would set up a proper salon in Paris.

"Well, old fool," he muttered to himself, "you are already basking in the admiration of the Francian nobles when the work is yet unfinished. Fah! What matter? As soon as the last stones are brought, the last will be but a few minutes work. You will make no blunders." He stared at the four major pieces. They were almost masterworks, but he couldn't really be certain. There was in each an open setting, a place of honor yet ungraced by gem. Mer-al had been given exact measurements for each special setting, the crowning touch for diadem, chain of state, scepter, and orb. When the last places were filled, then and only then would he know how great his accomplishment was—and ask for additional fee accordingly. "What will the center stones be, I wonder," the goldsmith mused. Then he consulted the old waterclock he affected in preference to the modern, mechanical devices now popular even in this corner of Iberia. "Ha! Midnight, more or less. Come on, then, where are you?"

As if in answer to his querulous mutterings, there came a soft tapping from the far corner of the back. Behind his workroom was a place of utility, with kitchen facilities, storeroom, and a little pallet as well in case Chasal decided to stay the night here. Of course the whole building was protected, and not by mere steel bars and iron shutters, bars and locks. Mer-al worked alone in the middle portion where bench, furnace, and tools were nestled. Surrounding this place were rings of mechanical and magickal alarms and traps. He methodically disarmed all the devices necessary to enable him to pass unhindered to the rear door. It took some time, and the soft tapping was repeated insistently all the while. "Yes, yes, I hear you!" the gemner finally barked. His loud voice cracked as he added, "Who seeks entry at this hour?"

"Four clear eyes," came the muffled response from the far side of the armored door.

Chasal Mer-al, hearing the agreed-upon password, muttered the cantrip disarming the protective magicks there, then began the process of unbarring. Then pulled and lifted top and bottom pins. At last he drew the great bolt and turned the lock. He held a long stiletto in one hand nevertheless. A thick chain still secured the door from opening more than an inch. Through this narrow crack the goldsmith hissed, "What do four eyes see?"

A woman whose face was obscured by a veil stood in the dim ray of light. Her clear voice said softly, "Celestial wonders." She stood unmoving as the door shut again. There was a rattle, and then the portal opened wide enough for her to slip in.

"You are late," Mer-al said testily as he went through the many steps of the process of re-securing the rear door. "Go into my workroom, there," and he pointed though it was obvious, "and wait. I must be alone to finish the wardings, eh?"

"Of course." Her voice was sweet and melodious. "Please don't delay, master goldsmith. You must complete your work tonight."

Mer-al stopped, stared coldly. "Then be more prompt in keeping appointments." She was unknown to him. He had made the arrangement for the work with a man. Chasal realized immediately upon seeing the woman that the fellow had been but her lackey. No matter, for he would brook nothing from either. He must not appear too eager. "Tardiness—" Mer-al cut his words off, for as he stared she turned and went into his studio.

He clamped his mouth tight, hating to have said even one word to empty air. It took only a minute to whisper the activations, a gesture, a release of heka energy stored in hidden pentacles, and the place was proof again against intrusion. The goldsmith had to restrain himself from haste. In truth, Chasal Mer-al was anxious to see the final gems, to finish the work, and collect his payment thereafter.

Her eyes were on the eight pieces as he stepped into the workroom. At the sound of his footfall she looked away from the jewelry. Mer-al was troubled, for he couldn't tell exactly what color those eyes were which now assessed him. He spoke a bit too harshly. "You have the four stones?"

"Why else would I come, goldsmith?"

She made that sound as if she had meant, "You are a fool." Mer-al sneered to hide his anxiety. "Then do not delay me further. Put them here, in this tray. I must see them, touch the jewels, *feel* them so as to be attuned. They are as I was told?"

The woman produced a small ivory box from inside her cloak. She pressed here, slid bits of ivory this way and that, and suddenly the top of the little coffer snapped open. There was a glow from its recess. Even though the box's interior was well-padded velvet, she was careful. With long, graceful fingers the woman withdrew each of the four gems one at a time from the box, nestling each gently upon the soft surface.

The goldsmith could not hide his awe. "Ahhh...." Chasal sighed, stared for a few heartbeats, enraptured. "Such color. What brilliance! Madame, are these truly...?"

"Yes, goldsmith. They are mahydrols." There was a hint of laughter in her voice as she spoke.

Mer-al noted that and paid no heed. He had seen her gaze caressing the gems as avidly as his own had. Each of the four was alike in color—bright blue turning to purest green at its heart, the transition creating a hint of deepest aquamarine where the hues met. Four jewels, scissor-cut but as brilliant as if they each bore a hundred facets. They were all of rectangular shape, graduated in size. The smallest was surely not less than seventy or eighty carats. Chasal reached forth tentatively, touched each with his fingertips, sighed again.

"Well? Are you going to fondle them or set them?"

"Do not attempt to rush me. I told you I had to attune my being to them." He purposely took more time than he really needed. He knew instantly that he could not fail with these stones. Mer-al had never seen a mahydrol, of course, even though he knew all about these gems of elemental water, crystals from the oceans depths where volcano fire and bursting magickal energy combined to turn that element into solid material. He picked them up, each in turn from smallest to largest. After examining each with his loupe, the goldsmith placed it next to the piece it was to complete. He stepped back, looked, and nodded. "They are suitable touches to my artistry, madame. I will begin now. But tell me, where did you obtain four such jewels?"

"You go beyond the bounds, man," she said with irritation making the music of her voice strident. "Your only concern is setting them. Get on with your work. I need all within an hour. Your fee depends on it."

"Fee? We'll see about that—whomever you are. Until I am paid, and paid handsomely, mind you, there will be no work, no delivery at all!" Chasal Mer-al stepped so as to place his body between her and the jewelry. "Mahydrols are indeed crowning glories for my masterpieces, but the work is mine, done under contract!"

"Do stop this behavior, goldsmith. I have your fee, will pay you immediately 'pon the completion of the pieces. Get busy!"

Mer-al was doubtful. "Such a sum as I am to be paid can't be borne by a slip of a woman such as yourself. Show me the coin now."

"No, goldsmith. You will follow my bidding, and do so now. I am here to place castings upon the gems as you finish the settings. You will be paid, but that is the secondary. To your trade, else I will depart with the mahydrols, and you will be left to explain your debts for the rest to the Lord Mayor's court. Do you understand?"

Her voice was now flat, as hard as her words. Mer-al reconsidered his position. "You make yourself quite clear, madame. I will now set each of the four in the prepared mountings. It is the work of minutes only, and have not the slightest doubt it will be perfectly done." Owing as he did, the gemner was not about to lose this commission. More importantly, he longed to have these masterworks complete, exhibited, talked about—as they surely would be, even if seen only on rare state occasions. Which throne these were to belong to was unknown to him, but Chasal Mer-al knew it was a major one. He would be famous, and soon. "However, the ensemble can not be released from these premises until I am paid. Say what you will, there are enchantments and guards only I can lift. Can you assure me of my fee?"

"Your concerns reflect the pettiness of your background. I am tired of this. A great master would accept a marker, but I expected such from you. Here." The woman slipped a silken pouch from her sleeve, began to undo its fastenings.

"Eh? Another stone? Let me see. It is no easy matter to get fair price for gems, and I insist on gold doubloons...." He trailed off as she opened the little sack and placed its contents onto the suede palm of her gloved hand. There lay an egg-shaped platinum box set with a rainbow of brilliant gems, a masterwork of incredible perfection. "So. Very nice. Lovely. Some noble lady might well pay a million reals though its actual worth is not a quarter that sum."

The woman's eyes glittered, and she shot the goldsmith a poisonous look, but her voice was again a musical chime as she said sweetly, "But you have not seen the contents, Chasal Mer-al. Now look!"

He watched as her delicate fingers pressed the little catch and the egg came into two halves, hinged so as to show twin oval cups lined with snowy satin.

Mer-al gasped when he saw the contents cradled in that interior. "Incredible! A whole cache of them..." A score and more mahydrols lay there before his eyes, the gems winking in blue and green fire, none under several carat-weight, and the least of them certainly worth ten—no twenty—doubloons anywhere. Five million reals at the very least, discounting the container. Mer-al did not discount it. "The box and stones are mine then?"

"I thought this would satisfy you, goldsmith," she replied with contempt. "When you have finished your commission the whole is yours."

"Then I am content. You will not find my work imperfect. Be so good as to set the box down, and then seat yourself. I don't like someone watching over my shoulder." Chasal ignored her then. He concentrated on setting the massive mahydrols, even as a part of his mind gloated. No paltry couple of million, no indeed. He could parlay the hoard of elemental jewels into ten times that by releasing them from smallest to largest. Every noble in all Æropa would soon be clamoring for jewelry made by Mer-al and set with a gem of pure, crystalized elemental water. Only the greatest, the select, those with the most funds, would be able to afford such a piece.

The orb came first. Mer-al's hand took the mahydrol with the shallowest pavilion, placed it into the pyramid-like mounting atop the sphere of gold and oricalcum. The gem was to be viewed from front and rear only. The fiery copper of the oricalcum was to clasp it fast. Other artists employing that metal needed great care, for it was harder and even more unresponsive than platinum. Chasal not only managed it with ease, he actually alloyed his gold with both platinum and oricalcum so as to make it more like both while retaining its wonderful color and luster. Mer-al had studied alchemy and heka forging both to accomplish this, and because he could bend magickal forces as well as bits of metal, he was a master jeweler. In truth, his vast expenses in this project had been more for laying enchantments and readying magickal forces than in buying metals and stones. He set the orb aside, nodding to himself.

"That took you nearly half an hour!"

"Be silent. Do not interrupt me. It was the most difficult piece. The rest is child's play— for one of my skill."

He took the diadem, selected the right mahydrol at a glance, lowered his loupe, began the process of securing the jewel. Next came the scepter, and then the central stone in the chain of state. Each required no more than ten minutes time to do. To work with speed and absolute precision was exhausting, but he managed it, spurred on by the reward awaiting just at his elbow.

"Dear lady, please behold. The agreed-to masterpieces are finished!" Chasal said. Not quite a full hour had passed.

"I see the four major pieces, but what of the others?"

Mer-al brought the other four and set them on the velvet so that the whole set was there for her to behold. He was disappointed that the veiled woman didn't gasp at the beauty thus displayed. More than a little acid was in his voice as he prompted, "As ensemble such as not even a Hindic potentate can boast of—or any monarch in Afrik or Æropa for that matter. Such beauty! Such perfection. These are crown jewels fit for an empress... which?"

"None you are aware of," the woman replied curtly. "You have suitable cases, I trust?"

"But of course."

"Then get them and be quick. I must leave now."

That made Chasal Mer-al's heart glad. All was well, and the two dozen mahydrols in the bejeweled egg his own. He pocketed the precious oval even as he hastened to obey her command. He brought forth the boxes he had commissioned, padded and velvet-lined, each suited perfectly to encase one of the eight pieces. Plain wood on the outside, naturally, so as not to attract attention, each with a cleverly sliding top which needed three steps to unfasten. Of course, these would surely be replaced by stronger and suitably ornate coffers by the monarch to whom they belonged. No matter. He worked swiftly, mechanically, opening and nestling the pieces, largest to smallest. Securing each lid, placing the cases one upon the other to form an oddly shaped structure there upon the table near his workbench.

As he laid down the smallest container, that with the ring, the woman stepped beside him. "What is this?" Mer-al shrank back, his voice quivering with tension somewhere between fear and anger. Behind her veil this woman certainly hid great beauty—her form was very shapely. The gemner wasn't affected by such blandishments, hated anyone at all close to his person when he had such wealth secreted thereon.

"No need to become agitated, Master Goldsmith." Her musical voice fairly purred reassurance. "I have something extra for you—you met my deadline, you see."

"Get back! Keep your distance, you wh—Did you say extra?"

She had taken a half-step back as he spoke. Her eyes smiled over the veil below as she held forth her gloved hand, fingers closed in a fist. "Do you wish to see?"

"No tricks, woman! I see a clenched fist. Neither it nor any charm you hold therein will harm me in this place." He felt trapped, and his upper body swayed back from her still-too-close presence, one hand meanwhile feeling for his dweomered hammer.

"Really, goldsmith! You are too suspicious. What I offer you is something truly special. Mahydrols aren't the only elemental gems, are they?" Her voice lowered to a whisper then, as she thrust her clenched hand before him, and she said, "Look what I hold, Chasal Mer-al," as her fingers uncurled to reveal that which was within the palm of her hand.

"Gods!" the jeweler exclaimed involuntarily, voice now hushed and reverent. He stared, unable to take his eyes from what he beheld. "It is an empyrium...."

She moved her palm, so the clear, hot hues of the incredible jewel seemed to explode in dazzling flashes. "Not just any empyrium, goldsmith. This is a gem amongst its kind. Look closely at it. See the vermillions, scarlets, and crimsons dance with the ambers and the apricot? The crystalline inner wind in this stone plays thus to make fluid the colors of fire, real and ever-changing."

"Yes, yes! Never have I seen its like!" Mer-al didn't wish to take his eyes from the jewel. "Why I—I discern hues therein which mortals have never beheld!" He began to reach for the empyrium as he said the last words.

"Not yet, goldsmith." Her voice held a command which made him hesitate in his overwhelming urge to snatch the jewel from her palm. "You must know this gem first so as to be able to hold it. There are supernatural hues in its heart. Watch them. They will reveal their nature to you if you but concentrate on them. Look deeply into the flame-heart, Chasal Mer-al."

"I do so now, and I begin to understand."

"Do you desire the stone?"

"Yes!"

"Will you agree to become possessed of it?"

A million thoughts and memories seemed to flash through Mer-al's brain. Only one thing was important. He drew a long breath, saying as he exhaled, "I agree, I agree, for it is what I desire."

"It is a thing of eternal fire, goldsmith named Chasal Mer-al. The jewel burns forever as living, elemental flame. Do you truly accept it?"

"With my heart and soul."

"Then you shall have what you ask. First, though, you must allow me to pass out of here without disturbing the spells and other wards with which you have hedged us in. I do not care to be blasted by heka, you know."

It took his whole will to tear his gaze from the empyrium. How he wanted that burning gem! "Give me the stone, then I will release my alarms, bindings, and guards."

"Let us be reasonable. I must needs remove myself and the jewelry. A compromise, Chasal Mer-al the goldsmith who has crafted eight masterworks in precious metals and gemstones, bestowed those selfsame works upon me this very hour, and accepted in payment therefor jeweled egg containing twenty and five mahydrols. As you unbar the rear door for me and I pass through with that which is mine, I shall give it to you."

"I deserve to have that empyrium now."

"Perhaps, perhaps. Yet the 'now' you speak of will be that time I depart, as I said."

"All right, very well. I yield," Mer-al grated. His eyes wandered toward the gem, then he forced his mind to concentrate on the demanding process of disarming his fortress, the knowledge that he would soon actually hold it enabling him to act. Never had there been such a stone! The mahydrols paled into lifeless lumps of rock after beholding that empyreal essence of elemental fire. Riches could be gained and lost—would be reaped in abundance from the disposal of those lackluster bits of blue and green fused elemental water—but the jewel of fire would remain forever his own. It didn't strike him as odd that he no longer cared to be recognized as the greatest artist in jewelry, had no desire to be the goldsmith to the crowned heads of Æropa. What he wished now was to be alone with the empyrium. Only then could he hold it, stare at the mystery within, contemplate eternity and be content.

Heedless of what the woman heard and saw, Chasal rushed through the formula necessary to deactivate the many castings which enveloped the little building. Thereafter he disarmed the several mechanical devices protecting the rear entrance. Dismissals complete and triggers locked, he began pulling the bars, bolts, and pins holding fast the steel-sheathed door. All were of no import. After she left he would simply walk out of the shop, leave it forever. Whomever happened to come in first could have all therein. Mer-al took the key from his girdle, slid it into the lock which was all that remained of the protections against opening the portal. "The empyrium—give it to me now."

"Only the key needs be turned for me to depart whole and safe?"

He gave the key a twist. There was a sharp click as it turned tumblers and the lock's mechanism withdrew the iron block into itself. "As you see," Mer-al growled as he pulled the door open a few inches. "I'll have that gem, woman!"

"So you shall. You have requested it, and I but accede to your wish. Open your hand and receive your reward."

The goldsmith complied, thrusting forth his blunt-fingered member as if he were attacking. Excitement made it tremble slightly. He watched as the veiled woman held her fist over his open hand, tilted it, and allowed the empyrium to roll into his sweating palm. The gem was warm, almost hot, to his skin, but there was no discomfort. "Get out!" he nearly shouted. Would this woman's irritating presence never be away? The goldsmith was wild with desire to be alone with his prize. "Begone. Go!"

"Help me with these boxes, please, Master Goldsmith."

"Manage for yourself," Chasal snarled, pushing at her with his free hand to force her outside. "They weigh but a stone or two, and you're young."

With a swift gesture with her free hand, the one which had transferred the empyrium to his hand, the woman touched his forehead. "To you the empyrium, and the empyrium to you," she hissed. "Two truly inseparable, forever fire, and you immersed in its eternally living flames forever—old fool!"

Chasal Mer-al tried to shriek as agony suddenly engulfed him. His mouth opened, but no sound emerged. The jewel he grasped flared into flames. He tried but could not loose it from his hand. Somehow the gem had expanded, and it now surrounded his whole hand—was his fist! "Help me," he managed to gasp in a tiny, piteous voice.

The woman was smirking. She touched Mer-al's chest. "Help you? No, I think not, you stupid pig! I shall help myself instead." Her hand fastened around the jeweled egg enclosing the satin-nested mahydrols.

He tried to stop her. First Mer-al attempted to strike with his left hand, but it wouldn't respond. Then he sought to bring the burning globe that was his other hand up to smash that firey member down upon the woman's head. All to no avail. The goldsmith could not move. He was paralyzed. Only his lips responded a little, allowed a moaning sound to pass, and his eyes stared at her in horror. The gloved fingers plucked the platinum container from the folds of his tunic, deftly placed the box within her own breast. Chasal finally managed to speak. "No! You can't..." The cry was but an agonized whisper.

"Oh, but I can. I have!" she countered with a merry lilt in her voice. "You see, you have no need of those sorts of things now, Master Goldsmith. Not where you are going. I do so wish I could have warned you about the empyrium. Pity.... Do you know that the mere touch of one of the mahydrols would counter the effect which consumes you now? No, I suppose not, else you would not now be in your predicament."

"What's... happening... to... me?" Mer-al's voice was faint, filled with ineffable pain.

"Silly thing! You are being devoured by an infernium—a cursed empyreal, dear old man. Isn't it just awful? I'll wager the process is agonizing too, and the best part is that it hasn't any end!" She laughed softly, watching his reaction to her words. "I prepared it especially for greedy fools like yourself, you know. But you had to have lust and greed and covetousness in your heart to activate the magicks. Only when you accepted it could the unbreakable link be forged. It has spread to encompass your whole arm now. In just a few seconds it will consume you entirely. Only your spirit will remain."

Chasal Mer-al's horrified gaze locked on her eyes. "Oh, goodie! You have guessed it! When all but your soul has burned away, the stone will have another tiny little flame dancing inside it—your spirit, goldsmith! Isn't it thrilling for you to know that you'll be in there leaping and prancing and adding sparkle to something precious beyond belief?"

"NOOO!" wailed Mer-al, as the sphere of rubine hue grew and spread over his head and chest. It was a cry of pain, despair, denial of the unthinkable. Had anyone normal heard it, the sound would have sent them fleeing in terror.

It brought another musical laugh, almost a giggle, from the woman who watched the terrible process with evident enjoyment. "But yessss..." she mimicked in contradiction. "And I so love it! Oh-oh—too bad. Finished already," she sighed a minute later. The fiery glow no longer bathed her face and illuminated the room in a hellish light. Where tongues of flame had danced there was now nothing but a scattering of powdery ash and a shining gem on the worn floorboards they covered. A vile stench filled the air. "Well, it was all too brief," the woman said lightly, inhaling deeply as if enjoying the fragrance of a garden. "Still, I have this small token to remember you by," and she laughed once more as she picked up the empyreal and replaced its silken case.

A push sent the metal panel banging open. Two shadowy figures appeared in the dim light spilling from the doorway, hurried inside the shop. She spoke harshly to them. "Get these boxes into the places prepared for them on the horse. Be quick about it."

The two muffled men obeyed instantly. They returned almost as quickly. "All is as you ordered, my lady," said one.

With that the veiled woman went toward the exit. "This place is now yours to loot, but set aside a tithe in a separate bag" she told them, giggling as she said the latter. With that she departed. As an afterthought she called back over her shoulder, "Do enjoy yourselves—I have!" Then she was lost in the gloom.

Neither man moved until they heard a horse snort, then the jingle of bridle and harsh clattering of hooves moving from trot to canter on the stones of the alley. Only thereafter did they dare get down to pillaging.

Chapter Five

THE SEVEN OF them had been together there for almost three hours now, with two breaks while Migueal and his partners performed their dancing. That entertainment was concluded now. Migueal—finished, too, with his proposal, and more than a bit tipsy—got up and headed for the jakes. It was nearly three hours past midnight.

Clarinda pressed her leg against Ferret's. "My room is nearby, Ferreet," she whispered.

What a sultry voice! Ferret loved the way she said his name, too. He glanced around the table. Raker was deep in conversation with the girl named Myrilla, and the two dancers were indifferent to him. Why not? He pressed back, smiled. "Let us drink up and go there then, beautiful lady!"

Splat! The slap she delivered to his cheek came as quickly as an adder's strike, and even the lightning reflexes of the lanky man were insufficient to avoid the attack. He stared at her in amazement, but Clarinda was looking elsewhere. Her glare forced the others to look away, go back to their conversations. "No, Ferreet, I am no *puta*—whore, as you say."

"But you asked me—"

"You should not listen to Migueal, not be involved in stealing and such things. You are a better man than that!' Her look defied him to deny that.

"But you hardly know me," Ferret stammered. "I have been a—"

"Silencio! Come along then. We will go to my room." Clarinda stood up, and watched as he hastened to follow suit.

At that moment a party of men thrust their way inside the Black Lion. At the head of a column of gray-clad soldiers in the maroon-and-yellow tabards of the watch was an officer clad in wine-colored doublet and cape, the arms of the city picked out in gold thread on his chest. At his side stood a cleric in long robe and scarlet mantle indicating he served Keganal, the Atlantlan god of destructive storms and warfare. Behind were eight soldiers armed with spontoons. The tavern fell into a hush, as does a forest before a great storm sent by the deity the grim priest served.

Ferret took it in at a glance. Already standing, he slipped back and away without seeming to move. His comrade too was performing a similar "fade," Raker somehow getting out of his chair and sliding toward the rear of the tavern. It seemed almost a staged display, a gavotte perhaps, with serving wenches and various others coming forward in time to a surreptitious backward evasion by select members of the troupe.

"HOLD!" The velvet-clad officer called out loudly. The growing babble stilled again. "Do not attempt to flee. There is a squad at the rear to prevent escape. We are not here to molest any save two—foreigners, not citizens!" That might have had some small impact, although nearly half of the customers of the tavern fit that description. The stealthy retrograde all but ceased, however, when the officer called out those words.

"What is it you want... or who?" Galvo bellowed. He stood behind the bar, face florid in anger. After all, he paid handsomely to assure the Black Lion was not raided in this manner.

"A Kellt—a Lyonnessian calling himself Ferret—and his associate, a Savoyard known as Raker."

"Never heard of either," Galvo lied. "Now unless you see them here, I demand you leave."

Myrilla and Clarinda had moved together, and the two hunted men slouched behind them. "The priest is doing something, Ferreet," the long-tressed dancer hissed behind her hand. "I think—"

His hand on her shoulder cut her short. Ferret was moving her aside, stepping between her and Myrilla. His lean body seemed taller than his actual height then. The square-shouldered Raker followed, moving from Ferret's wake to a position at his comrade's left as the two made their way through the scattering folk between them and the law officials.

"What are you *doing*, chum?" Raker asked in soft but urgent voice. "Have you lost it?"

"The cleric, my friend, is along to suss us out," Ferret answered so that only his comrade could hear. Then he called loudly, "Ho there! I am the man you seek, and my companion, Raker, is likewise here. How may we serve your excellencies?" The last question was posed from but two paces' distance, as Ferret looked from officer to priest. The former was a short, darkly handsome man with a vapid but arrogant expression probably betokening some old aristocratic family of Dertosal. On the other hand the priest was tall and sharp-visaged, his expression reminding Ferret of one who has just bitten into something bad-tasting. What an unpromising duo!

One hand resting on the hilt of his rapier, the officer eyed the two men from crown to sole and up again. He sneered languidly. "Your *service,* dogs, is to hand over your arms and proceed to the citadel under my guard. I arrest you in the name of the Lord Mayor!"

Neither Ferret nor Raker moved when the swarthy officer spoke. Ferret wore a pair of very long, fancifully quillioned dirks, right and left on his belt, the blades of these weapons nearly equal to those of small swords. Raker's own blade was a heavy rapier counter-balanced by a main gauche somewhat shorter than his comrade's daggers and also heavy of blade. As the pair stood unmoving, a large space opened around them. The soldiers, sensing trouble, tilted their staff-pikes with whitening knuckles.

The cleric spoke up. "But of course Lieutenant Don Filberto means that figuratively, don't you, Don Filberto?"

"Eh? What's that you say? What do you mean?"

"That you were informing these two men that they must symbolically disarm themselves by pledging not to draw their weapons. Isn't that what you said?" The cleric's hatchet-face turned sufficiently to allow his deep-set eyes to fix upon those of the lieutenant. Don Filberto looked away in haste, cleared his throat, and nodded. "Now, give us your word, and let us away to police headquarters."

Raker smiled thinly. "You actually expect us to—"

"Thank you... pious excellency," Ferret broke in without seeming to. "May we inquire as to the nature of our arrest?"

"Call me Intensity—Intensity Elfuego—the proper honorific for a senior priest of Keganul, or any serving the pantheon of Atlantal, and the latter part is my own name, of course. You understand?" When the lanky man nodded slightly, the cleric continued. "Fine. Then come along. As to charges, let us say that you are wanted for questioning."

"We have committed no crime in Dertosal," Raked retorted boldly.

"That is good. Being so, you should have no hesitation in complying with the demand Lieutenant Don Filberto has made. Innocent men have nothing to fear in Dertosal." Raker laughed, and Ferret showed his canines in the mirthless grin he reflexively made when things were tense. "I see no humor in that," the sharp-visaged ecclesiastic said. "You are trying my patience!"

It was plain to him that Raker was about to draw, so Ferret acted quickly. Something about the senior priest's expression in the last exchange reassured the thin man that there was truth in his otherwise ridiculous assertion. "Very well, your intensity. I take your word as a true servant of Keganal—whose worshiper's word is a bond as strong as iron heated in the fiery forge, is it not?" He stepped past the cleric. "Coming, Raker?" he queried without looking back at his comrade, moving so as to place himself squarely between the two files of soldiers.

Raker slammed his partly drawn blade back into its scabbard, cursed under his breath, and followed after.

"Squad, about face, quick march!" The angry tone in the officer's voice was unmistakable. The little nobleman was evidentially disappointed that the two men had not put up a fight. Don Filberto could not, of course, remain at the rear of the column, and he hurried ahead on short legs to take his proper station in the lead, leaving the priest behind. He thought Elfuego a boor at best. You will be sorry for this night, the officer fumed mentally. How dare that fool counter his orders! No matter if the colonel had said they were to be brought in for questioning, Filberto knew better. Their informant had stated these two were guilty, so if the foreigners resisted proper arrest, let their blood flow. Resistance was admission of guilt, death the penalty.

"A pleasant night for a stroll, eh, my friend?" Ferret said softly.

Raker smiled at his old comrade. "True, true—but I would rather we had those two pretty women by our sides. Methinks this glaive-beaked priest and the popinjay prancing afore us a sorry second choice..."

Ahead, the little officer was ruminating on past events with growing anger. They had gone fully a hundred paces from the tavern when the lieutenant finally remembered the rest of his detachment. "Squad halt!" he almost screamed in his frustration. Rather than blaming himself for being too lost in thoughts of revenge to command properly, he took it out on his subordinate. "Serjeant Mendez, are you a fool?"

"No, sir."

"No? NO?! Then where are the remainder of your men, serjeant?"

"With corporal Garzal, sir, at the rear of the Black Lion—where you ordered me to post them, sir."

Spittle flew from the officer's mouth as he screamed, "I? No, serjeant, YOU! I clearly ordered you to see to the posting and recall of those men. You are to blame. Tomorrow I am placing you on report for failure to carry out orders. Now, before you embarrass yourself further, get corporal Garzal and his detachment here instantly."

The serjeant opened his mouth to protest, thought better of it, saluted. "Yes, lieutenant," he barked. As he turned, though, he couldn't fail to hear stifled snickering from the two men he and his squad guarded. Prisoners or not, Mendez smiled to himself in thanks to the outlanders. He sent them a mental wish for luck. They would need that after insulting Don Filberto as they just had. If the pair were not guilty and released, the lieutenant would surely demand satisfaction and challenge them to a duel.

Don Filberto Segoria was the finest swordsman in the city, possibly all Aragon.

Indeed, the young officer was thinking just that. He had hoped to run the two foreigners through back there in the tavern. Now he pledged he would do it on the field of honor. "I heard that sound you made, dogs!" He spoke in a low, hard voice without turning, knowing that his words carried well enough. "You will answer to me for such insult—if you survive questioning and don't hang!"

The laughter from Ferret and Raker lasted until the noise made by corporal Garzal's returning squad drowned it out. The hatchet face of senior priest Elfuego was aimed at the pair, but he showed no sign of emotion. As the clattering boots of the corporal's squad sounded behind him, Elfuego slid past the two prisoners and stepped beside the irate young lieutenant. "My lord Filberto, may I suggest—"

"You may not, priest. Company, forward march!"

Intensity Elfuego shrugged mentally. He could ignore petty insults from an insignificant man who was a useful tool. In one way he was glad. He needed his wind for the long climb up the ridge to the citadel overtopping the city's center.

Chapter Six

THE FORTRESS OF Dertosal was even more thickly walled than the city, while its blunt towers stood starkly above the community it shielded—and dominated. The citadel flung out a curtain wall to encompass barracks and a marshaling yard, disdained the neighboring structures. To its left as one approached from the city streets below it, a secondary stronghold was evident. Mayor's palace and various moderately sized buildings of city government were clustered together, conjoined by wall and tower, to form another, lesser compound. On the right of the citadel were a great temple and a handful of smaller religious structures, built where they were undoubtedly because those who constructed them felt that height increased proximity to the divine. These, too, were formed with walls surrounding them that made them minor strongholds.

Lieutenant Don Filberto led his soldiers and prisoners straight to the massive main gate of the citadel. Both torches and witch-lights illuminated the area surrounding the fortress in unpleasant light. "Open in the name of the lord mayor," the officer bawled.

"Who goes there?" came the response from the guard above.

"Lieutenant Don Filberto, bringing two prisoners to Colonel de la Cabarro as ordered." The response sounded flat and harsh. The little nobleman was still full of rage.

"You may enter. Guards, open the gate for Lieutenant Don Filberto and his company," came the cry from the corporal of the guard on the rampart. There followed the faint sound of hastening footfalls, a grating of metal upon metal, and a creak and a groan. The small door within the rightmost gate swung inward, and brighter light showed inside.

The lieutenant and serjeant Mendez's squad entered first. Thereafter Intensity Elfuego ushered the two prisoners through the narrow portal. "Come, gentlemen, let us follow the lieutenant. Please hurry." The priest added those words because Don

Filberto was already halfway to the office of the commander of the guards, Colonel de la Cabarro. The little idiot is going to try to make me look the fool he is, the sharp-visaged cleric thought, but that notion contained nothing of concern for himself. Elfuego was the chief cleric of the city, secure in his position, self-confident. Still, regarding other matters, he was less sure. He strode ahead as he uttered his urging, leading by example, as it were.

Ferret and Raker followed silently, trailing the flying cape of the velvet-garbed officer. What choice had they? There were now another dozen sentries in sight. "Active place considering the hour," Ferret remarked to no one in particular.

"The heart of Dertosal never rests," the priest informed him.

Ferret wondered if he had detected humor in the man's voice. He couldn't be certain.

Up a flight of stone steps paralleling the face of the central building of the fortress, in through a thick, iron-studded and bound door, along a wide hall, into a cluttered room.

"Colonel de la Cabarro!" Don Filberto nearly shouted his words as he stomped into attention, then bowed curtly. "Sir! I have brought you the two dogs, as ordered—despite no little interference from Intensity Elfuego, I must say."

The man addressed was big. That was evident even when he was sitting behind a large table, as he was now. His head had been bent over a sheaf of papers, reading. Colonel de la Cabarro looked up placidly as the lieutenant banged in, went through his show. He looked at Ferret and Raker, smiled at the priest, before directing his attention to the little officer stiffly at attention before him. "Thank you, Lieutenant Don Filberto. You may go."

"Go? I have been belittled, insulted, my re—"

The colonel stood up abruptly, towering over Don Filberto, face frozen in hard lines. That was sufficient to make the little man chop off his protest.

"As you command," he said, nearly choking on the words. Filberto did a smart about-face, glaring in turn at the two prisoners and Elfuego as he left.

The non-commissioned officer still remained in the room, immobile and at attention by the entrance. The colonel smiled at him. "Be so kind, gentlemen, as to give Serjeant Mendez your sword belts and arms—a matter of protocol, you know. Serjeant, take their weapons."

When the two men uncertainly complied, the colonel nodded. "You are also dismissed. Close the door when you leave, serjeant," the big man said in a sonorous baritone. A smile fleeted across Mendez's lips as he saluted and obeyed. The door closed with a solid thump. "Better," the colonel said to himself as he resumed his seat. Then he placed one hand under his chin and regarded the three persons remaining in his office.

"Intensity, I offer you my apologies. Do have a chair. Have you anything to add?"

"Not at this time, Excellency," the priest said, casting a meaningful glance at Ferret and Raker.

The big man looked at the two standing at ease in front of his desk. He scowled as if to let them know that such relaxed posture was an insult to his rank. Both could not fail to note that expression, but neither reacted. "Do you know who I am?"

"Colonel de la Cabarro of the Dertosal guard, yes?" Ferret said it lightly but without disrespect.

"Not merely colonel, jackanapes. I am commandant of the citadel and chief of security for his grandness the lord mayor. Just in case you don't follow my words well, that means I am in charge of police and the watch as well as guards. Is that clear?"

"Whew!" expostulated Raker, wiping his face as to remove worry. "I am happy to be so intelligenced, colonel. For a minute there I thought we were being conscripted in the—"

Ferret was about to elbow his comrade to make him stop when the big man reacted.

"Silence!" His stare brought Raker to a cold realization which was heavily underscored by the colonel's next sentence. "I can have you summarily executed."

"Ah-ha-hem… Your Excellency, I believe…"

"Oh, do be quiet, Elfuego," the commandant boomed without heat or force behind his admonition. "Give me more credit," he murmured as if in apology. The cleric sat straighter, hands folded, and said nothing in response.

Colonel de la Cabarro tapped the thick sheaf of papers before him. "I know a lot about you two. The list of crimes you have committed are sufficient to hang you each a dozen times over!"

"We have broken no law in Dertosal," Ferret said mildly. His mind was racing, and there was a chill weight in his gut. "In fact, we have been in your fine city for but three weeks, all the time paying in good coin for what we—"

"Pirate, highwayman, thief, gambler, imposter, burglar, assassin, traitor, confidence man, bandit, seducer, counterfeiter, murderer, forger. So much for you, master Ferret.

"And your associate, master Raker, you are also a true specimen of the worst of men! Outlaw, extortionist, thief, brigand, looter, strong-arm man, arsonist, robber, kidnapper, killer. This last incident with stolen jewels and trollops is typical of your villainy. A sorry list of crimes, is it not?"

Raker looked innocent. "I counted only ten charges, your excellency, not a dozen. Besides, I am not guilty of—"

"Any of them," Ferret interjected. "I, too, vehemently deny ever having assassinated anyone, the most flagrantly false of the spurious accusations brought against us."

Colonel de la Cabarro rolled his eyes heavenward. "You are not in court. Not yet. You are here to answer questions. I am now going to ask those questions. When I do, each of you will answer *truthfully*—not as you have just now done. Try that again, and we will adjourn to the vaults beneath this place. I will not hesitate to use torture if that is the only means of eliciting correct responses."

"Correct? Does that mean the truth… or something else?" Ferret spat back. They were in it now, so there was no sense in trying to mince words.

"May I, Excellency?" the priest asked.

"Of course, Your Intensity."

Elfuego stood up and stepped close to the two prisoners. "I am here to see to it that truth is spoken, knowledge revealed, facts made plain. I will use heka to determine things thus, if my own facilities are insufficient. I must add that His Excellency Colonel de la Cabarro's own acumen in such matters is acute. I urge you to take this warning to heart."

When they both nodded, the colonel said, "Then no more frippery. Stand at attention. Answer fully, one at a time, after I have asked a question." He motioned the ecclesiastic back to the corner chair, paused for a moment as the senior priest of Keganul readied certain things. Then Colonel de la Cabarro stared hard at Ferret and Raker. "Have you ever heard of the name Chasal Mer-al?"

"No," said the lean man before him.

Raker shook his head after frowning in thought for a few seconds.

The colonel glanced at Elfuego, then looked back at the prisoners. "Have you stolen anything since being in Dertosal?"

"Absolutely not," Ferret responded.

"Not so much as a bit of liquorice," his muscular comrade confirmed with real sincerity in his voice and puzzlement written on his face.

"Where were you last night?"

The response came in unison: "At the Black Lion tavern."

"All night?"

"Yes," confirmed Ferret.

"From the middle part on, anyway," came Raker's correction. That surprised the lanky man, but he said nothing nor showed any sign. "There are many who were there who will confirm that."

"Rats protect their pack," quipped de la Cabarro. "I want the truth."

"You have it," Ferret said firmly.

Again the colonel looked over at the cleric. Then he directed his gaze to the two men before him, his craggy features set, betraying nothing as to what he was thinking. He examined the lean man called Ferret. Three fingers under six feet tall, narrow and lean, but with movements which betokened sinewy power and speed, not unlike that of the animal whose name he bore. The man had odd hair. In the light it showed silvery glints as if the tips were colored thus, in shadow it was dark. So, too, the fellow's complexion, pale in bright light, seemingly the shade of old leather in dim illumination. How much of a chameleon is this man? de la Cabarro wondered. He had no question as to what he had read in the report—knew a little of the thief besides. Before him was one of the most clever and dangerous rascals alive.

"You are from the Avillonian Isles, correct?"

"I was born in Lyonnesse," Ferret answered. "But it has been years since I was anywhere near there."

"Fourteen years, to be exact," the colonel supplied with a trace of superiority which failed to raise any reaction from his subject. He shifted targets.

The one named Raker was less of a puzzle to him. Although only a bit over five and a half feet in height, he was undoubtedly a dangerous opponent. Square shoulders, corded arms, and his bearing told the commandant clearly that this was one who possessed many deadly skills. Handsome, with silver-blonde hair, striking gray eyes, and a little scar at the end of the left eyebrow to intrigue the ladies. Certainly a rogue, swordsman, and a hit with females—common and aristocratic alike, the colonel wagered mentally.

"And you were born in Savoy, leaving there a decade ago to join forces with your associate, Ferret."

"Well, it has been about ten years since I left Turin, but it was not to meet *him*. You should have seen the woman who took me to Nice. She had the—"

"Yes. Corrupt since youth. Now tell me, what have you done with the goldsmith's body?!"

He stared hard at both. Neither man flinched, sweated, or gave the least sign of guilt—or comprehension.

"Goldsmith?"

"What body?"

"Guard!" The door seemed to fly open, and two soldiers stood there with ready spontoons. He saw the prisoners tense at that, using the corners of their eyes to try to see what was happening. "Send in someone with the evidence," the colonel snapped in their direction. One disappeared, returning in a minute with another uniformed man whose knees were bent under the load he carried. Both entered Colonel de la Cabarro's office. The man bearing the heavy box set it on the floor where the commandant pointed. Then both saluted. "You may go," he told them. They were careful to close the door as they exited.

"This condemns you. Confess."

"A box?" Ferret's expression was incredulous.

The colonel used his foot to flip aside the lid. Inside was a jumble of silver and gold, raw metal, wire, ingots, and jewelry. "Not the box, dolt, its contents! Here is the evidence which condemns you."

"I've never seen the junk before. Have you, Raker?"

"Never!"

"What nonsense! Give it up, you two. One of my men took the lot here from your room at the inn. It took my men an hour to discover where you'd concealed it. Very clever misdirection casting you placed upon the hiding place."

Ferret opened his mouth to protest, looked at the colonel, and thought better of it. He snapped his jaws shut. Raker, seeing that, likewise remained silent.

"Where is the rest of the loot?" demanded the commandant.

The senior priest finally spoke up. "Undoubtedly shared with cronies, given away, spent, sequestered elsewhere—what matter, colonel? I believe it is time to see justice done.

"Your Intensity is correct. Guards!" Again the pair of eager soldiers appeared in the doorway. "Bring manacles and shackles. Do not allow these two out of your sight for an instant after they are secured in chains. They are to be taken to the vaults and locked in separate cells in the lowest level, and a pair of guards is to be on duty there at all times." Colonel de la Cabarro stretched his heavy body, smiled wolfishly at the two, then looked back at his men. "They are dangerous felons, but we have them fast. It is the axe or the rope for them, and we've solved the problem of the goldsmith's robbery, too, with or without a body.

"Shit!" Raker said. It was the only word either of the two captives uttered as they were cuffed arm and leg and led away with a rattling of steel links.

Chapter Seven

THREE DAYS IN solitary confinement in the deepest, darkest, chilliest dungeon Ferret had ever experienced and hoped never to see. There was a dim, magickal luminescence coming from the stone ceiling, but that was the only amenity. So far meals had been but twice daily and consisted of a little bit of bread, thin broth, and unidentifiable mushy stuff. Thank goodness there was no hard labor. Ferret's stomach rumbled when he thought of food, so he stopped thinking of it. On a somewhat positive note, he and his friend had found a means to communicate. The wall between their cells was not thick, and one particular stone seemed to carry sound well. Just then he heard something.

"Tap-tap. Tapity-tapity-tap. Tap-tipity..." The faint clicking went on for some time. "Do shut up, old chum," Ferret murmured, as he got the drift of Raker's coded message. His comrade was now complaining about being prevented from fighting when they had the chance back in the Black Lion.

Just then a guardsman paced close. "No talking in there!"

At least that made Raker quit his rapped and tapped bitching, Ferret thought glumly. Not that there wasn't reason to complain. For the hundred crimes they had committed and gone scot-free there was now one of which they were innocent but which was to spell their doom. Or was it?

"Tip-ta-tap-tap." Ferret's mind was racing, and he sounded a fast reassurance to his companion. "Wait. We aren't dead yet, and won't be." Wishing he was really certain of that, wondering what it was that made him doubt they'd meet the executioner soon, Ferret racked his brain. "Is it that dream?"

"I said NO TALKING!" screamed the soldier peering in through the little grate in the cell door.

A laugh came from the adjoining cubicle. The guard's face reddened, and he stamped over to shout threats at Raker. Good man! Ferret thought to himself. He stood up from where he had been crouching on the mouldering little heap of straw that passed for a bed, began pacing back and forth, three to the door, three to the solid rock of the rear wall, short steps at that because of the leg chains. Hours passed. At last Ferret formulated what he had only vaguely felt. The solemn cleric and the big commandant had been too abrupt. Some higher official had to be told. This was obviously a set-up to send them on a greased slide to their deaths, thereby hiding the real culprits.

He began to send another rapid but far more lengthy message through the ashlar wall to his comrade. "Tappity-tip-tipity... We are set up. Must tell lord mayor..."

"That would be a big mistake, my child," a soft voice said from behind him.

Ferret sprang up, spun around, his face registering the shock he had just had.

Intensity Elfuego smiled serenely, his hatchet face homelier still in that expression. The priest stood inside the cell, one finger at his mouth. The cell wall at his back showed a small opening. Elfuego withdrew the finger from his lips to point it at that opening. Then he bent over and exited.

Ferret followed as quickly as his fetters allowed. He found himself in a narrow passage, a secret way. A hand moved him back a step. There was a slight grating sound, and the dingy illumination from his cell was blocked as the stones closed to make the wall seem unbroken. It was utterly black in the narrow space. Then a rosy-hued witchlight grew overhead, and he was able to see again. "This is not a normal part of confinement," he drawled as he gazed at Elfuego.

"You are perceptive. Follow me." The black-and-red priest turned his back and moved along the passage, the rubine witchlight floating over his head as he moved. The passage made a right angle. They passed a cramped flight of ascending stairs, proceeded to a place where another way allowed them to go to the left. "Wait here. I will fetch your associate, Raker."

Ferret watched as the cleric moved a few steps down the little adit, bent, lifted a catch, snapping his fingers simultaneously. The magickal glow snuffed itself at the sound, but almost immediately thereafter there was a growing patch of dull light. He heard a hissing call from Elfuego.

"Master Raker. Make no outcry or noise! Quickly, now, here to this escape way."

"Trick or no, I'm coming," the broad-shouldered swordsman whispered loudly as his head appeared in the opening.

"Hush!"

"Sorry, I forgot..." Raker said very, very softly.

Total darkness. Then the rosy glow of the witchlight again sprang into being overhead. "I am here too, Raker."

"Ferret!"

"Both of you be quiet! I'll tell you when you can speak." Elfuego squeezed past the lean Ferret, headed back the way they had come. Raker needed no instructions as to what to do. He was on his friend's heels as Ferret trailed after the priest. At the top of the long spiral, they came into what seemed to be a normal room, save that it was almost bare and had no windows or discernable means of exit. Even the way they had entered was now blank wall. "Get your arms secured, gather your belongings, and then sit on that bench and stay there."

The two freed men looked with surprise to the corner that Elfuego had indicated. There in a heap were all of their worldly possessions, including their daggers and Raker's sword. They quickly buckled on belts, the gray-eyed swordsman slipping on his baldrick thereafter. Raker grinned and said, "Quite a turn of events, just as you told me, Ferret. Thanks, priest... priest?"

They both scanned the chamber. "We seem to be alone," Ferret murmured to his companion. "No matter. Let's sit and wait as the good cleric suggested."

"I mislike being in such a trap!"

"Stop pacing and sit. This is less a cage than those cells Elfuego was kind enough to free us from. Besides, my friend, I see three means of egress."

Raker sat down heavily beside Ferret. "You do?"

"Certes. There is the way we came in." He pointed to a place on the opposite wall. Raker stared, stroked his spade beard, peering intently. "To our right is the way by which the priest must have exited. If you will use your eyes, the cracks which give it away are plain enough to see." Again his comrade stared, saw nothing, and this time tugged at his whiskers. "And finally, my dear Raker, 'ware the floor just... here!" Ferret had stood up as he spoke, and with two strides came to the place he cautioned against. "I'll bet you ten to one that this bit of floor falls away to send unwanted guests into some oubliette—though then again it might be an escape route. Care to see which, Raker?"

"No thanks. I'll wait quietly as Intensity Elfuego instructed."

"So meek? You are the firebrand! Where are your strident urgings to action? Those hot and hasty—"

"Leave off, Ferret. I was nervous back there in that cell—headsman or hangman and all."

Before his friend could devil him further, Raker was saved by the entrance of the priest, now following none other than Colonel de la Cabarro. "All ready, I see," the big commandant said heartily. "I imagine you both have some number of questions—No! Hold them until I have finished speaking."

"The dossier on you two which so conveniently arrived on my desk was a signal to me, but I gave no sign. Did you know that Lieutenant Don Filberto brought it in? Of course you didn't know that," he hastened to add when he saw the pair about to answer. "I asked that only rhetorically. He tells me a secret contact gave it to him. So, what did the material contain? Too much! It was headed by a note warning that there was to be a murder and a robbery performed, naming you, Ferret and Raker, as the perpetrators. This most knowledgeable informant even gave us the name of the man who was to be done thus. A most useful missive, that, adding in its contents your address, the Noble Traveler Inn, even while warning that you'd probably not be there.

"Unfortunately, and surely by purest chance," the colonel said with heavy sarcasm, "the whole batch of material arrived only just before midnight. As usual, I was not in my office at that time. The able lieutenant sent a man to fetch me, but meanwhile acted on his own initiative and ordered a squad to search your room, simultaneously leading a detachment to round you up at the Black Lion. Can you believe that? His informant correctly predicted you'd be there!"

"This is obviously a put-up job."

"Quite. But perhaps more insidious and clever than you might suspect."

Ferret slapped his hands together in anger. "You are right, sir! Even I didn't know we would be at that tavern until I managed to stumble upon it that night. That was at ten or eleven o'clock..."

"Why bother to finger us?" Raker blurted out. "We haven't done anything here—don't even know anyone!"

"Men such as you two surely have enemies everywhere," the priest supplied in his sonorous voice. "You should reconsider your paths...."

De la Cabarro jumped in to prevent his exposition from degenerating into apologies, doctrinal arguments, justifications, and who knew what else. "You'll have plenty of chance for that another time, Intensity. Now is when I must get to the bottom of this pressing matter."

"Pardon, excellency."

"Of course. To continue: I have played along with this charade as I have to discover who would dare such a shallow ploy. My intelligence is insulted! A heinous crime has been committed, and while you two are outlaws, I do not believe you are the perpetrators. Also, I must now examine my apparatus here. Do I have traitors? Spies? Is there a conspiracy?"

"I hate to spoil an interesting story, Colonel de la Cabarro, but what does that have to do with us? Police matters are hardly our line of work...."

The big man seemed amazed. "No? Even without the detailed dossiers I received on you two, certain things have reached my ears. Yes, even here in this remote backwater," he asserted when he saw the two exchange glances. "Have you not at times performed certain services—for nobles or even governments—in order to avoid embarrassment or worse?"

"Well... yes, but..."

"Let us return to that later," the official said with a meaningful look and firm tone. "To conclude my reasoning on this matter, I accepted things as they were on their face—as far as everyone beside myself and the honored Intensity Elfuego there. There is a desultory search for the corpse of the missing goldsmith, Chasal Mer-al, but as far as Dertosal is concerned, the two culprits are imprisoned awaiting trial and execution."

Ferret ventured, "Don Filberto might—"

"Don Filberto is not overly bright. I actually suspected him for a time, but in the last two days have come to the realization he is naught but a dupe."

"A very dangerous swordsman, mind you. He is the finest in Dertosal, possibly all of Aragon," the senior priest cautioned Ferret and Raker. "Do not give him further cause for taking offense."

"Not bloody likely while we rot in prison," Raker grumbled.

His comrade let it pass. Instead he queried, "Why do you free us clandestinely? I assume we are about to be set loose."

"I'm coming to that. Do not be impatient. Patience is a necessity for success in most things, including solving crimes and uncovering secrets."

"Not much of a concern of mine..." but as he said that half-heartedly, Ferret knew better, and his trailing off indicated the fact clearly enough.

"You two can in no way be connected to the goldsmith's shop. You have a history of theft, but neither of you are killers for the sake of removing a potential witness against you, as your records so clearly state. Why, from what I can tell, about half of the lands of Æropa and North Afrik seek your arrest. No. A paltry few thousand reals loot and a missing proprietor? The loot conveniently in your room at the inn? Bah! No investigator worth the name would connect you two with this crime."

"Thank you," Ferret said with sincerity.

The colonel was solemn. "Don't thank me yet. Segoria, were he in my place, would have you done for already. Don Filberto is the man most likely to succeed me, for the lord mayor owes much to the Segoria family, likes the young don personally, and plans to marry his daughter to him.

"If Don Filberto learns you are free, he will run to the lord mayor, and I will be in trouble—you, too, if you are caught. Nobody save us four can know what is going on, and there is a time limit for me to conceal things. This is where the good Intensity comes in. Elfuego...?"

The sharp-faced man stood up, cleared his throat, and inclined his head to de la Cabarro. "His excellency is a kind and generous man. He believes in justice, is insulted by one who supposes him to be a fool. You two do not know it, but I am both the principal cleric of this city and also its most able practitioner of heka. Thus, I sit on many councils, and I assist in matters of police investigations as well."

"You are a man of many talents," Raker said without japing.

Elfuego paused, looked at him, actually smiled a little. "Thank you. That was sincere. You see, I can tell much about people—when they lie, evade, or speak truth, as long as no counter-heka is employed to foil me.

"I scrutinized the shop of Chasal Mer-al. There was a great magickal residue there. Impressions of things too horrible to ponder, but no other clues. Magick was employed, and more castings to wipe away anything useful to those seeking a solution to the crime.

"Neither of you is a consideration in regards to the wielding of heka. In my estimation, neither of you has any considerable skill in regards to any major field of practice." He held up his hand as Ferret looked a little skeptical. "No need to say anything, for I know both you and your associate can use some limited castings and possibly have certain minor powers. What I read at the goldsmiths was great power of the blackest sort—*sorcery!* "

"Round up all the sorcerers in the city, and you have your man," suggested Ferret.

"There are none in all Dertosal," Colonel de la Cabarro shot back.

"Oh...."

Intensity Elfuego continued, "Now you begin to get the picture. I have augured, and there is no doubt in my mind that a conspiracy brews nearby, one involving this city and more."

"You think we have something to do with this heka-divined plot?"

The colonel shook his head, answering for Elfuego. "Yes, Master Ferret, but not in the way you imply. I am sure the two of you were made targets in order to remove you from the scene. Whomever did away with Chasal Mer-al wanted you two dead and gone from Dertosal. The nexial point just happens to be the goldsmith's."

Raker looked at his comrade, shook his head. "I don't understand any of this. If you know we didn't do it, why imprison us, then secretly free us?"

"What his excellency means," the senior priest of Keganul told the gray-eyed swordsman, "is this: Something of potent sort was prepared at the goldsmith's shop, and undoubtedly by Mer-al himself. Then he was eliminated so as to prevent him from telling anyone of it. Investigators have learned from questioning neighboring artisans that the fellow was doing something 'special'—he was an alchemist and heka-forger as well as a jeweler, and he left debts, a high amount. I also was able to read a little there at the scene despite the force of the concealing wash of power."

Ferret wasn't satisfied. "Well and good, but where do we fit in?"

"You two are the only lead we have left. We are setting you lose to track down the guilty ones. If they wished to be rid of you, you know something!"

"We don't, colonel. That is the truth."

The cleric agreed in part. "Not consciously. Perhaps you will recognize one of the conspirators, or maybe some greater force is using you as an agent without your knowledge. Whatever may be the case, you two are the key, I think."

"Great," Raker muttered. "Just great. As soon as we leave here the word will be out, so we'll be on the track of an enemy who knows us but of whom we know absolutely nothing at all. Come on! That's a suicide mission. We'd be better off just riding off as soon as you let us go."

"Noble of you to point that out," smiled Colonel de la Cabarro. "You and your friend could do that, in fact. All we have to encourage you is the fact that we're risking our positions—possibly even our lives—to free you now... and the reward..."

Ferret and Raked exchanged glances, then both men looked at the commandant and spoke in unison: "Reward?"

"There is precedence, is there not? You have done similar assignments, if your dossiers speak truth, for others. Carried out your missions, and been paid in coin as well as pardons. I am personally guaranteeing to pay you each fifty thousand reals when you bring in the person or persons responsible, alive preferably, but dead with sufficient proof of guilt," Colonel de la Cabarro averred. "In addition, the city will grant you free passage here for as long as three months' time whenever you should choose to visit. A very useful thing for those in your... chosen field, shall I say?"

Again the pair exchanged glances. Ferret spoke for both, saying, "A fair sum and indeed a handy advantage, as you say. Still..."

"The Temple of Keganul would be most grateful as well," Intensity Elfuego said in his sonorous voice which was so incongruous with his appearance. "I can give no large sums, but we do have a very special blade, a rapier of exquisite design, forged of the finest alloys, and dweomered to enable its wielder to strike swiftly and true."

"Take me to see it!" Raker said with enthusiasm.

The priest actually laughed at that. "Impossible. When you leave this hidden room, you must go directly from Dertosal. I have managed to chart the flow of magickal energy from the shop of Chasal Mer-al. The course of the disturbance went from here in the city across the Ebro to Roqueta, then to the northwest. The path it took was plain for sufficient time to enable us to give you this much. Of course the trail has now faded away, but the direction and distance make the likely destination plain."

"Suppose we agree," Ferret spoke slowly. "How do you explain our 'escape'? And when we come back to get our payment, won't we be seized and incarcerated again? This sounds too much like another set-up."

"Nonsense!" The big colonel was truly angry upon hearing the lean man's words. "Haven't I given you my word? I will—"

"Your pardon, excellency," Elfuego interjected. His voice was as sharp as his visage. The priest was anxious not to have this whole plan disintegrate now. "I have laid ritual castings on both cells. As far as anyone will know, the pair of you will be rotting there below, awaiting the convening of the high court of Dertosal. That gives you eleven days to perform your mission and return—safely! You will both be given written passes and a signet ring as well when you leave, so that if there is any trouble when you return, those things will assure you safe passage back here."

"Well, just for the sake of argument," Ferret said, "suppose we accept. Then we are stymied. No culprits can be found in the time alloted. That means we have no reason to return, so we ride away. Where does that leave you two?"

The commandant inclined his head toward Ferret. "Very noble of you to consider that, Ferret. My esteem for you grows. Naturally, if you fail you cannot come back to Dertosal. We don't ask or expect that—don't want you to. It would put your lives at extreme risk, and such an act would likewise compromise us entirely. Allow me to say that we have carefully prepared for such a contingency. It is most unlikely that the ruse will be discovered or our positions here compromised. Thus we will be no worse, nor better, off than we are now."

"Not bad," Ferret said.

"But hardly good," Intensity Elfuego corrected.

Raker was meanwhile busily mulling over what he had just heard. He liked what he discerned from the information Colonel de la Cabarro and the chief ecclesiastic of the city had given them. "I say we can't turn down this offer, Ferret." As he spoke he used small, secret signs to emphasize and explain his words.

"As my friend says, this is an offer we can't refuse. To stay is death, and by accepting the mission you propose we gain freedom and the prospect of reward. We agree."

"Then you must have this map, this purse of money for the journey, and the rest of the information we have. Solve this case, bring back the criminals responsible, and you will have also my eternal gratitude." The colonel spoke with moving sincerity.

The senior priest's expression was not filled with such warmth as de la Cabarro's. His deep-set eyes fastened upon Ferret. The lean man looked away as if concentrating on what the commandant was about to tell them. Raker was likewise studiously ignoring Elfuego, his mind set only on carrying out the mission. "Before his excellency concludes your briefing, then, *gentlemen,* I must do one more thing." That made both of the would-be agents shift a bit nervously, exchange glances before looking at him. The priest was very astute, and he doubted that even the colonel noticed the small signs he did, for the pair were very controlled and careful.

"I told Master Raker it would be impossible to go to the temple to see the weapon I pledged as a part of your reward. That was misleading. I apologize now, for duplicity is bad, is it not gentlemen?" Elfuego watched their reactions, slight as they were. His hatchet-face seemed to hover as an axe over their heads as he went on. "Truth is all. I now give you this, Master Raker." He produced a roll of velvet, discarded the cloth, and held forth what it had enwrapped. "This is the sword I mentioned, a rapier not dissimilar in appearance to your own, but far superior in every way. Take it now. You will need it in fulfilling the mission you have pledged to undertake and fulfill as ably as you can."

"I... I am most honored, Sir Priest...." Raker hesitated only a moment longer, then stood up, taking the sheathed weapon in his two outstretched hands. He carefully inspected the hilt, then slowly drew the rapier from its scabbard, lovingly inspecting the engraved length of silvery blue adamantine steel blade thus revealed inch by inch. "May I?" he asked when the sword was freed.

"Be my guest," Elfuego told him, stepping back to give the short man space.

Raker bowed the blade, and as it sprang back he flashed into a series of passes—cuts and thrusts, blocks and parry moves. It was plain to all who watched he was a natural swordsman and fencer. Fast, sure, and with a greater reach than might be expected for one his size as his arms were long and his athletic ability enabled incredible extension of leg and body. "This is the finest weapon I have ever seen. To hold it is a dream come true!"

"Consider it yours. Whatever occurs, neither I nor my temple will ask for its return."

"Then I am your humble and obedient servant," Raker said as he gently slid the rapier back into its silver and leather scabbard.

At that the cleric smiled. "I had hoped that all along. I am glad to hear you now truly accept. Find out what powerful forces threaten Dertosal, and bring back the guilty ones."

Chapter Eight

"NOW WHAT MADE you go and do that?!" Ferret wasn't angry, but he was plainly upset.

"You have no honor," Raker retorted. He kicked his mount so that the horse moved at faster pace, leaving his companion in the dust kicked up in the process.

Ferret urged his own genet ahead so as to regain a position beside his comrade's stirrup. "We owe them nothing. They admitted we were innocent, that the whole matter was one of false accusation. Why be stupid? We risk our lives in a hopeless quest for what? Some imagined cabal! Some hope of promotion for policeman and priest!"

"You are despicable."

"Is that so? You were bought and paid for by a sword, and you say I am base?!"

Raker reined in his steed. He sat staring at his companion until Ferret brought his own horse to a halt, turned it, and walked it to where he waited. "Let us speak no more of the matter, friend, else a long camaraderie be sundered. We are going to seek out the felons, lay them by the heel, and return to Dertosal. That is that."

Ferret sighed. "I give up. Insane, but I agree to your demand—but only in the name of friendship, mark you, Raker! Despite all, those two play their own game. Probably it is against the villains described to us, yet the two sides contend over something we are ignorant of, so while they engage each other thus, we are mere pawns."

"Pawns? Never. In your own terms, Ferret, I am a knight. In fact, bearing this blade the good priest was so generous as to bestow upon me, I am perhaps a marshal."

The lanky man opposite him shifted in his saddle. Raker referred to Fidchell, a game Ferret often talked his comrade into playing, for few could outmaneuver and win against Ferret, and he never ceased teasing the blond-haired swordsman about losing. "Just because I love the game doesn't make me love this work. But tell me, old friend, if you are knight or marshall, what piece do I equate to?"

Raker reflected a moment. "Jester," he snapped as he spun his horse and set off again.

"Aptly said, Raker!" Ferret called as he cantered to a position beside the swordsman. "A piece similar in move to a knight, not so far ranging but deadly in close—not an unimportant man at all. You struck the center squarely. Now let me remind you that the jester is there to bring sense to the rash when they attempt to themselves play the fool."

"You call me fool?"

"I say that I was troubled much even before all this befell us, just as you said you were."

"No. I said—"

Ferret cut him short. "No matter. Have I been wrong in the past when foreboding came? Hasn't that special sensing saved both of our lives more than once?"

"Yes, but—"

"But now you gallop off as if you were a knight errant seeking a blessed relic! You lead us into the pit prepared by those who sought to have us executed back in Dertosal and think yourself a noble warrior."

"High time we did something good."

It was quite an unfair thing to say. Ferret's mouth drew down in a scowl, then he shrugged. "So. The jester has shot his bolt and will now be silent. Lead on, cavalier."

"You make it sound as if I am *being* cavalier," Raker shouted.

"You are, but I'm with you. Somebody has to protect the foolhardy when they blunder into danger."

Raker didn't respond further, keeping his eyes on the road ahead, maintaining the cantering pace so that their steeds covered the ground rapidly. Soon, however, the gradually rising slopes and hills became less gentle. Ahead the land hunched higher, old mountains beaten down to but steep tors by time and elements. "We rest here and eat a bite while these mounts have a breather."

"You are the horseman, friend, and leader of this dance too."

They sat a while on a rock, ate a little, and drank. Neither spoke. Both men thought about what had happened. After supplying them with a map, showing the path of magickal movement read by the priest's own heka, and pointing out the most likely destination, Colonel de la Cabarro and his clerical associate led them out. Via secret door and unused hallway, the four came to stables. There, equipped and ready, were two fine Iberian horses, genets.

"Keganul guide you," Intensity Elfuego had intoned.

"I count on you to be back before the deadline has gone," added the commandant, "for much depends on the success of your mission."

With black cloaks of the priesthood of the storm god muffling them, the two had left the citadel by its postern gate. The hour was that before dawn, the dawn of this very day.

Raker broke the silence. "The Penumbratos are desolate. It seems a likely place, don't you agree?" It was his way of letting Ferret know that he was no longer angry, bore no grudge. It was honor, not greed for the sword, which made him resolute. Raker hoped his comrade apprehended that fact.

"Torenegro—I think that name was in the dream...."

"That's twice in the last hour you've returned to that old theme. Have you at last recalled it?"

Ferret ignored the sarcasm. "No. Just snippets of things, maybe mere hunches, but quite enough to make wary. No help for it. We are up to our necks in dung, and you would have us wade further. Well, over our heads or not, I'm with you. Mind, though, blondie, that I'm the taller besides wiser. When your head slips from sight, don't whine to me about immersion in mire."

"How could I speak with my head in a sea of turds?"

That made Ferret laugh. "All right. This *is* better than trying to track down the pair of thugs the astute priest was able to describe for us—they who did the looting of the goldsmith's and placed the dregs of their work in our room at the inn."

Raker hadn't really considered that. "What makes you say so? I'd suppose you would want those two for some persuasive questioning. Knowing you, detailed information should be at the top of your want list."

"Pish. That they could be described indicates the pair are a false trail. Consider their descriptions, not unlike our own, eh? It would take days to find them even in a place as small as Dertosal. My guess is that they have fled the city by now. Anyway, they are a blind alley. We are more likely to locate the true culprits where we go—and I mislike that greatly!"

"You, afraid?"

"I fear to lose my life on so useless an errand," Ferret confessed. "What we do now is attempt to find the toad who placed warts on us, even though we know that cold monster has a poison bite."

That made Raker stand up in agitation. "That is aptly put. I, for one, resent those warts—bumps which were meant to make us lose our heads or stretch our necks! Toads can be stuck!"

"And the fine priest gave you the tool to manage that."

"If you would have this a toadsticker, so be it." Raker was again becoming heated.

Ferret suddenly smiled, stood up, and slapped his companion on the back. "You are a gem, Raker, a veritable savant!"

Raker eyed the lean man suspiciously. "You say that to mollify me. Don't think to turn me from my purpose."

"Turn? Never. Not now. Hells, no! We must ride to Torenegro."

"What on Ærth has come over you? This is too much of a change."

His words fell on empty air, for Ferret was already mounting his horse. "Come on, slackard! We are on a quest to right a desperate wrong."

"That I know. Who dragged you this far?"

Ferret ignored the barb. "It was both waking sight *and* dream which troubled me until just now. No longer. The memory has returned."

"Joyous. Momentous! Prithee say on," Raker said crossly, vaulting into his saddle in a show of superiority. "You know who the guilty party is, right?"

"Recall the witchy beauty in Tangier, she who did us out of the Phonecian's hoard?"

"*Neva,* that bitch! She nearly did for me then. I bear the scar still where she stabbed me."

Ferret laughed. "Near your heart. She'd never have been so close save you were thinking to have her, chum. I don't make light of your wound, but it is that which made all clear."

Raker's face was a study in puzzlement. "A scar on my chest is the key to the dreamgate—ivory or horn?"

"The gate of horn, my friend, but no. Not the scar. It is the act which gave it to you. That vile but gorgeous woman struck you with her poniard as if you were a toad, don't you see?" Ferret broke into rolling laughter as he finished.

"I see no humor in that whatsoever."

"It is your Teutonic heritage."

"I am a Savoyard."

"Your mother—was she not from Bern?"

The gray-eyed adventurer took another tack. "Get to the point." He waited a moment for Ferret's renewed guffaws to subside. Their horses were now laboring up the steep and snaky road. He had plenty of time. "You remembered my being stabbed by a nasty, conniving trull, and this makes you want to recall what troubled you, want to seek the ones who—"

"Very near. I saw her in Puertal Mago, only it didn't register. She noticed us sure enough. I think now it was she who put the guards onto us, not your carelessness with stolen gold. There's more, though."

"More?"

"Yes, it was after that, in Dertosal, that some dream-like sending came to me. In it there was a woman who turned to a demon, dragged you and I into fire. When I remembered Neva's being there in Puertal Mago, then the whole locked-up recollection came rushing back. Toadsticker... a fine nickname!'

Raker did not rise to that bait. He patted the hilt of the rapier, nodded. "So I shall call it, for the nonce at least. With it I'll skewer that murderous harlot Neva."

"Safer that than with the weapon you originally thought to employ 'gainst her. Most unchivalrous, but I counsel a fast strike, my friend. That one can toss castings about as a juggler does balls. If my rede is true, she is in the thick of the affair, too."

"How so?"

"Who else to remove the goldsmith and his wealth in such fashion? Magick and death, the good priest told us. Neva is the answer. She would have us removed for many reasons, not the least of which is that you and I would recognize her *and* her handiwork."

That made Raker feel good. His companion seldom was so inclusive in his lauds. He could certainly identify her, relate of her prowess with hidden weapons, but as to heka recognition... The Savoyard shrugged mentally. I can outride, outfight, and outromance Ferret on any given day, he thought, but the lean man is a better thief, more clever, and knows far more about the esoteric lore of heka practice than I do—has greater innate abilities of that sort too, such as his quasi-dreams and hunches. "So we know who the culprit is, and where, too—Torenegro!"

"Perhaps, old comrade, perhaps. She won't be alone, though, for this is some great and deep plot she is part of if our Iberian benefactors in Dertosal spoke truth. No, Neva will have henchmen... and a master, methinks."

Ferret's voice was heavy as he spoke the last phrase. For some reason Raker shuddered even though the midday sun was blazing.

Chapter Nine

THE SWOLLEN SPHERE of fiery orange that was the setting sun altered its color as if a chameleon as it sank against the jagged skyline. To scarlet, then an angry crimson, the mountains old blood and maroon, the scattered clouds madder and lake.

"Torenegro is more distant than this map shows," Raker said with irritation.

Ferret glanced at the parchment in his comrade's hand, then looked at the road ahead as it corkscrewed upward in the distance. "We view it as the falcon, not the fox. The way is as looping as an old river's course. Had we wings or a Farzian flying carpet, we would dine in Torenegro tonight. As it is, my friend, we have before us the prospect of cold food, hard ground, and a ceiling of stars. We are still at least a half-day's hard ride from our destination, which lies in the vale on the other side of that mountain."

"We should keep going...." Raker's gaze had been on the sepia and gray of the far distance. But as he spoke the upper rim of the sun was swallowed by the horizon. Shadowy places became black voids, and his range of vision was pushed back to a tithe of its sun-aided range. This sudden change was only a little surprising, recalled his own home, save the alps were far more rugged than these worn peaks, and darkness more swift still. "Never mind. This is a fair place, so we camp for the night." With a creak of cuir bouille, Raker swung from his seat, grabbed the sword and both pairs of saddlebags, strode to the most sheltered place around, set down saddlebags and weapon, tossed his hat atop them, and returned to the horses.

By then, Ferret, too, had dismounted and removed the saddle from his steed. His friend did the same. Their location was acceptable indeed, with a low rock wall nearby and some grass and shrubs for grazing. As Raker first groomed and then hobbled the horses, the lean man effortlessly carried saddles and pads to the sheltered spot. They were at a sufficient elevation that the night would be cool, cold if a wind blew. He set his burdens beside the other gear, began searching in the fast-fading dusk for firewood. Soon he got a little bonfire crackling, water heating, and prepared their scant supper.

They ate in silence. After an hour thus the fair-haired man spoke. "I am for sleep," Raker said tersely. The play of little flames marked the dwindling of the big chunk of branch to embers and charred remainders. A jumbled collection of twigs and sticks lay near the fire—wood for making morning tea. He stood, walked three steps to his bedroll, and began stripping off his leather and horn armor, a gift of Colonel de la Cabarro.

First came the broad collar studded with pieces of horn, with its attached lamellar shoulder wings also of horn plates and hardened leather. Then he unbuckled and set aside the thick, high leather girdle which covered any gap between lower body armor and that protecting the upper while helping to support the latter at the same time. Next came the shell-like cuirasse, front and back slightly overlapping on the left side, wide shoulder straps to both protect and further distribute the weight. Long experience enabled him to undo the laces with ease, pull it up and over his head. Off came the undercoat of padded cloth with arms and short skirt of leather. High boots with bone splints and jutting knee guards were tugged off; pantaloons of leather reinforced with the curve of tough animal horn at critical places between their double layer were last shed.

During this process, Ferret had put the only other large log he had found near their campsite into the heart of the embers, then used a stick to move ashes and even some dirt around and partially atop it. That would help guarantee it would not burn totally away before they arose next morning. Finished, he came to his own sleeping place. "Phew! You need a bath!"

"It's all this damned armor," Raker said. "I feel as if I'm in the military again."

"Perish *that* thought," Ferret responded, recalling their brief stint as mercenaries in Khaziria. He too undressed, his lighter leather and padded armor being fashioned more like normal clothing than the protection favored by his companion. "You should rely more on speed and less on that bulky stuff."

"You have a goatish odor, too, chum," Raker said as he rolled over and got as comfortable as saddle pad mattress and stony ground allowed. "You'll voice a different refrain when a dozen foemen surround you."

The lanky rogue finished stripping off his outer garments before saying more. "I fought my first battle when you still wore your chamber pot as a rag round your buns, youngling," he finally responded. Raker sent back only a soft snore. Ferret grinned to himself, lay down, pulled his traveling cloak over him, stared up at the stars a moment. The sky glittered, the jewel-like stars reminding him of the robbery and likely murder of Chasal Mer-al the goldsmith and gemner with alchemical skill and heka-forging ability. What had that man wrought to bring what then occurred on his head? Ferret sighed. A wolf howled, a far distant keening which went unanswered. Tomorrow would be time enough to think further on their mission. He was tired from the hard and hot ride, and the night air's damp chill made Ferret feel snug beneath heavy wool. He slept.

A cold sweat had sprung out on his head when Ferret awoke with a start. He had a fleeting impression of a chittering bark, undulating motion nearby, but that didn't bother him. His whole body was tense, but anyone watching him would not even have known the lean man was no longer sleeping. He even retained the slow, regular breathing of one asleep. His senses of hearing and smell were on full alert. Ferret didn't bother to try seeing anything, for a quick peep had revealed nothing save ground and the dark glow of the fire's few embers.

No strange odors assailed his sensitive nose, but his ears detected a deep growling coming from some distance. The sound lasted only a second, but it triggered his memory. He had heard that in his just-ended nightmare, a gristly dream begun with howlings and concluding with slavering fangs at his throat. Everything fell into place in his mind. How much time? Seconds!

"Hsst! Raker, we are about to have company," he called so softly it might have been a soughing of the wind.

Raker's fingers stole out to grasp his sword's scabbard, but he was silent and otherwise motionless.

Ferret counted to thirty-three, then he heard small sounds—a click of pebbles, the rustle of foot against grass. He was up in an instant, twin daggers naked in his hands as he stared into the darkness toward the source of the faint noises.

"Please don't harm me, wayfarer!" The soft cry of alarm was in a throaty female voice, and after those words the speaker appeared. Hair a bit disheveled, clothing showing wear and tear, feet bare and dusty—all no matter. It was a beautiful girl whose wild mane of dark hair showed silvery glints like Ferret's own in the pale light of a sickle moon. Her face was exotic, teeth perfect white, form supple and pale where bare flesh was visible. "I am lost, hungry. I've been seeking your camp for hours—ever since I saw the light of your fire. Help me!"

"Of course, ma'am—and pardon my companion's attire. My own, too, for that matter. We weren't expecting company." Raker was up now, smiling toward the pretty stranger.

She came slowly toward them, smiling in return. "Thank you."

Ferret could detect a faint scent now, a spicy musk coming from the girl who was but three paces from the blond-haired swordsman now. Without a word, Ferret stooped, set aside his twin blades, and began rummaging in his small pack. Only then did he say, "If you are in need of sustenance, senorita, I'll have the answer for you in a moment."

Meanwhile, Raker smiled still and smoothed back his hair with one hand. Then, evidentially noting her perfume too, told her, "An alluring fragrance, ma'am." With a flourish and bow he gestured to his own pallet. "Do join us—sit on the bedding there, and use my cloak as a shawl, for the air is chill here in the mountains."

"The Penumbratos are dangerous at night," she agreed, not moving. "I am called Lupe; what is your name, pale-haired man?

And what is yours?" she added as she looked uneasily toward Ferret where he was crouched, still getting something from the pack.

Raker took a step toward her, was about to tell her his name, ready to guide Lupe to his place. At that instant his friend bounded up and cried out: "What matter names, señorita? Your own included! Here, have *this.* " A second long stride placed the lean man between Lupe and Raker. Ferret thrust out his left hand, its contents thus before her face. The woman expelled her breath in a whoosh, sprang backward and was gone. "Your blade, Raker!

"I've never seen reflexes like that," he murmured, moving as if he were a somnambulant.

"Godsdamnit, HURRY!"

The shout galvanized Raker. He no longer pondered anything, but reacted. With a scrape and plangent ring the weapon was free, glinting silver-blue in the moonlight. "You fear that girl?" His comrade's urgent demand had removed his sudden lethargy, but Raker had no idea as to why Ferret was acting as he did. "Or did you not want me to—"

"Shut up! Get over to the rock, keep your back to it." As Ferret urged his friend thus, he kicked the smoldering fire into little flames. The fire flared immediately. Ferret added twigs and sticks, so that the flames licked up, grew. Then he added all of the sticks, even the thick piece of limb. Now the bonfire was bright. A dance of ruddy illumination and gray-black shadows now surrounded them. From beyond this circle of growing brightness came a terrible growl followed by three ear-shattering howls. "We're going to have company again in a second," Ferret called frantically to the sword-armed man who now stood in tense expectation where his friend had told him to take position. Even as he spoke he was tossing the herbs he had had in his left hand, that "gift" which had sent the woman, Lupe, away in a flash, upon the burning mound.

"From that hellish belling, chum, I think it's a visit we could do without."

"Pray the priest didn't embellish the blade's dweomer," Ferret shouted back as he dug frantically in the parcel from which he had gotten the leaves. "I'm not much of an apotropaist nor magician, but here goes—" He chopped off his words, busily drawing something on the ground with his right hand, left sprinkling some powder. The work was done quickly. Then he fanned the smoke from the blaze so that it swirled round him, eddied throughout their little hollow. Just then three dark shapes sprang into the firelight.

One came straight for Raker. The long rapier was there to meet the fury of the attack.

The second headed for Ferret, coming fast, jaws agape. It was a black wolf as large as a man. The lanky adventurer moved as it charged, diving so as to have the fire intervene between himself and the creature. The thing whined involuntarily as it encountered the thick smoke, yelped as it leaped over the flames.

The third huge animal refrained from immediate assault, slinking low, its feral gaze shifting between its two fellows.

Raker's point took the leaping wolf in its open mouth, a fanged maw which seemed to laugh. If so, that humor was of the blackest sort, for the beast's teeth were huge, the muscles of those ravening jaws capable of crushing bones, ripping muscles, tearing sinews, severing veins and arteries.

Many men would have supposed the attack was by werewolves, sought silver to slay these monstrous killers. Ferret perceived otherwise, for although his free use of wolfsbane had strong effect, he knew that they were under assault by weretherios, animals able to alter their bestial form to anthropomorphic ones. The wolfsbane hurt them because they were lupine, forced them from human to their actual shape, but the herb would neither keep them at bay nor slay them. The weretherion which leaped over the flames to savage Ferret was blinded by the herbal smoke, but invulnerable to any non-magickal weapon the lean man might wield.

Meanwhile, the leader of the trio slunk into the center of the camp. The one who had named herself Lupe sent forth a moaning sound from deep in her throat, a keening noise which impeded the thought processes of humans, making them easier prey.

That sound availed the weretherion attacking Raker not at all. It was not a matter of planning or brainpower. When the huge male wolf charged, leaped, the rapier was ready. Raker drove the point with all of his innate skill and powerful muscles. The enchanted blade struck through the mouth, passed through the palate, pierced brain, and showed a foot of bloody metal beyond. The force of the leap continued to drive the beast on, so that the whole length of the blade protruded, as wolf and man collided and went down in a heap.

The creature bent on slaying Ferret missed its mark despite its incredible swiftness. The man was to one side of where the wolf thought he would be, and as the beast turned its head and slashed with its great canines, a loop of wire was there. "Bite now, dog," Ferret growled as he yanked and the iron circle shrank to a small hoop. He moved, tugged, and twisted. The thin strand of metal circling the creature's snout had the wolf's jaws locked shut—but only for so long as the lanky man could maintain his hold on the other end of the wire.

The weretherion caught thus was likewise a male, as large as the one thrashing and kicking its last atop the stunned Raker. It was as powerful, and cunning, too. It sprang at Ferret, knowing that any slackening of tension would enable it to jerk back its muzzle and free its jaws. It growled horribly as it came, the furious desire to tear out the throat of the man who dared to hinder it thus blazing from its burning eyes.

Ferret saw the attack, tumbled backward, sent the beast caught on the end of his steely strand high with his upturned legs and feet. Holding fast to the turns of wire punished him cruelly, for the metal cut as the weight of the wolf jerked against his hands. Wishing for his gauntlets, but nevertheless gripping fast, Ferret ignored the blood, the pain as he twisted right. As fast as any true ferret he was on his knees, upright, hauling back on the strand of wire. Half stunned, the weretherion wolf was a fraction slower in its reactions. Still trying to roll from its back where the throw had brought it in a jarring arc, the beast's head was yanked hard left, then the wolf was dragged muzzle-first along the rocky ground. Such punishment hurt it only inconsequentially. The constraining wire was still looped fast, but the beast was unrelenting in its fury. With a heave of massive muscles its body convulsed and jackknifed. The move brought it from back to side, and in a second its legs would be under it, and the wolf would be ready to attack again. This time it would use a series of complex motions to gain the slack it needed to free its jaws, tear the man to red rags.

As if reading those bestial thoughts, Ferret himself howled in fury as he hauled the struggling wolf into the fire. "No use, monster! Bite flames!" The effect was gratifying to the man, gruesome for the weretherion. Fire consisting not only of burning bits of wolfsbane but a powder of magickal materia ate at it. The heka energy from the powder Ferret had thrown into the bonfire gave the flames an enchanted intensity which enabled them to set alight the beast's hair.

The great wolf scrabbled round, finally managed to get its legs under its body, dashed free from the fire's heart. Heedless now of the iron loop holding its jaws, the monster ran. It trailed tongues of flame which grew longer, hotter as the wind of its rushing flight whipped them so that they consumed hide and flesh beneath. Like a meteor the monster went, vanishing from sight in a heartbeat, followed by tiny sparks which winked out as swiftly as the passage of the weretherion. A horrible cry fading from the distance marked its long-deserved death.

"Ferret?!" The shout came from Raker as he at last managed to heave the weight of the dead monster from atop him. Stunned as he had been, the muscular swordsman had needed a few seconds to recover, then shove the carcass off his chest, free his blade.

Those words brought the lone surviving weretherion's attention to him. The beast who called herself Lupe was filled with hatred, frantic with bloodlust and desire for revenge. The slain had been her mate and their offspring. Her keening changed to a growl as she crouched, muscles bunched to spring. Yet she hesitated to attack, though his back was toward her, for the man had the terrible sword whose metal tongue had drunk the blood of her mate, was smeared from quillions to tip with that stuff now.

The hot gaze of the wolf bitch made Raker's neck hair horripilate. He spun from looking at his friend to face the sensed threat. As he did his point came instinctively before him, feet in guard stance.

"Come, wolf-thing," he called mockingly as his pale eyes met Lupe's blazing ones, "I have a special present for you. You hunger for man-flesh, don't you? Well, my blade is thirsty for beast blood!"

The weretherion moved belly-low, creeping forward, preparing to attack the moment she saw advantage. Sword or no, she knew that her reflexes were faster than the human's, just as her nerves and muscles were superior. Once inside the range of the long blade, her teeth would be free to rip, the rapier's greater length a handicap then. Inch by inch she came nearer.

Raker backed, came abruptly against the rock wall. He saw the wolf's skin ripple as muscles bunched, knew she was about to spring, tried desperately to get his weapon set so as to stop that assault short. He was far too busy now to speak.

Just at that moment a pair of objects flashed into the scene before Raker's eyes, struck the crouching beast's flank, buried their lengths deep there in the hard flesh of the weretherion wolf. Lupe's deep growl gave way to a startled yowl of pain. Her spring changed too, its direction now turned aside from the man. Off she went into the darkness, leaving spatters of blood to mark her trail, sending back to the men's ears the yipes which told of her pain from the wounds just inflicted.

"I'm almost sorry for that," Ferret said softly as he listened to the cries fade in the distance.

"Me too. You could have aimed for the heart," Raker called sarcastically. "But thanks anyway for saving my life there. That damned wolf almost had me!"

His friend grinned mirthlessly. "Those were not mere wolves, chum. Look at the size, the teeth. You slew a shape-shifting wolfkin, Raker, a weretherion. The one I sent flying was the 'woman,' Lupe."

"What a vicious bitch!"

"You said it there."

Raker shuddered, face pale. "I hate to admit it, Ferret, but shape-changers of any sort give me the shivering fits. Gods! Beasts becoming like humans are the worst of the lot!"

"Weretherios worst! Man-killers for certain, but otherwise nothing much worse than many denizens of Phæree."

Never having heard before the correct plural usage of weretherion, the gray-eyed swordsman was careful when he responded, "Well, I wish those *weretherios* would stay at home, leave Ærth to men."

That made his companion shrug. "I'd be not surprised if you heard the same thing about humans from many residents of Phæree, yet the two worlds are linked by magickal portals, my friend. We will forever be exchanging residents thus."

"Two at least won't trouble us more, either. That devil that leaped for my throat wanted to reverse such happy circumstance, but my sword deemed otherwise."

"Well, he didn't get to you... did he? You're all covered with blood!"

That made the blond man pause, check himself for wounds, then laugh. "No, nothing more than a couple of scratches from his claws. The blood is that of the dead beast, not mine, chum. The priest wasn't lying about this blade," he said gleefully as he brandished the rapier, danced about the dying fire. Raker was experiencing a sort of counter-shock reaction. "Ya-HAAAH! We cut them down, sent 'em flying!" Then he stopped his victory celebration, looked at Ferret. "How did you know we were about to be attacked? What did you do to...?"

"First I had a dream, old friend. I know that always makes you doubtful, but that's the way it was. In it I saw a woman, was attacked and slain by a wolf. Something woke me from that horrid vision, and I heard a noise, knew that the dream was a warning. Thus I awakened you.

"As for the other, a few tricks with apotropaism and heka, Raker. I sensed that Lupe was no true woman the moment she came near. Her smell was all wrong; her looks and actions and words weren't quite right—almost but not quite."

"You saw her for what she was?"

"Not exactly. The dream guided me to logical conclusions. I spotted her for a shape-shifter though, and because of the scent I thought her a weretherion rather than some other sort. It didn't matter as long as I knew she was lupine. Stupid of her to use that name, wasn't it?"

Raker scratched his beard, looked a bit sheepish. "I suppose it was... but you haven't told me how you—"

"Took care of the other one—and the bitch, Lupe—without a heka-enhanced weapon?"

"Right!"

Ferret smiled, began to gather his things back into their proper place in his bag. "I cheated, you might say—created my own enchantments with a bit of dweomercræft and a dash of apotropaism."

There was a long silence as Raker waited for his comrade to complete his sorting and arranging. "Quit that and explain," Raker finally said.

"Okay, but only if you'll clean that gore from yourself and your sword too," Ferret responded with irritation. "You know I hate that sort of mess." When Raker got his waterskin and a rag, began to wash, Ferret launched into a brief account of what he had done. "The powder was magickal, materia to make fire affect substances not normally subject to that element. I knew I'd have to rely on it for more than smoke of wolfsbane—a mere hindrance, though painful, rather than deadly deterrent. I grabbed the snare wire instinctively for a defensive weapon, and by great good fortune managed to encircle the beast's muzzle. It was a devil of a time keeping it fast and getting the monster into the fire!"

"What about the bitch? You wounded her with your daggers?" Raker was puzzled, for he knew his comrade's dirks were not enspelled.

"Just a couple of my little throwing points, not daggers, my friend. There is a casting which empowers iron nails and spikes against things malign. It is an advanced casting, one I wasn't sure I could manage under the conditions, but you delayed her long enough for me to try. I thought those weapons were sufficiently akin to spikes to serve—as admirably they did! The result is for warding or offense. I, of course, used the pair as missiles, throwing true, for the distance was negligible, the wolf still and unsuspecting, and the flank large. Surprise and fear did the rest. Such a beast surely suffered no more than minor wounds from the two points."

Raker scowled. "We must warn all we meet. That weretherion must be hunted down and destroyed."

"True indeed, though the thought somehow seems repugnant. Never mind." Ferret started to turn away, then looked back at Raker and smiled wickedly. "At least this night proved one thing."

"Indeed? What, may I ask?" Raker recognized that look and was wary.

Ferret waved his hand. "Observe your state of dress—undress, rather. No armor was needed to best that wolf-beast. My opinion on undue armoring stands vindicated."

"Crap! Come here and observe the runnels in my flesh caused by the claws of that devilish brute—better yet, sew up my blouse, it is in ribbons!" He studiously finished cleaning off blood, using the remnants of his aforenamed garment to complete the process. "Had I my armor, friend," he called over to the now prone and covered Ferret, "none of this mess would need tending to now. By the by, have you a spare blouse?"

Chapter Ten

IT WAS JUST after dawn, and the two were mounted, riding from the scene of the fray. After a bit of discussion they concluded that the trio of weretherios had not encountered them by accident. "Sure it is, Raker, just as you say," the lean adventurer concluded, slipping unconsciously into a bit of Kelltic brogue as he spoke. "Those beasts were lying in wait."

"For us, you mean."

Ferret shook his head rode along beside his comrade. "Not likely, is it? I mean, after all, how could they know to expect you and I? No, what I think was that the pack was set here to waylay any travelers appearing to be, well... a threat."

"Armed men. Followers. Trackers."

"Right"

Raker seemed unconvinced. "A company of cavalry from Dertosal on the track of the witchy Neva would have been stopped by three wolves? Weretherios or not, I can't believe that. You say that their wailing muddles men's minds. Fine. Their heka-charged Phæree blood makes them proof against ordinary arms, well and good. No force rides the wilds without some counter to such. You yourself pointed out that there are ever incursions of goblins into our world. Priests and magicians always accompany a force of soldiers, Ferret. How then would those weretherions—weretherios, I mean—have been triumphant?"

"Excellent point, Raker! Let me think.... Waylay or warning, of course! The surviving bitch will be making tracks straight to her master—or mistress. Come on, old rakehell! Let us spur on to Torenegro so as to get there before the bitch's warning has allowed them to fully prepare for our arrival."

The gray-eyed man mulled that over for a moment, reined in, and began to look carefully around. "Come on, Ferret!" He called to the lanky fellow's back. "Stop galloping off, and start searching for sign."

Ferret was there in a minute, saying, "What are you doing now?"

"Making our job easier. You wounded the bitch wolf, and then she ran off this way, right? She's bound to have left a trail of blood, of course!"

"In this terrain? You'll never see anything."

"You're wrong." Raker jumped out of his saddle, got down on his hands and knees, then stood and pointed. "There. Those marks are from her running, and that spot of rusty brown is blood. Maybe you can't track such tiny spoor, but I can."

That statement irritated Ferret greatly. It was a slight to his name; besides which fact he was a better hunter than Raker. He said nothing, though, for he mentally had to admit he had been too busy trying to spot the intangible elements of this problem to consider the prosaic, material ones—that which would aid them here and now. Raker was again mounted, bending low and peering at the ground as he moved his steed ahead at a slow walk. Ferret, still unspeaking, stared at the land ahead. Then he urged the genet to a canter. Even a weretherion wolf had to follow some track; a wounded one must certainly take the easiest and shortest to its destination. That meant no matter how they hurried, the foe would have ample warning. Assuming he was correct, then the route the weretherion took would be a path which led directly to some stronghold in or near the town of Torenegro. Ferret's keen eyes had spotted a goat track going up into the mountainside, a way which seemed to more or less parallel the road, only following the shortest, not the least steep, path.

Raker saw him, shook his head, and went back to his careful examination. "Don't get lost," he called, without looking up.

"I'll see you in an hour," Ferret called back, and he laughed.

It was only about three-quarters of an hour later when Raker came over the little ridge that marked the summit of the old mountain, steed toiling, man with reins in hand, studying the ground. He swore, looked up. Ferret was there, relaxing with feet propped up on a little boulder. "Smart ass!"

"Ain't I, though! Thought for sure you'd spot my mount's tracks, even though I did my best to stay to the far side of the tail."

Raker looked around, went to the north and looked down. There in the big valley below lay the town. The road that they had been following, had deserted in favor of the rough trail, was apparent from this vantage point. It looped around the eastern shoulder of the burg, then continue to curve so as to enter Torenegro from the direction of the sunrise. "This way is five, maybe six miles shorter."

"At least—but impassable to wheeled vehicles and laden pack animals. See the small gate there in the south wall? Herdsmen and some of the locals must use this way from time to time, but only locals know it, so the map shows only the main route. When you began following the bitch's spoor, I figured she'd be likely to take some game trail of track like this."

"So you just rode on up here, checked to see if there were signs of her passing, and rested yourself," Raker murmured in disgust.

Ferret chuckled, arose, stretched. "Well, yes, I guess I did, didn't I? Had to get some satisfaction for your out-thinking me back there. Hey, chum, you could have paid more heed to what I was doing. Don't be sore at me for figuring this out."

"Me, bear a grudge against a pal like you? Ferret, I am shocked to hear you say such stuff." Raker looked sincere, innocent too, as he mentally vowed to get even. "Mount up, and let's get on down there."

"No hurry, Raker. We're sure to lose the sign left by that wertherion down there in the traffic. Besides, assuming we're right, and she entered the town, it will have been in human form. The lot of those shape-shifters probably have a cache of clothing to slip into when needed."

"Point well taken. Lupe certainly didn't have any garments when she attacked and fled in her true form."

They ate some of the hard bread and cheese from their supply of trail rations then, washing the dry stuff down with the sour wine from Ferret's goatskin flask. "Sun's just past overhead," he observed as they finished. "Hot too. Let's take a little siesta in the shade there, and head down in the late afternoon."

"Sounds fine to me," Raker said, heading for the likeliest place to nap. "That gives us just enough time to get to Torenegro before they shut the gates. How do we find her in the town? There must be about six thousand people inside those walls. Even with liberal distribution of coins, it doesn't seem likely we'll find anyone who'll remember her."

"You *are* being astute today, Raker! I'll never accuse you of being all muscle and no mind again," Ferret lied. "Consider this. If there's anything shady going on in a town that size, who's most likely to know?"

"Everybody."

That droll reply made the lean man flinch. "Okay. How about if I put it this way: where would the greatest amount of real information be?"

"Thieves' guild, of course."

"We'll go there. If the culprit who took care of that goldsmith back in Dertosal headed this way, he's here in this town, and the guild will know all about it."

Raker thought to protest. A few coins wouldn't buy them anything in the way of information when it came to the members of such a criminal organization. Then he clamped his mouth shut. After all, both he and his companion were themselves accomplished thieves. Thinking of that, he remembered he had been a belted and spurred cavalier at age 15, the "wonder" son of a petty noble family—a mother and father desiring greater advancement, employing him as their tool. He would rise, become a great man, and after would come his family. Naturally, Raker had rebelled at the prospect, spurred on by all the harsh demands placed upon him. No love, only ambition, discipline, advancement, scheming. At first he had merely been a rover, so to speak. Then he met Ferret. He smiled to himself. How *that* had altered his course!

He knew the cant and the silent signals, could be as at home amongst the hardest criminals as he was mingling with the aristocracy. Ferret had instructed him in much—learned, too, from his pupil. Together they were outlaws of the highest renown in underworld circles, yet they could easily pose as foreign gentlemen, officials, or even nobles in order to work some illegality or other to make a score. What awaited in the rustic community down there couldn't be too challenging—at least compared to some of the adventures he and Ferret had been through.

What was Ferret planning? Raker lay down, pretended to be asleep as his mind sorted through the possibilities. His boon companion had admitted once when well in his cups that he was a bastard, the son of a country squire and a peasant lass. That his father had virtually raped his mother, then thrown her off his lands when he saw she was bearing his child. Ferret had grown up an outcast, dwelling with bands of masterless wanderers, in the slums of cities. Ferret would handle the minor criminals of this little place with ease. The underworld in Torenegro would certainly be wise as to the direction of the wind, so to speak. If there was some mighty plot brewing, the local boys would be alert, ready to take advantage. Now what could the clever fellow have determined already…?

"Wake up."

Ferret came to his feet at those words, blades ready. Raker was looking at him from the other side of his already saddled genet. "I have to take a piss," he called over his shoulder as he walked a little way away. "Saddle up my horse, and I'll be ready to ride in a minute."

"We're going to have to walk our mounts most of the way down," Ferret corrected with irritation, even as he did as his comrade asked.

Ferret was still grumbling when the blond swordsman came back. Raker laughed, took over the chore of cinching the saddle just to make sure, then swung up into it. "A good horseman can make the descent in comfort, old boy. You walk if it pleases you, but I'm going to ride."

Of course Ferret stayed horsed as Raker led the way downward. After a couple of miles the grade was more gentle, and from there on they made much quicker progress. The sun was still visible when they covered the last, level mile of land from the base of the old mountain to Torenegro's walls. Farmers and other peasants leaving the town glanced at the two men, then looked quickly away. Strangers were always trouble, and this pair looked like sell-swords.

"Notice that?" queried Ferret.

"That the locals are wary of us? Sure, but so what?"

"A bottle of the best vintage in the town, Raker, that Torenegro happens to be full of mercenaries right now."

"You're o—Not so fast! No bet, Ferret. That would figure, if there's any truth to what the Colonel de la Cabarro and Intensity Elfuego told us."

A bit disappointed, the lean adventurer snapped, "As you say. Don't use those names again here—unless you want your throat cut."

"Less than I want to stand you an expensive bottle of wine," Raker jibed. Then they came to Torenegro. They barely had room to ride side by side through the unguarded gate. The way opened into a small plaza with three streets leading out of the market, none broader or more auspicious than the other. "Which way, all-knowing one? We could wander 'round, but with but nine days after today..."

Ferret had been surveying the place. "Don't worry about that deadline. We've ample time. Look, up the street ahead, that sign is surely a tavern—yonder is a stable. Let's stall these animals, then wash away the dust in our throats."

The sign proclaimed a wineshop, the Grapes and Barrel. Horses safely boarded, the two entered that establishment, finding it more a saloon than its advertisement admitted. It had a sprinkling of drinkers at tables, a handful of more serious imbibers standing in a clump near the heavy bar. As the pair entered, everyone stopped and stared, then resumed whatever they had been doing.

"Want something?" demanded the landlord as Ferret and Raker halted before his station in back of the thick board where cups and bottles had left a thousand signatures over the years.

"Wine," Raker said, biting back a sarcastic comment he considered in response to the truculent barkeep.

The landlord looked at them for a moment, turned slowly, took up a big, straw-wrapped jug, and from it filled a couple of pottery cups on the back board. He wheeled around, plopped the drinks down without spilling too much of their contents, and said: "That'll be five reals, hombres."

Raker paid over a copper coin, picked up his wine. The knot of men nearby left, heading for an open space near the rear. "Not a very sociable crowd you cater to here," the gray-eyed man said.

Again the barkeep eyed the two. What he saw made him a trifle more friendly, a forced joviality. "No, we don't see strangers here—until recently. You two hombres here to sign up with Grandee Pendeccho, I suppose?"

Ferret looked a bit startled. "Grandee who?"

"PEN-dec-cho," the fat landlord said carefully. "You don't speak Iberian so good, huh?"

"No, I speak it quite well, thank you," the lanky adventurer corrected. "I wasn't listening the first time, and I caught only the last. I thought you'd said—"

The barkeep's laughter cut Ferret off. "Oh, sure! That's okay. A lot of guys call—" Then the fellow recalled that the two were strangers, mercenaries probably, going to serve the nobleman. He shut up and turned a bit pale. "No disrespect for my betters," he finished lamely.

"Where's the grandee's place?" Ferret said with a hard note in his voice.

The fat proprietor tried to smile. "You are about as distant as you can be and still remain inside Torenegro's walls, señor. You see, this place is at the southwest of the town, and the castilla of the grandee is in the northeast, just by the great gate."

"Then we are in the lowest part of Torenegro?"

"By no means!" the landlord protested without much force. "Why just the next street over," he told them, waving toward his right, "is a very den of cutthroats and…" Again he stopped himself, this time trailing off into nothing as he gaped at the narrow stranger. Never had he, Diego, been so foolishly free with his tongue—and with no coins to so loosen it! "No more! If you are seeking information, I am not your man!"

Raker almost burst out in laughter, controlled himself. "What are you jabbering about now, landlord?! It is directions my comrade is asking for, not gossip, eh?"

Diego looked pained, swallowed. "You have what you need, then… unless I may pour you more wine?"

"Drink up chum," Ferret said to Raker, and set the example by quaffing off the contents of his cup, even though the stuff was something between vinegar and grape juice. He set the empty container down solidly, smiled at the barkeep. "Pour, my good fellow, pour! Make it a better vintage, and have one for yourself." As he instructed thus, the dark-eyed adventurer clicked a silver coin down on the battered oak board.

Leaving a happier Diego at his station, Ferret steered Raker toward a nearby table. "This stuff had better be drinkable," he murmured as he sat down and prepared to take a sip.

"Hadn't we better get going? We haven't a single clue as to where to look for Lupe or whomever that monster serves."

"No hurry now. Evening is just the time to make inquiries, so let's enjoy the half-hour we've got. Aaah! Pretty fair!"

Raker tried the wine too then, drinking slowly, savoring the stuff. It was passable. "The 'den of cutthroats a street over'?" When his friend nodded, looking not a little surprised, Raker drank again. The reference by the landlord was said with such emphasis as to have meant only one thing. "You think that the house of the 'brotherhood' is the place where Lupe headed?"

"Not at all," countered Ferret with a relieved expression. "For a moment there you had me worried, Raker! We'll go over to the place just to double-check what I suspect." With that he turned a little to survey the patrons, leaving his comrade to ponder what he knew that Raker didn't.

Of course the swordsman wouldn't ask further. He nodded, looked as sage as he could manage, and likewise observed their fellow drinkers. "I'll be ready with my rapier, old sport, just in case you rub fur the wrong way."

Neither of them liked thieves' associations. Not at all. Both were certainly accomplished in the vocation, knew most if not all of its broad fields, specialities, and odd branches, too. They, like some few others, however, held there to be a considerable distance between those who were employees or agents of an organization and the free spirits who chose to roam about where they saw fit, gaining riches illegally as they went. The former were thought of as second-rate hoodlums hiding behind the facade of a "guild," the latter elite rovers—rascals, perhaps, and rogues—completely *adventurers* in the sense that they traveled, deceived, experimented, gambled, tended toward rashness, and were held by many to be ignoble.

Abandoning the wine shop before darkness fell, the pair strolled in the general direction fat Diego had inadvertently indicated. In ten minutes they had spotted the place he had meant. It was a building whose sign read "Commoners' Liberation League."

"Wretched little dump, that," Raker said in distaste.

"Pay off the common town officials so as to be free to 'liberate' the money of those bourgeoisie and free folk who are spotted as being well off. Same old deal. I wonder how often the top dogs here have to toss the law some wretched member?"

Raker snickered. "Not too often, I'd say. The locals probably get caught in the act often enough to make the watch look like they're taking care of things. I'd hate to be the member who offended the masters, though. 'Justice' is likely to be rough in Torenegro. That's bound to keep the population of footpads, cutpurses, burglars, and robbers to a manageable level!"

"The peasants don't object to the thieves, the aristos are paid off, and the freemen, in the middle as usual, are the butt. Well, serves them right for being so damned money-grubbing." Ferret sounded as if he didn't mean it. He only stole from the very wealthy, rich bankers and merchants, nobles. Ferret looked hard at Raker. His companion looked disinterested. "Onward then, Raker. Let's see who's on duty."

"Sumthin' youse want in here?"

The flat-voiced inquiry came from a flat-faced hulk sitting behind a battered table whose top was empty save for a little bell. Next to the dull-eyed thug a cocked crossbow leaned against the dingy adobe wall. He was playing catch with pair of hatchets, juggling them after a fashion. As he made his inquiry, an ape-like associate, whose beetle brow suited the rest of his physiognomy and physique perfectly, shuffled around behind Ferret and Raker, skulking rearward and hefting a bludgeon whose end was weighted with a spiked ring of wrought iron.

Ignoring the obvious threat, Ferret advanced on the seated giant. "Is it raining outside?"

Flat-face automatically ceased his hatchet play, craned his neck to peer through the door, then caught himself. "Hey, smartass! If its trouble youse want—"

"Never mind that. The trouble we're looking for you can't supply. I'm called Ferret. He's Raker. We're here for information."

The no-neck with the morningstar thought his stealthy movement to get closer to the two was undetected. Neither of the two strangers seemed to notice he was now just two paces from them. The spiked club rested on his shoulder, but he gripped it with both hands. He smiled evilly to indicate to the other man that he was ready.

"Let's cut through the shit. Who is the master of thieves?"

"Huh? You're fartin' in the wrong direction, asshole. Dis here's a legit association fer the betterment of woikin' folks, see? I resents yer woids. Get outta here, and now, else I'll be forced ta trow youse outside on yer arses!"

The gorilla couldn't help laughing at that. "Ya! Right out bouncin on yer skinny lil' butts. Ahee, ahee, ahee!"

Flat-face shifted his threatening scowl from Ferret and Raker to his fellow. "Shaddup, Raoulito!"

"Uh, sure, Jorgal. Sorry. . . ."

At that moment Raker moved right, Ferret left, as the latter said, "Now we're making progress." As he said that he flashed in thieves' sign to the man behind the table, "Life threat. You. Use your wit. Listen."

"He means it, you can be sure," Raker added ominously, using the thieves' cant. "Who is the boss here, Jorgal?"

The flat-faced hulk raised his three-hundred-plus-pound body from his chair. The hatchets he had been holding slammed down on the table. He towered over everyone in the grimy room. He glowered still more, dull eyes narrow. "Dat's it!"

Raoulito took his cue, swung the morningstar, aiming for Raker's head. He knew that Jorgal could crush the skinny guy with his bare hands, and he wanted to finish his man off in a hurry so he could watch the fun.

To his surprise, the pale-haired head he was sure he was about to smash wasn't there. His massive roundhouse blow whooshed through empty air, and his weapon nearly flew from his hands. Apish visage a comic study in consternation, Raoulito spun in an involuntary pirouette. Just before the turn was fully completed, a long blade bit his throat.

At the same instant as Raoulito attacked, the giant launched himself at Ferret. He meant to dive across the table, grab the lean man in his huge paws, and choke the life from him slowly. Outsiders, thieves or no, were fair game, and this was the kind of sport Jorgal relished. Ferret had anticipated just such a move, glad that the giant had abandoned the wide-bladed hatchets in favor of direct contact. The hulking man telegraphed his intent to the keen-eyed adventurer, and as he moved Ferret had already begun his own counter.

The table seemed to soar upward of its own volition. Jorgal impacted its now-vertical surface with a thud, and there followed a crash as table and man tumbled to the floor together. His reaching hands had saved his face and head from full impact, but

Jorgal's nose and lips were mashed and bloody anyway. He was raging as he scrabbled there under the table, grabbing up the hatchets he now wished he'd used in the first place. "Dirty little sonnabitch! You scrawny shit! You rotten prick!" He stopped as he found his weapons. With a heave he tossed the table off of his back, started to get from knees to feet. "Now, you fuc—" Jorgal stopped in mid-threat. Raoulito was lying dead in a pool of his own blood, and neither of the two strangers were in the least hurt. In fact, the blond one's sword was now pricking his side, while the lean man who said he was called Ferret had just placed a pair of long daggers before Jorgal's eyes. One inch, and he was a blind man.

"Drop the hatchets."

"Sure, sure." The two weapons clattered to the floor. "Now what was dat youse wanted to know?"

Chapter Eleven

"WELL, JORGAL?"

The flat-face was covered with sweat. "Hey, youse can't 'spect me to just blab 'bout da organization. Gimme a break, huh? Ain't we brother priggers?"

Raker moved the point of his rapier to the man's groin. "If you're a prigger, I'm a cull, but seeing as how you're not, neither must I be. But—and mark you well, dolt!—you'll be a capon in an eyeblink unless you say the name of the man who is master of thieves here."

"Okayokay! Shit, I thought youse guys was ribbin' me, see?" The glittering tip of the blade swished through the air, and the old-fashioned codpiece of Jorgal's breeks suddenly showed a lateral slash. "It's Xebal!"

"Stop shrieking lies," Ferret admonished coldly.

"Ain't a lie!"

Ferret laughed derisively. "The guildmaster is an Atlantlan prince?"

"Naw, he's an all-right guy from 'round here, see? Xebal is just his name, like… ah… ol' Raoulito over dere, or like youse got—Fairass, right?"

Ferret struck the lantern jaw with the pommel of one of his daggers. "Don't try to be cute, asshole," he grated. "The name is *Ferret*. " Jorgal rubbed his chin, not really much the worse from the blow. The lean man thought at that moment how very glad he was that this giant hadn't managed to come to grips with him. Ferret's face betrayed nothing but hardness, however.

"Got it, Don Ferret. Whatever youse say. But da boss's name is still Xebal."

"Just where is he now?"

The flat-eyes of Jorgal clouded. "He…? Oh, sure, youse mean Xebal," the hulk rattled off the latter quickly as Raker started to move his rapier again. "Da boss is at da grandee's place. Youse know, da big castle what's over to da udder end ah town."

"Your Guildmaster Xebal must be a very important man here in Torenegro," Ferret said with mock awe.

"An' youse is messin' with one of his best boys!" Jorgal nodded. "Da grandee has plans fer da boss, don't make a move widdout consultin' him foist. Say, youse two can join up. I'll square it wid Xebal, so's youse'll get in on da action."

Ferret shook his head. "Nah! We're big-time. This place hasn't got enough in it to make a worthwhile haul." He looked around spat. "No way, Jorgal. Too bad, though, because I was beginning to like you."

"Huh?"

"We aren't going to hang around until your boss comes back. He'll be upset at the mess we made of Raoulito and his floor."

"So what? Youse hate goodbyes er sumthin'?"

"Sort of. We don't leave witnesses, Jorgal. It's goodbye to you. Kill him, Raker!"

Jorgal panicked. "No! Wait! Please!" He was near tears. "Youse ain't heard da good part. Da fac' is pretty soon da Association is gonna be all over da place—all us guys'll be bosses then. An' youse can't get inna action widdout me vouchin' fer ya," the hulk added with a smug finality.

"Horsecrap!"

"Hold up, Raker. Maybe he's telling the truth."

"I am, I am," Jorgal said with fear in his dull eyes.

Ferret slapped the huge man's back. "Sure, pal. But prove it to my friend Raker. Just how big is the Commoners' Liberation Association going to be, and how soon?"

"A prig like me don't know dat kinna shit—'cept dat da boss said alla Aragon an' Mago, an' even Castile inna while."

Raker whistled when he heard that. "No way the Duke of Mago will allow such a thing, let alone the kings of Aragon and Castile. He's lying to save his skin."

"Are you, Jorgal? I'd be very sorry if you were, but I'd still be breathing, unlike you!"

The hulking fellow gulped. "It's all true, honnes' it is! Da grandee is gonna take care of alla it. Don't ast me how, 'cause I don't know. Sumthin' ta do wid him bein' rightful ruler er sumthin'."

"You know, Raker, I believe him." Ferret said. Jorgal sighed in relief as the blond swordsman withdrew his rapier to a more comfortable distance. "What say we check out the story with the grandee?"

"What about Jorgal?"

"He'll have to stay put and be a good boy."

"Youse can count on me!"

Raker smiled. "I'm sure of it."

"Hold. Let's have a drink on it." Ferret set aside one of his dirks, pulled a silver flask from inside his vest, handed it to the giant. "Best Francian armagnac—like brandy," he explained just in case Jorgal didn't know what he meant. "Seeing as how you're our new chum, you get the first swig."

Jorgal unstoppered the flask, sniffed, then tipped it up and drank fully half the contents. After swiping a paw against his mouth, he handed it back to Ferret with a smile. "Hey, dat's pretty goo—" There was thud as the meaty thug hit the ground.

"Goo? Ho, ho! It's goo'night, oaf!" Raker laughed.

"What he swallowed off is enough to make a dozen men sleep for a day," Ferret observed as he replaced the flask, then tucked his daggers into their sheaths. "Considering his constitution, though, I'd say he'll come to tomorrow sometime. Still, that's plenty of time. Let's be gone"

Night had fallen. When they departed from the rundown headquarters of the local thieves' guild, the two used the back way. Once in the narrow passageway there, they followed the crooked route between dilapidated buildings to where the walk accessed a filthy alley. That gave onto a lane in turn, and this enabled them to get their bearings.

"Not bad," Raker observed as he craned to see the sky overhead. "That way is north, and the lane ahead seems to twist generally eastward too as it runs in that direction."

"Let's see for ourselves then, comrade. All we need to do is get to a wall street and we can't miss the grandee's fortress."

Before that transpired, though, their route brought the pair of adventurers into a main thoroughfare, a wider street which was relatively well-illuminated, lined by open shops, and had many pedestrians. Worse, the boulevard angled off to the west northwest.

"We'll not be particularly noticeable," Ferret said after watching from the lane's mouth for a few moments. "Plenty of foreign mercenaries."

"Yah. Too damned many for a little town like this. Something is up for sure."

Ferret nodded, stepped into the light and began walking on, Raker beside him. Nobody paid any attention to them, save for a couple of beggars and the usual shopkeepers outside their establishments trying to drag customers inside. After a hundred paces or so, Ferret said softly, "A brisk bit of trade going on. So far I've counted about two-score locals and twice that number of hired soldiers. It's the latter who are spending. Coin in the purses of common mercenaries means either a successful battle's been fought or some prince has opened a deep coffer."

"Heard of any wars here recently?"

"Nope."

Raker nudged his companion over toward a side street. "Then the grandee's spending a whole lot of money paying men-at-arms to hang around in this dumpy town. That's crazy. This street takes us back eastward."

"So I noticed." They angled off the thoroughfare. There was still a fair amount of foot traffic on the darker street that pointed toward their desired direction. "I also see that we've really blended into things."

"How so?"

"This whole way is full of men like us wearing swords. By the Apis Bull's balls, Raker! There must be a thousand or more soldiers in this godsforsaken town."

The shorter man seemed pleased to hear that. "You're right as usual. Now who is going to notice two more, tell me?"

Ferret didn't respond. There was no need. They continued on, and despite a couple of jogs and a zig away, the street zagged back and brought them to the place they had sought. They left the street, went to a shadowy place and loitered as if in conversation as they observed the castle. Before them was a wide crescent. On the far side of the paved swathe of ground lay a deep ditch with stone scarp and counterscarp, and beyond that the first of two walls. "Big one, considering," the lean adventurer drawled.

"Barbican protecting a single town-side gate with drawbridge and portcullis. First wall ten yards high, second twenty. Flanking towers on the double curtain wall, all outer wall towers and bastions backed by the higher wall's own. The enceinte is large, so there's certainly room inside for several hundred horses and a thousand troops—three times that number by packing them in for a short time. New work aplenty, including ashlar block batters, machicolations, bartizans—new loopholes probably mean there've been casemates recently carved into the walls. With the pierced merlons, shutters, and who knows what else inside, I'd say that they're aiming to make the grandee's castle here in Torenegro one of the strongest fortresses around."

That rapid assessment made Ferret cock a brow. "You know your stuff, my friend. It doesn't add up though."

"I'm not mistaken."

"Didn't say you were, Raker. What doesn't make sense is this fortress. No matter what, it's still just a town citadel, subject to all that entails. Next, it's a stronghold in a small, out-of-the-way community. No real strategic or tactical meaning—unless the Castilians are about to attack this portion of Aragon. That we'd have heard about for sure, and Torenegro would be swarming with royal engineers and troops. The work you mention has certainly been done by the local lord, the grandee whose name we still haven't learned, but even a full-blown duke in this part of the world doesn't have so much spare cash as to do that and hire a small army—or any call to."

"Rebellion."

"With a couple thousand mercenaries and the handful of troops likely to be in regular service to the grandee? Even with all the levies of this area as fodder, the array would be too small to do aught but skulk about in the hills. Once a royal force took the field it would be all over."

Raker tugged his beard. "Our flat-faced pidgeon mentioned Mago and Castille..."

"I say we cease idle speculation for the nonce, what? Care to accompany me for a stroll through the citadel there?"

"Lead on, Ferret—there's a stout heart!"

Laughing together, the two walked toward the townward gatehouse. This first line of defense for the citadel's main gate consisted of a pair of horn towers about twenty-five feet high, tied together with an upper wall above the outer portcullis and gates. Battlements twenty feet above jutted out, leaving space to drop or discharge things downward to the base below. The prow-like turret fronts made assault by battering difficult. The entryway was wide and flaming cressets and glowing magickal lights made the outwork and its vicinity bright. As they neared it, Ferret and Raker merged with a group of singing mercenaries evidentially headed back to their barracks. These were veterans whose garb was not dissimilar to that worn by the two strangers, and the men accepted them readily enough.

"Hey there, bring a bottle back?"

Raker said, "Naw—out of money."

"Well she-it, boy! Jes' like us!" The whole group roared at that witicism. They came to the gate, and the leading man in the little band began singing, "How come they call us sell-swords, when we'll sell anything *but* our swords!"

"HALT! Who seeks entry to the castle of Grandee Armando del Vargos?" The demand was from a soldier clad in chain mail and a black brigandine. The sleeves of the tunic over the mail showed vertical stripes of black and aquamarine. He held a heavy-headed glaive-fork at the ready, but there was no tension in his stance.

"Brave men of the Nubiferous Advance—the light company and scouts for Bassano's Tercio, in case you didn't know!" That made the party break into more guffaws.

The sentry gave them a look of distaste, but lowered his polearm and shouted, "Enter, men of Bassano's Tercio. You are recognized as friends."

"Friends your ass, boy!" someone near the front shouted. "We're the meanest and baddest fighters in the whole land! Give us some of your wine, and we'll tell you some tales… won't we, lads?"

The guard turned away, waving an arm. "If I want to hear fables I'll have my granny tell 'em. She's probably won more fights than you. Now get on into the castle, or else I'll put you all on report."

With a few catcalls and grumblings the near-dozen proceeded on through the passage under the upper floor of the barbican. Arrow slits on the walls and a big, square murder hole in the ceiling showed that contested passage along this way would be deadly. Nobody loosed missiles, and no defending soldier assailed them from above. In ten paces they were out of the tunnel-like place and onto the bridge over the ditch. There was a shoulder-high parapet walling off either side, the stonework creneled. Any crossing of the ditch right or left of this work would expose the attackers' flank to archery.

Ferret pretended to weave, stumble into an embrasure. As he righted himself, the lean man looked down. The stone-faced ditch was at least fifteen feet below, and it contained water, but whether by design or from some recent rain he didn't know.

"You okay?" Raker said as if checking on a tipsy buddy.

Ferret nodded vigorously, as if he were indeed in his cups. "Fine!" Under his breath he murmured, "Deep son of a bitch—maybe twenty feet, but I'm not sure. Water in the bottom."

"Who mentioned water?!" The derisive shout came from one of the mercenaries next to Raker. His voice must have carried.

"Drown in that stuff," another of the soldiers observed. "O' course, could drown in wine too, but who'd mind that?"

Still laughing drunkenly at such a fine jest, the band clumped over the thick planks of the drawbridge and into the entrance of the citadel proper. Ferret and his comrade were now in the lion's den.

Chapter Twelve

ANOTHER COUPLE OF bored sentries, witnesses to the initial check just thirty paces distant, waved the little clump of men through their station. It was essentially a replica of the barbican, only the gatehouse was no isolated work but a part of the outer circle of wall. Neither Ferret nor Raker were surprised when they found themselves in a sunken lane walled in smooth stone as they exited the gateway. The route from outer and inner gates lay some fifteen feet below the earthen fill between the two curtain walls of the fortress, an area called the *lines*, which was a half-bowshot across at this point. Above their heads were yet more ramparts where defenders could rain down missiles upon any attackers who managed to breach the first gatehouse. The way angled upward, but as the lane rose, so too rose the span from cobbles to the base of the crennelated battlements above, so at all times there was a feeling of being hemmed in, trapped. The rather steep incline made some of the drunken mercenaries stagger and pant as the party ascended. "No wonder I like leavin' this place better 'an comin' back," the scar-faced fellow next to Ferret said as he spat. "Downhill all the way to have fun, jes the opposite reportin' for duty."

"Duty?" the lean man responded with an alarm he did his best to hide.

"Well, shit!" the man muttered defensively. "All we got is 'bout six hours before it's our watch. Good as duty, if ya ask me, goin' to quarters fer too damned little sack time."

At the base of the inner wall they had to enter one at a time through the small door in the left-hand gate. There were several soldiers on duty, but they merely jested with the returning mercenaries. "Better shag asses there, boys. Captain Dietzmann doesn't like it when his troops are late!"

"Screw him."

"Screw you!"

"What are you, another Teutonic prick?!"

"I've got one. Have you, dearie?"

"He's lying."

"The captain's busy kissing nobles' asses up in the high hall."

"Where do you kiss 'em?"

And so it went. Security was lax, for there was no threat. The fortified gatehouse was simply a larger version of the outer one. The entrance was below the level of the ground inside, so the lane continued its upward incline as it passed the thirty feet through the construction and ended in the outer bailey. This area was a great yard of rectangular shape. Three sides were porticoed, and underneath their covered walkway were rooms as well—stables, barracks, storerooms. Atop them was an alure, a continuous walkway accessing the casemates in the wall and at various places ramped upward to the parapets at the top of the inner curtain wall.

Across the exercise and marshalling yard was yet another wall, one higher than the other three, for it formed the enceinte of the inner bailey as well as the fourth side of the outer ward. "There's the way we need to go," Raker whispered to Ferret.

"You in the west barracks?" asked one of the soldiers.

That made another pause. "Ya, what unit you guys from, anyway?"

"Lavisor's Banneret," Raker said immediately.

At the same moment Raker responded, "Roybell's Company

"Never heard of 'em," both mercenaries shot back immediately, suspicion beginning to grow. Their pause made their associates turn and begin to gather around the two strangers.

"Not surprising, seeing as how we're brand new to Torenegro," Ferret supplied smoothly. "Say, keep this under your hats, huh? Nobody's supposed to know about the regiment. It's being slipped in bit by bit. Our formations just arrived." At that the others turned and began to drift away toward their barracks.

The initial questioner was still unconvinced, however. "Then where are you quartered?" he demanded.

Raker was getting nervous, but his comrade was expert at just this sort of thing. Ferret reached inside his vest, pulled out a folded paper. "Good question, pal. The major gave me this to deliver to Grandee... del Vargos personally."

The man took a half step back, eyeing the two. "Funny, but you don't look like officers to me."

"Officers? What? Are you trying to be funny?! We're the real leaders. I'm grand serjeant Ferrel, and he's arminger serjeant Rochette—but who the hell are you to be asking us questions?"

The fellow breathed out a sign of released tension. "Oh, sorry serjeant. Corporal Gar*mumble*," he snapped off as he turned and hurried away, ostensibly to catch up with his mates.

"Nice, Ferret, very nice!" Raker said with suppressed mirth. "Did you hear that junior noncom trail off on his name so we couldn't understand it? Great stuff."

"Lax, but shows there's still discipline and lists. Let's see if we can't get through to the inner ward and locate the high hall. That's where we'll learn what we need to know."

Raker shook his head. "Risky, old chum, but it's now your show. Lead on."

Their route was through a great round tower, broad and thick-walled, but not as high as the other similar structures forming the great enceinte walling off the furthest third or so of the citadel from that toward the town. Obviously, the place was the last bulwark against attack. Again the main gate into the tower was shut fast and barred. The lanky adventurer rapped smartly on the little door set in the greater one. A little window with an iron grille over it opened, and a pair of eyes looked out at them.

"Who goes there?"

"Serjeants Ferrell and Rochette of Bassano's Tercio."

The eyeballs rolled. "What business do you have herein?" their owner barked.

"Urgent communication for Captain Dietzmann."

"Dietzmann?"

Ferret let irritation come into his voice. "Yah, like the only one by that name in the whole godsdamned castle. You know, the one in command of the Nubiferous Advance Company."

"Har, har, hah! I love to hear you chumps pronounce the name of that outfit. What a hoot!"

"Ain't it. Are you going to open up so we can carry out our orders now, or do you want to explain to Colonel Bassano later on?"

The little shutter banged shut. There was a rattling, thumps, and a creak. The eyes belonged to a soldier in the black and aquamarine uniform sported by all the regulars employed by the grandee. "Don't smart off to me, merc, or I'll have the officer of the gard on *your* asses. Now get inside so's I can secure this gate again!"

They stepped over the thick portion of the gate in which the door was cut, walked on along the usual passage for such a place. "Thanks, sentry," Raker drawled.

"Up yours—and who gives a buzzard's butt about your colonel?"

The two exchanged glances of amusement as they proceeded, but neither returned the insult. It was a hundred feet through the big tower, but at the far end of the corridor the gate was open and unguarded. Within this part of the fortress there were many more lights. In addition to the usual torches, lanterns and witch-lights there shone brightness from dozens of windows facing the inner bailey. The yard was a trapezoidal space, narrowing toward the northeast. In its center stood the donjon, and they had to skirt that massive structure to see beyond. Across the shortest part was a huge building which had to be the chief hall. Flanking it were several lesser structures of nonetheless considerable height running off at the angle of the wall. Here was the seat of the grandee and all that went with it—guards' barracks, armory, temple, storehouse, and the rest.

"That's the place we want," Raker said as he slowed a bit so as to give them as much time as possible without seeming to be not going about some important business. "Its a massive one. The 'high hall' we heard about will be on the first floor, I'm pretty sure—grandee's personal quarters and those for important guests above that. Where we come in will be all guardrooms and minor chambers, maybe a small audience hall, and the lord's kitchens."

Raker didn't turn as he said out of the side of his mouth, "You hungry?"

"No, just showing off."

"Thought so," Ferret jibed smugly.

"Are you badgering me?"

"Dare you call me weasel?"

Raker persisted. "You suggested I was a glutton, polecat!"

The verbal play made them both relax, so that this last and certainly hardest test they had to face seemed less oppressive. Where the lord of the land abided, the sentries would be alert.

"Here goes," Ferret hissed, picking up his stride and wrapping himself in an air of easy confidence. He went with sure strides up the broad flight of stone steps leading toward the entrance of the hall, a structure whose fortification was less than a castle, but stronger than a palace. At the head of the stairway was a sort of porch, open doors to the interior, and guards with pole-axe-like voulges. Those weapons dropped to bar their progress as the two made to enter.

"Serjeants Ferrell and Rochette of Bassano's Tercio on orders to report to our colonel."

The heavy-headed weapons withdrew. "Pass."

"I'll be boiled in batshit," Raker murmured in admiration, once they were safely out of earshot.

Ferret was depreciatory. "No credit to me. This is a sloppily run stronghold for sure. The head guy here must be really second rate or awfully sure of himself."

They crossed the antechamber, ignoring doors to either hand, entered a deserted hall with a grand staircase. Distant echoes of sound reached them. The lean man was about to ascend when his friend pulled him aside. "Let's try here first." Raker pushed open a door, entered with Ferret at his heels.

"What are you looking for?"

"Something to make us less conspicuous. Our garb is a little rough, shall we say." He slanted across the room, opened another door. It was pitch dark beyond, but it took only a moment for him to find his magicked garnet kept safe in a little box. He flipped open its lid and sunset illumination sprang forth. "Here we are!" Raker had discovered a cloakroom or wardrobe of some sort. "Grab something you like."

Ferret chose a dove-gray cape edged with dark fur of some sort and found a fancy cap which went well with it. He placed the bonnet on his head at a roguish angle, threw arms akimbo to show off the cape. "Suitable?"

"Most," Raker said as he fastened the cloak he had selected. It was a fine garment of black velvet lined with turquoise-hued satin. He tossed it back over each shoulder so as to display the lining. "I believe this is appropriate for an officer of the guards."

"'Pon my word," Ferret said with admiration. "It's probably the commander's own!"

Laughing, Raker pushed his comrade from the closet. "Then I'll lead the way—only I hope you're wrong about it being the top officer's property. If so, we're done before we begin. This will throw 'em off should it be true." He produced a fancy plume he had found in a hat in the wardrobe, stuck it on his own. "Now I'm ready." A glance showed the hall to be empty still, so they exited in haste, went up the stairs looking as important and purposeful as possible. The flight went up beyond the first floor, but the two intruders ascended no further.

Here was a gallery lined with many doors, those at its ends were double. It ran along the central axis of the building's length. "High hall has to be to our right, some grand salon to the left," Raker hissed under his breath. There were armed men at both places.

"Go right then, damnit! Lead the way, will you!" Ferret muttered back.

No longer hesitating, the blond swordsman headed for the guarded twin doors at the right end of the broad passage. His boots made no sound, for there was a thick runner to preclude just such disturbance. He stared at the men on duty as he approached, frowned as if noting something wrong in their bearing or uniform.

Raker would have smashed face-first into the oak panel had not one of the guards jumped to swing it inward. Both snapped to attention as the two strode past them into the room beyond. "Whew!" he breathed once inside.

"This is the high hall, alright," his comrade murmured as they slowed and went from officious to unassuming poses so as to fade into the throng that was there. Throng indeed. The place was huge, broken by columns and buttresses, and had almost as many doors along its walls as did the gallery by which the two had come. Aristocrats in bright costume, begowned ecclesiastics in glittering vestments and plainer ones too, military men sporting an array of a dozen different dress uniforms, merchants and other businessmen in more somber apparel, though costly and indicating great wealth, were everywhere. Hurrying back and forth, coming and going through the many doors, were servitors and pages, messengers and soldiers on duty of one sort or another. To the far left, where the scene was less hectic, and few people stood, was a platform. Upon this dias was a great armchair, a half-dozen lesser seats, and a long table with a handful of occupants around it.

As there were clumps and knots of people scattered along two-thirds of the hall length, Ferret and Raker simply moved purposefully in to their right, pretending to be deep in important conversation. Once away from the main entry, they drifted to where they were sheltered from most observers by one of the massive columns supporting the ceiling high overhead. "I don't like that upper gallery walkway. Some sharp-witted young lieutenant or minor functionary might spot us, but it can't be helped," Ferret said as they relaxed a bit.

"There sits the grandee," Raker said softly as he gestured back the way they had passed. "He holds a strange court this night."

"Aye. I say he's planning, from all those maps and papers spread about. This must be the whole of his following—nobles, clerics, knights, men of money and position. We arrived just in time, methinks. The plot is about to hatch."

Raker stroked his moustache. "Odd that we're here to uncover it because of someone doing in a goldsmith in Dertosal...."

"Too odd by half. Something we haven't discovered is at work in this, but let's bash ahead anyway even as we keep alert for the unexpected element. Come on, time to move." He stepped away from the column, headed to the wall, walked to the far end of the room.

A pair of nervous burghers stood there whispering together in hushed voices. When they saw Ferret and Raker the two were anxious. "Are we to speak with his grace the marquis now?"

"That is his lordship the marquis," Raker responded automatically in a clipped voice. "Better to refer to him as the grandee—or else say the Marquis Penumbratos, or his lordship of Penumbratos," he added in an almost pedantic manner.

"I meant not to offend," said the pudgy fellow, wringing his hands. "Allow me to introduce myself. I am Estaban, a freeholder of some considerable lands and a breeder of fine horses. My associate is Sebastianol, likewise a landlord and rancher. Please, sir, in what way do you address the noble grandee?"

Raker drew up, peered down his thin nose. "I? Usually as Lord Armando, occasionally as Don del Vargos, but that is only when we are alone or in company of our peers. Here? I would bow low and say 'my grand lord of the Penumbratos,' of course."

"Oh, thank you sir...?"

Raker ignored the attempt. "So, Master... Estaban. You will supply the steeds our lord requires, yes?"

"That is why I am commanded here, of course, sir. I fear my available animals will displease his lordship, though."

Raker looked startled. "Do you? What is the most you can furnish?"

"No more than a hundred stallions, although there are ten times that number of geldings and mares."

"Your associate can provide as many?"

Sebastianol dared to enter the exchange. "Perhaps a few more seeing that the price offered is so—"

"Sebastianol!"

"Sorry, Estaban. My apologies, sirs."

Raker looked bleak, and Ferret turned aside a bit as in distaste. "You are correct to apologize, for gentlemen must never speak of money in such a place as this, unless Don Arm—his lordship happens to bring up the subject.

"Now we are doubly in your debt."

"Think no more of it, Master Estaban." Raker made as if to turn and walk away, then paused. "Perhaps there is something you could do for me in return. You see, I am in charge of special security, shall we say. Tell me everything you know about the plan."

Both men paled, but the blond swordsman's commanding stare made them speak, albeit hesitantly.

"I... we know nothing that isn't common knowledge amongst all the better sorts of people, and we say nothing to anyone we don't know," the pudgy Estaban asserted. The hard stare still fixed him. The man looked to his associate, eyes pleading for help.

Sebastianol tried. "We know, great sir, that in the veins of our overlord, the grandee, runs the blood of the ancient rulers of Iberia."

"But of course," murmured Ferret in his ear as if trying to assist the fellow out of a difficult situation. "You need to be more specific in order to please the... noble inquisitor, shall I say?"

At that Sebastianol gulped, and Estaban, overhearing, began to sweat. The latter looked down, then said, "We have heard that his lordship has at last recovered the long lost emblems of empire."

"What?" snapped Raker.

"The ancient enchanted regalia of the the conqueror king which will reunite the separate kingdoms into one mighty empire as in the days of the wars between Atlantal and Rome," whispered Sebastianol in conspiratorial fashion. "Not many who are not nobles know that, eh?"

"No," Raker said unsmilingly, "I would think not. Now what other rumors and information have you? Come, come. Be quick!"

Sebastianol, not wanting to be outdone, told the gray-eyed swordsman, "We know that many of the other great lords around have sworn fealty to our grandee. With the aid of Mago we will soon see the coronation of a new sovereign. Then Aragon will regain Granada, Castille—eventually Leon, Navarre, and even Portugal—as her own. The empire will be restored!"

"Not so loud," hissed Ferret, looking around nervously.

Sebastianol's face fell, and he nodded. "Of course, sir.... But all here surely know—"

"Dare you answer back to your better?!"

"No, no! I—"

Raker came close to the two men, frowned. "As loyal servants of his lordship of the Penumbratos, I forgive you, trust you. But never speak again so openly to another, save the grandee or his highest officers. Of this conversation you must tell no one. Understood?"

Both men were eager to get away. "On our honor," they said almost in unison."

"On your lives," Raker corrected. "I will, naturally, repeat all of this to Lord Armando. Your cooperation and truthfulness will not be overlooked." He was about to say something more, but at that moment a page came near.

The lad was examining the faces of everyone in the high hall, occasionally stopping and inquiring. He looked nervous. When he came to the four of them the page asked frantically, "Are any of you masters the ranchers Estaban and Sebastianol?" Both of the named men responded in the affirmative. "Then hurry now and report yourselves to his lordship. He doesn't like to be delayed, and soon he will want details on horses—you are raisers of horses, aren't you?" The lad was tugging at their arms, so the two ranchers left without any parting words.

"That was most enlightening, my friend," Ferret said when the three were out of earshot. "Excellent performance."

Raker was fidgeting. "Thanks. Let's discuss it elsewhere, shall we? Never did I dream such revelations would spring forth so easily. Here is sedition and treason mixed with lies and legends in a brew bound to foment trouble for all. Should we be discovered here, a quick death would be welcomed, methinks."

"I concur. Those two fools will probably slip and blurt out something about our conversation, too. Back the way we came, and as quickly as decorum allows. Attention is the last thing we need now."

Raker slid his hands along the cloak so as to make its bright lining no longer turned out. Then he and Ferret began to stroll toward the door, speaking in low tones, seemingly paying heed to nothing around save their important conversation. Without seeming to they managed to remain behind a screen of various clusters of folks there, and thus they made their way to the center of the hall and to the exit.

"Out is always easier than in," Raker said as they came to the double doors.

"Quite. Allow me," and so saying Ferret reached toward the nearer handle. Before he could grasp it, though, the portal was opened fully by two guards on the other side, and a woman swept through. It was none other than Neva.

Chapter Thirteen

FERRET AND RAKER froze in shock. Neva in a fancy gown stood squarely in the middle of the wide entry. Behind the beautiful woman who knew them all too well were several armed men, cavaliers of the grandee's court, undoubtedly. She who called herself Lupe was to one side, nearer, dressed as if she were a lady in waiting.

Neva's big blue eyes opened wide, assessed what she saw. Her delicate, childlike face showed not a trace of a wrinkle even as she cried in a surprisingly loud voice, "Spies! Take them!" One bare, milk-white and rounded arm pointed toward the startled pair, as Neva's dainty finger swung right and left so as to leave no doubt as to whom she referred.

"Holy shit—it's that witch!" exclaimed Raker.

"Run!" screamed his comrade, grabbing Raker and yanking him rightward. Ferret's long shanks were already moving him at considerable speed toward the least-crowded area of the huge chamber. Before he had taken three more strides, both of his long daggers were in his hands.

There were shouts of alarm and the clatter of running feet as guardsmen rushed to take stations along the overhead galleries to either side of the hall, ran to seal exits and protect their lord.

When he saw where the lean man was heading, Raker thought for an instant that Ferret had gone mad. Then he realized that this was no panicked flight but a planned act. Once past the portion of the hall nearer the main entrance, there was nothing between them and the dais except a handful of men and a dozen scattered guards. The latter were converging on the grandee, trying to form a human wall to protect him. This rush had already created chaos as the others there sought to get away from the place. A bystander was cut down by an overeager halberdier, and two of his fellow guards were down in a tangle of arms and legs brought on by collision with none other than the pudgy rancher,

Estaban. Raker's sword came hissing from its scabbard as a soldier came at him with a leveled voulge.

As the spear-like end of the heavy-bladed weapon pointed at his heart, the blond swordsman shifted his weight to the right, moving aside a fraction thus, twisting his body in such a fashion as would bring an "olay!" from the spectators in a bullring. "Hah!" Raker cried as the voulge and guardsman brushed past, and his rapier cut the man deeply across the back of his unprotected thigh. The fellow tumbled down. He won't trouble us further, thought Raker as he leaped onto the low platform.

Ferret was there on the raised portion of the long hall ahead of him, twin poniards flashing. Fully a half-dozen guardsmen were barring his path, but the lean adventurer was too fast for them. Inside the reach of their pole-arms, the daggers wrought terrible execution. Helmeted in morions and partially armored with full steel cuirasses with armguards and greaves, and mesh of mail too, the soldiers were protected over much of their bodies from missiles and most blows. At close quarters—and Ferret was close—the exposed areas made the guards as vulnerable as any unarmored man, and their heavy plate and chain links slowed them. Face, throat, armpit, buttocks. Nobody who saw his work could believe the thin combatant could move so fast, attacking with left and right hands with equal precision and speed. Two of his foes were dead in the space of a few heartbeats, two more wounded and crumpling.

"Stop him! He's going for the marquis!" a tall cavalier cried out as he interposed himself between the oncoming Ferret and the big chair in which the grandee still sat. The courtier had his sword drawn, ready. His name was Don Javier. He was a blood relation to the grandee, and alone stood between Grandee Armando del Vargos, Marquis of the Penumbratos, Lord of Torenegro and the desperado with blood-dripping blades who seemed unbeatable. Courtier or no, Javier was brave.

Coming on Ferret's heels, Raker had a clear opening onto the dais, for none of the soldiers to either side had yet had time to react. Some were attempting to plug the gap in their line, others were now beginning to fall back to guard their master. As if to further the bedlam and confusion, buzzing quarrels from arbalests discharged from the galleries above began to crisscross the area. Most buried themselves in the planks of the dais's floor or bounced and ricocheted harmlessly off. Most. Here a stray bolt pierced a bystander's leg, there one left a red runnel along another's cheek. A particularly poorly aimed quarrel thudded into a guardsman's shoulder where solid plate and chain armor met, while another bolt, almost as ill-sent, pinned a soldier's hand to the shaft of his voulge. Both soldiers were out of the contest. Raker was two long strides onto the platform when the hail of missiles began. He crouched, knocked aside a thrust from a nearby guardsman's weapon, slashed at him to force him back, darted past. "Ferret!?"

"Left!" His comrade shouted back without turning. Ferret had his hands full with the courtier, as the fellow was a superb fighter. It required all of his skill to ply his pair of daggers to keep the aristocrat's long blade from running him through. He didn't concern himself with Raker, knowing his ability in such a melee, and trusting his friend to stay close. When the courtier extended himself in a lunge, Ferret caught the blade in the guard of his right dagger, twisted and raised his arm, and sprang in. He brought his left weapon in a roundhouse swing as he closed, and the steel hilt smashed against the side of the aristocrat's head. "I'll kill you another time," Ferret panted as he continued on past the stunned fellow. A shove sent the dazed man stumbling toward a knot of advancing guardsmen, and Ferret was away. A bolt knocked the fancy bonnet from his head, but the lean adventurer hardly noticed.

"Help!" cried the frantic nobleman as he saw the lanky man with gory poinards defeat his nephew, Don Javier. He was already on his feet, and with a desperate effort made off at best speed for the door nearby.

Their lord's sudden flight made the guardsmen crowded along the galleries halfway up the high hall's sides cease their shooting for fear of striking their master. Ferret had in fact counted on just such a thing, although proximity to the marquis rather than the movement of the man had been his objective. Seeing that there was no hope of taking the grandee hostage, Ferret simply stayed on the fleeing man's heels. Lord del Vargos had at least five steps' lead, though, and the nobleman was but another five from his goal.

Raker saw what was occurring, guessed what his companion was thinking, and realized that the grandee would get through the door and be able to bolt it fast behind him before Ferret could reach the portal. There was another door only a few feet to the left of the one for which the grandee was reaching, so Raker jogged aside, lunged for that one. "Come on, Ferret!" he cried as he managed to get the heavy door moving inward. He leaped ahead, moved so that he was at the back side of the thing.

A quarrel clattered on the stones just inside the door. A split second after it came Ferret. "Slam it!" he gasped. Raker threw his weight against the wood, and the door banged closed. "No bar!" his frantic comrade cried. Ferret slammed his twin dirks into the planks, reached with now-empty hands for his throwing blades.

Without hesitation, Raker had meanwhile backed to set his square shoulders against the wooden portal, bracing himself for what was to come. There was a great thump as a couple of soldiers threw themselves against the door. It moved an inch or two, then the pressure of the blond man's legs and body slammed it back against the stone jamb again. "Hurry up!"

Ferret had a short, thick throwing knife in each hand. "I... am... HURRYING!" he shouted the last as he drove the right-hand blade head high into the wooden frame. Then in a swift motion, he stooped and sunk the other deep in the oak at his knee. "That'll hold for a few seconds, let's—ah *crap!* "

"What's wrong?"

"Nothing but stairs up. That's a crock of shit for sure," Ferret bawled, but despite his great displeasure at what he discovered he didn't hesitate. He began racing up the steps three at a time.

Raker came after, managing the climb as quickly as did his friend. "What's wrong with up?" he managed to pant.

"There's a godsdamned company... of crossbowmen... and no way out... that's what!"

"Windows?"

"Jump down that far?"

"Well..." Raker thought of the deep ditch, all the unyielding granite, and ceased speaking.

They were evidentially on a private stairway, probably one used mainly by servants. As Raker spoke the last word they came to a landing. The flight continued upward. He paused, but Ferret went on dashing up the steps. Raker had to extend himself to catch up. Neither was saying more for two reasons. First, they didn't want to alert anyone not already aware of it that they were here. Also, both men needed to save their wind. Running up stairs after a desperate dash and fight was demanding in the extreme.

"Now we... duck away," Ferret muttered between gasps of air. There were yet more steps upward, but this third-floor landing was as high as he wished to go. He jerked the door there open, sprang into the hallway beyond with blades again ready. Raker likewise came through the portal with rapier high. No foe was there to assail them.

"I hear voices, shouting."

"They have raised a hue and cry throughout the whole building," Ferret snapped. "We're trapped here, too, for if we couldn't leap from the story below, this one is certain death. Let's move!" He trotted down the hall, trying to use the muted cries to guide them toward the least-populated portion of the huge structure.

Raker heard calls and the sound of running feet behind then and instinctively ducked into a narrower side passage. He was now leading, Ferret coming behind quickly. The blond swordsman ignored the doors immediately to either hand, went on a few more paces to the one at the far end of the little corridor. "You'll love this," he called softly over his shoulder as he stepped ahead.

The dim light was gone as Ferret shut the door quietly behind himself.

"I do indeed," Ferret agreed as he felt his way forward, then followed his comrade down the cramped spiral of steps Raker had led him to. "Sometimes sheer luck can succeed where all the intelligent planning in the world fails."

They were going very slowly now. The darkness and wedges of stone disallowed haste, demanded one step at a time, so with right shoulders rubbing the wall Raker and Ferret wound their way back toward the lower floors of the great building. After a time it became apparent that the shaft was one that had no egress to the second or possibly even the first floor. Raker brought forth his magicked stone again, and by the light shed from the garnet in the now-open box, they moved more quickly down.

When he realized that they were about level with the high hall and still no sound of pursuit came from above, Ferret spoke. "I repeat, luck!"

"You imply you had a plan? Well, my skillful leadership is saving us from that disaster."

"I think I had better move to the fore."

"Don't try it, stoaty. I'm in charge now." Raker took the steps more quickly to prove his mastery, then slowed. "The wall here is damp," he hissed.

The lean adventurer peered closely, saw condensation on the stones. "We're below ground level. This might be one of the grandee's escape routes."

"I told you my ability would get us out of the mess you made," Raker taunted. As if to belie that boast, the spiral suddenly ended in a little room. The place was bare and empty, save for an iron grate on the floor. That grate was padlocked. "Oh-oh!"

"Stop staring at that drain and shine the light on the walls, Raker!"

He did so, and when the red beam played upon the furthest it revealed two doors opposite each other at the corner angle. "I knew there'd be some way out."

"Sure thing. Try the left, I'll take the other."

"Locked," Raker reported.

Ferret found his to be likewise held fast. "Pick the lock, quickly," he commanded as he bent and began to work on the one before him. He used a small tool taken from inside the top part of his boot. He inserted, poked, twisted, jiggled. He felt three tumblers drop, then he turned the metal bar and the lock's bolt clicked back. Ferret eased the door open a crack, sniffed the air, then shut it again.

"Got it," Raker said in triumph as his companion turned to assist him.

"Gently," he hissed as Raker began to swing it inward. "Test the air, listen." Both men did so, that being their only recourse as the way beyond was pitch black. "Close it, but don't relock it. I have a better plan."

"Not another one!"

Ferret's voice was a rasp as he said, "Don't be an ass. Shine the beam on the grate again. Let's see what's below it. When his comrade did so, the lean man smiled. "Look you, there's some sort of tunnel not ten feet below. There's our way out!" He used his pick and had the big padlock open in a trice. "Move the grating aside just far enough to enable us to slip past it."

As Raker heaved and brought the iron crossbars up and to one side a bit, Ferret carefully placed the open padlock in his belt, hasp hooking outward.

"How's that?" asked the blond man.

Ferret paused, peered upward. "Ssshhh. They're at the top of the stairs. Down you go, lad, be quick!"

Without any hesitation, Raker dropped to the floor, set his witchlight on the floor, swung his legs into the opening, lowered himself until Ferret could see only his fingers, then dropped completely from view. A muffled bump indicated he had landed below.

"All right?"

"Peachy," came the soft reply from the shaft.

Ferret was moving as swiftly as he could. The sound of descending men was plain to his ears now. He fell prone, sent the box with the glowing stone down for Raker to catch. He did, for in a second the red ray was shining up on his face. "Look out, here I come." The lean man slid over the edge and was down lightly at the bottom in a single motion. "Set the light on the floor, then give me a leg up, fast! The pursuit is nearly here."

"What the—"

"Just do it." Raker locked his fingers together, and Ferret's foot seemed to appear in them instantly. Then he was standing on the blond man's broad shoulders. "Steady now. Ah, just as I'd hoped."

Sudden great weight pressed down on him, and Raker almost staggered. He steadied his legs, reached up quickly to hold on to his comrade's.

"Thanks!"

Then Raker heard a metallic clunk and the pressure was relieved. There followed immediately a slight rattle of metal on metal and a loud snap.

"Let go, damnit!"

Raker took his hands from Ferret's legs, and his friend leaped clear, silencing his fall by using Raker to slow the descent. "What did you do?" the shorter man asked.

"Replaced the grate and padlocked it again—quietly, too. It was when I had to pick it up and lower it down that you almost lost your balance. Now they'll think we went through one of those doors and never think to look for us down here where we've escaped!"

As he stooped and picked up the dim little witchlight, Raker said, "Lost the pursuit, you mean. Escaping remains to be accomplished."

"Quit bitching and let's get away from where we can be spotted. There are a half-dozen guardsmen up there just about to come off the stairs."

Chapter Fourteen

THE TUNNEL WAS four feet wide, twice as high at the center of its arched ceiling. There was a small stream trickling along the stone floor, and where the blocks had settled stood shallow pools of stagnant, slime-filled water. It stank. Ferret had led them along the flow.

"We are proceeding downward at only a very gradual angle," Raker said after observing the slow trickle. His comment came in a whisper. Any loud sound sent disquieting echoes reverberating along the passage. Both men continued to step cautiously, almost tiptoeing as they had done initially to make sure the searchers didn't discover their ruse. "This isn't an escape tunnel, it's a godsdamned sewer!" Raker had just noticed where a waste pipe emptied into their passage.

"Can be one and the same, chum. Uh-oh."

"What's 'uh-oh'?"

"Don't you hear it?"

"No, what?"

Ferret's senses were far keener than average, better even than his blond companion's excellent ones. Sometimes he forgot that normal sight or hearing or smell did not allow others to detect what he could. "There's a bigger flow up ahead. I can hear water moving. Ugh! Now I smell it. It's not a mountain freshet, old boy."

After a few more paces Raker began to note what his companion had sensed. He used the witchlight to probe the blackness ahead, but the rubine beam showed nothing until they had walked another fifty or sixty feet. Then its light showed a portcullis-like grate barring their path. "It figures," Raker muttered in disgust. "Let's try the other direction."

"Ah, don't bother. I'm pretty sure that all we'll find is a dead-end tunnel into which pipes can empty. We're going the right direction."

"Right? Up and out is right. Maybe the other end has a shaft to the surface."

"Doubtful, Raker. We came in by what seems to be the main service entrance to the system."

"Well then we either have to remove the minor obstacle in our path or else go back up the way we came down."

Ferret went to inspect the grating. He kept at a distance, for such an obstruction was likely to have magickal deterrents of nasty sort. Not only were the bars there to prevent tunneling besiegers from entering, but it also served to keep certain things dwelling further below ground from doing likewise. There was a labyrinthine system beneath, and most of what lived there could be viewed as dangerous to life and limb. The lean man frowned, made a couple of passes, and murmured a series of strange-sounding words. "Let's see if that hasn't taken the stings from it. Grab hold of the chain there, Raker, and see if you can't raise the thing."

"Me?" Raker eyed the bars, shrugged, and grasped the rusty links of the chain which hung in a loop near to him. Somewhere above the tunnel's roof was a system of pulleys, gears, and counterweights which would enable the grating to be raised and lowered by this means. "Uff! Won't budge."

"No wonder," Ferret said as he surveyed it from closer range. "Sliding bolts need be withdrawn first. See the place there? Right at eye level next to you, chum. Just grab that and pull it back, then cross and do the same over there," and he pointed to the second opening in question.

Without letting loose of the chain Raker shook his head. "I'll haul away on this when you've drawn the bolts, weasel."

"Coward," Ferret spat. He gingerly reached in and felt for the handle of the horizontal rod of metal that doubly locked the portcullis in place. When his hand touched the big ring he winced, but no terrible result occurred. "There! Nothing to it," he said with relief evident in his voice. "Next time perhaps you'll trust me."

"Not likely, chum. A wizard you're not. Now quit preening and pull the other pin. We'll be here all night otherwise."

Ferret grinned at him, stepped across, nudged Raker aside a little, and heaved so as to draw the bolt. Blue sparks danced on the grate, and the lean man let out a squawk as he was thrown down on the seat of his pants. "Arwan's ass! That discharge almost stopped my heart!"

Raker was laughing. "How's your own ass, Ferret? You sat down pretty hard—heh, heh, heh!" He chuckled. "Try to get me to test for that sort of thing for you, ah? Well, as I said, my friend, your skills at manipulating magicks might need some upgrading."

With a wooden face and great show of mettle, Ferret arose, grabbed the metal loop once again, and released the pin by tugging back the rod. Nothing happened, save for a rusty squealing of metal and a slight rattling of the bars. "Be so good as to now perform your part of the work, Rake."

"Up she rises," the muscular swordsman grunted as he used his weight to haul away on the chain. Every yard or so of links which Raker pulled down moved the heavy grating upward by only an inch, so it was heavy and rather long work before the long-spiked bottom of the bars was brought a couple of feet above the conduit's floor.

"Hold there," Ferret commanded.

Although he stopped his work, Raker was all for raising the portcullis higher. He watched his comrade crawl under the deadly points of the grille, not letting loose of the chain. "I'll pull it a bit higher for myself," he announced.

"No. We might have to return this way and return the bars to their former position. Just go under as I did." Ferret didn't say so, but he was thinking of what nasty things they might encounter on the far side.

Raker made a sour face but loosed his hands and with an easy motion dropped prone and rolled through the gap. "Slime or no, a bit of ordure is preferable to being skewered by those spikes!"

"Bah! The gate is held firmly in place until someone on the other side drags round that chain to shut it."

THLANGGG! Chita-chita-chita-ch-ch-ch-chang. Shhh-WHUMP! The first metallic sound was removed, muffled, but the dissonant clatter of the wildly whirling chain gave it meaning. Both men were well away from the partially raised portcullis when it plummeted closed. Reverberations of metallic protest played along the passage, making their ears tingle.

Ferret stared in shock at the bars. "How in the hells?"

"Good call, Ferret," his companion said bitterly. "That could have happened while I was crawling under it!"

Tinkling laughter came down to play over them. "True, Raker-the-Lucky. I had hoped to do just that." It was a woman's voice, Neva's.

The two began to back slowly from the fallen portcullis, keeping a wary eye on the place beyond. No one was to be seen.

"You wonder where I am, don't you? Did you think that I could not divine your location? Stupid little men! And foolish Ferret. Thought you not that there was access to the mechanism raising and lowering it. I am there now, and the guardsman with me knocked free the ratchet at my command."

"Big deal, Neva you bitch!" Raker shouted back in defiant anger. "You missed me again—and by a long way this time!"

"Save your breath," Ferret advised in an undertone.

"No need to whisper—I can hear and see you." Neva's sweet-sounding mirth sounded again. "He's right, you know, Raker. You both had better save your breath, for you'll not give up easily, I'm sure."

Ferret cleared his throat and spat. "Give up? Hells, witch. We're here and that which bars our way back stands immovable between you and us. See you around... and thanks!"

"Don't be so quick to thank me, Ferret. "There's no way for you now but down, you see. And just in case my little spell and the noise just then weren't sufficient to call attention to your arrival to those who lurk below, well—watch your feet!" She laughed viciously now, the horrid sound trailing to silence as if she was moving away from her overhead niche above the ceiling stones.

"Feet?" Raker peered down, rubbing the back of his rapier-holding hand against his cheek. "Befouled but sound. . . . "

The lean adventurer sniffed the air. "There's a new stink, Raker. Blood! Our red-hued light won't show it, but I think Neva meant for us to observe the runnel there at our feet."

"Blood?"

"They must be sending it down through the drains. Its reek will draw who knows what manner of foul scavengers."

"Then let's head to the right, up this tunnel rather than down where the gore runs."

His comrade shook his head. "No good. It's surely but another dead end—or barred along its way like the passage we just left. We would then be trapped for sure. Our only chance is down."

"Some chance! Neither of us are delvers." What Raker said was all too true. Both had explored a cave or two, even been in the upper, so-called Shallowshadow subterranean maze once, perforce. Now they were about to have no choice as to a second such sojourn, it seemed. Inexperienced, ill-prepared, and lacking equipment, they had to attempt it.

"Don't worry, if we can get down and to someplace where there are branching passages we'll be able to work our way back upward again. There we won't be in a cul-de-sac, either."

Biting back a foul remark, Raker turned from the iron grillwork and began trudging along at a brisk pace, red witchlight waving into the gloom before and one eye cocked so as to avoid stepping into the now-broad channel filled with sluggishly running waste and flavored with blood. The tunnel was wider than the one from which they had come, and a little higher, its bottom concave to provide for flow. The slippery slant made movement on the sides difficult, and after any distance it would prove tiring. Besides, a misstep might send one tumbling and offered opportunity for injury.

"Damn you, Ferret," Raker grumbled as he gave up and went splashing into the center where the going would be a little easier and a lot safer. "Ugh! Piss! Shit!"

"To name just a few of the ingredients," his lean comrade responded as he, too, took to the middle portion of the passage. "But what's the crap about damning me? You wanted to get into the castle as much as I did."

"I didn't even want to go to Dertosal."

"Then you shouldn't have screwed up back in Puertal Mago!"

"Who said 'Let's go to Mago' in the first place?" Raker used a high, effeminate voice to underscore the quotation.

Ferret in turn used a scathing tone as he rejoined, "Was it the asshole who got us hooked up with that Lybbosian conjurer?"

"Hey! We made a—" He cut himself short seeing his friend suddenly yank a pair of throwing points from his vest, body tense. Raker stopped his slogging and stood stock still, holding his breath to get as quiet as possible.

From somewhere ahead came a wet, snuffling sound. That nasty noise was followed in the space of a few heartbeats by a faint rattling and a clicking. "Company's coming," Ferret mouthed. "Looking for the source of the blood."

"Swell," Raker whispered back, drawing his sword as silently as possible. "Let's rush whatever the hells it is and get it over with."

"Not so fast! Maybe I'm no wizard as you say, but I think I can get us an edge." He was about to try something when a deep bellow came booming up the tunnel, accompanied by the sound of many feet running through the wetness. It seemed that whatever had come calling had a plan similar to Raker's own.

Chapter Fifteen

THE MATTER WAS decided, of course. When the thing charged, Ferret had no time to employ any special magick or other sort of complex heka casting. His keen eyes saw a dark shape rushing toward where he and his friend stood. The two steel blades he held were launched in near-simultaneous flight. Without waiting to see their effect, the lean adventurer drew his long daggers, and only then tried a desperate dweomer.

Raker was able neither to throw any missile nor to employ both hands in a melee. He held the only source of light. Without the dim red rays of the enchanted light the two of them would be lost. He wished now the box was set in a band round his forehead or otherwise secured so that he could use his familiar main gauche with the rapier. The sword alone would have to suffice, so he assumed a fighting stance, aimed its length toward the fearsome sound coming up the passage, and pointed the witchlight there to allow them whatever advantage that illumination might provide.

Just as Raker readied for the onslaught of the subterranean carnivore coming at them voicing its ferocious snarls, Ferret tried the only thing he could think of to aid them in this desperate situation. He rapidly repeated a couplet as he willed energy from himself into the enspelled garnet.

Both men were startled by the effect of that casting. The rubine beam changed in an instant, grew stronger, and its light changed from the dim red to which they had been accustomed. It now blazed forth in a white violet which made their eyes smart and water. The effect had far more impact on their foe. The charging monstrosity hauled up short, crouching and snarling not more than a half-dozen paces distant. What a thing it was, there revealed in the harsh glare of the reversed-spectrum witchlight.

If in nightmare the fevered mind of the sleeper combined the forms of such terrors as a mad mastiff and an attacking adder the monstrosity before them might begin to be explained. It was as heavy as a black bear, but its six legs were stumpy and its bristled body long and low. Waving wetly in their direction was the thing's proboscis, a trunk-like snout as long as a man's arm and thicker through than Ferret's own waist. That snout ended in a sphincter-like orifice filled with a double ring of shearing teeth, and that disgusting mouth dripped thick saliva as the trunk which bore it waved this way and that, questing for prey. Behind the proboscis was a huge head displaying four putrid yellow eyes in a line above its snout, those organs now weeping matter as the light struck them. It had fan-like ears which stood out and up, unfolded so as to catch the slightest sound. Set all round its neck and shoulders were a bristling growth of spikes like those of a hedgehog, and the ugly body showed a mangy coat of corpse gray which sported patches of these same short quills. A maroon streak of the thing's weird blood indicated that one of Ferret's knives had inflicted a negligible wound on its flank. The second point could be seen caught harmlessly in the bristled protection of its mane.

"What the fuck is that?" Raker whispered in shock and revulsion.

"Nothing I'd bring home as a pet," Ferret replied laconically. "The light has it confused, chum. You know what to do."

The blond swordsman knew, all right. He sweated in nervousness, not fear. It was kill or be killed now, and his part was the critical one in the drama of their attack. Raker watched, tense and ready as his comrade began to inch sideways so as to get as much distance between them as possible. The horrid ears twitched in response to the movement, and the snout curved to point at the moving man. One foreleg raised slowly, as might a big cat's as it prepared to charge. Raker saw that the limb had two claws and three sucker-like pads behind.

Despite the painful outpouring of radiation the beast felt, it was hungry and determined. It could smell the rich aroma of flesh and blood, feel the warmth of the two food sources before it. Soon it would satisfy its belly in a delicious feast. Wincing, not willing to close its eyes to escape the great discomfort, it used its oculars in separate pairs to fix the locations of the two radiant heat sources as its ears twitched to triangulate the place of the moving prey. Just a fraction closer, and it knew it could take that one in a single instant rush.

Ferret wished for a bow or even a pike. The pair of dirks he held were far from what he wanted to employ against the monstrosity he faced. To close with that thing was inviting a horrible death, but foot-long daggers demanded he do just that. "Hee-yah!" he cried loudly, swaying his upper body forward as he shouted, arms shooting ahead and crossing in the process.

That triggered the creature's attack response. Its bunched muscles released as would a spring, and it shot ahead on six churning legs. Its foe was fast, though. As its snout lashed out and its circular maw bit, nothing save empty space was there. No, not quite. Scissoring blades had flashed in the space a fraction of a second. The monstrosity bellowed as it felt the two deep slashes on its leathery proboscis. It came on, slowing not in the least despite the defense displayed by the prey. It knew such small wounds would heal quickly.

"Mangy monster!" Raker shouted as he lunged. He sank the point of his sword deep into the thing's side, jerked back as quickly so as to avoid having the weapon torn from his grasp. The attack elicited another roar of pain, brought the creature instinctively to a spinning turn so as to face this sudden threat. "Eat this, you filthy bastard!" Raker cried aloud once again, driving the point of the rapier toward the eyes behind the weaving snout that now moved toward him.

The beast was too quick, and the thrust missed. It now sprang toward Raker, but that attack was thrown suddenly askew by the weight of Ferret upon its back. Bristling spines or no, the lean adventurer had hurled himself on that elongated torso, and he meant to stay. Both daggers were buried to their hilt in the monster's shoulders, and with hands holding fast to hilts, legs gripped and squeezing tight around the belly, Ferret rode the beast.

Middle pair of legs notwithstanding, the creature wasn't built to bear such a burden, Besides its feral brain was flooded with rage at the attacker which harmed its body, and which further dared to cling to it. The monstrosity flung itself on its side, then rolled to crush beneath it the foe on its back.

Their attack hadn't been planned this way, of course. Neither man was capable of predicting such an encounter. It was a matter of opportunity, skill, and cooperation. As the beast thrashed wildly to free itself of Ferret, Raker stabbed and slashed and stabbed again with his rapier, The point punctured the beast's chest, its edge brought a gaping wound to the exposed belly, and then the length of the sword was buried in the thing's awful snout. Terrible teeth clashed against metal as the muscular ring in which they were set clamped tight. The hilt of the rapier was jerked from Raker's hand in a flash.

Raker fell back, managing to avoid the frenzied flailings of the beast. The sword had penetrated the length of the snout, passed along the gullet at a gradual angle, and transfixed the six-chambered heart inside the barrel chest. Nevertheless, the monster died slowly, and its death throes were terrible. When the convulsions ceased Raker moved closer, playing the beam of light over the still-twitching corpse. "Ferret. Ferret! Are you alive?" There was real fear in his voice as spoke.

"If you call this living," came a croak from ten feet away. Ferret hauled himself up from where he had been thrown into the stream. "When you managed to strike a mortal blow, Raker, that thing convulsed so that it tossed me here… into the shit, so to speak." He was wiping away muck from his soggy leather garments as he said the last.

"Out of the shit, you mean," his friend countered with a grin of relief. "You seem unhurt."

"In, out. All I know is that I'm covered all over with nasty ooze and bruises beneath. That godsdamned devil weighs a ton! Lucky for me there were few of those spines where I lay and this leather's so tough, else I'd be a pincushion right now."

Raker kicked the disgusting body. "Sorry you got the brunt of it, chum. Be glad it's only bruises. Hey, stop scraping that stuff off yourself and give me a hand, will you? It's still got my sword in it, and what if there's a another like it coming?"

That made the lanky man cease his fussing and hasten to his friend's side. "Morrigu! What a maw on the filthy thing. Those nasty teeth are still locked fast on the rapier's blade. What a stroke to send it down that trunk—how did you manage?"

Raker ignored the question, tugging at the hilt of the weapon. "Can you loosen the teeth while I pull?"

Ferret looked, nodded, and bent over. The beast was lying on its left side, and one of his daggers protruded from the right shoulder. Tugging it free, Ferret wiped the blade on the thing's horrid hide, then moved to its fore. He slammed the pommel of the weapon against the base of a couple of the triangular teeth. One broke. He hammered several more times, and this resulted in knocking out or shattering a few more.

"Leave off and let me see," Raker instructed. Ferret stood up, and the blond man yanked with both hands. A tooth splintered and the blade came free, withdrawing with a wet scraping. Following that came forth a weapon almost as deadly as the blade. It was the thing's horrid tongue, pointed and horn-like, showing protrusions like a wood rasp. "That'd free flesh from bone!"

Ferret spat. "Gods, man! That tongue could pierce leather and muscle, too. It's a weapon worse than those teeth!"

Raker hacked down and severed the appendage. "I want some small trophy from this kill," he murmured as he rinsed the ugly thing, then tucked it, still dripping, in his belt. Blood of dark hue and disgusting odor came running forth from the leathery snout, trickling downward to merge with the sewer's main stream. "Maybe that'll discourage any fellow horrors that think to make us prey," Raker mused as he stared at the gore.

"I can't fathom you somethime. The tongue! To each his own, but do stop staring at the thing, and clean your blade, old boy. That's a most precious weapon you bear!"

His comrade used the beast to cleanse the worst of the mess from the rapier just as Ferret had done with his dirk. "Don't credit too much to heka-forged enchantments, Ferret. My own skill was the main cause for the success of the stroke."

"I had hoped as much, chum," Ferret told his friend, giving him a slap on the back to underscore the faith he felt in Raker's swordsmanship. "Glad to hear you say that. Now it's your turn. Let's roll this bastard over so I can recover my other blade—I'm lost without matching dags, you know."

"Yeah," Raker grumbled, not wanting to touch the monstrosity. He lay the sword down carefully, then grabbed the beast's left foreleg, lifting and turning it as he did so. "Push!" he commanded.

Ferret had gotten into position at the middle, and used his hands to force the flank up and over far enough to show the protruding hilt of his other dagger. As Raker maintained his hold, the lean adventurer thrust a knee solidly against the flank, then with hands free reached over and worked the weapon loose. "Dinged up the pommel and scraped the shit out of the sharkskin grip, but otherwise undamaged and ready for the nex—"

"Don't say it! Come on, let's get out of here."

Side by side the two men resumed their trek down the middle of the sewer tunnel. They had gone only fifty yards when they saw a rat dash past, heading back from where they had come. Soon there was a stream of the big rodents skittering past them, hugging the walls in fear but unwilling to let that fear keep them from the feast the intruders had provided for them. At about the same time they both felt small things slipping past their booted feet, too: slimy, sinuous things that struggled upstream in an instant's passage. "What a great place," Raker grated.

"At least there won't be carrion stinking it up—not for long, anyway."

"Who'd notice the smell of a rotting corpse down here?"

Ferret voiced a grim chuckle. "Rats, those eely things just passed by, and who knows what, old boy. Methinks we need to find a side passage pretty quickly."

"Oh, crap! You're right. Let's move!"

"No, keep on as we have been, Rake. Commotion brings the curious." His comrade calmed, slowed his pace to the steady walk that Ferret maintained. They continued thus, unmolested, for fully a half an hour. The walls to either hand were broken only by small drainpipes. They had only one route to follow.

"How far down do you suppose we are?" Raker muttered.

Ferret considered a moment, then answered, "Not so deep—say maybe thirty feet or so below the surface. This tunnel has a gradual slope—makes me wonder."

They slogged on a bit before Raker asked, "Wonder what?"

"Wonder where this actually goes. I think we'll find out pretty quickly, though. Hear the clamor ahead."

Raker couldn't detect anything except the sloshing sounds of their progress, but he kept listening as they trudged along together. "What does it sound like to you, Ferret? Clamor doesn't actually describe it...."

"It's a rush of water and the echoing of its fall, isn't it?"

"Maybe so," his companion said uncertainly, even though he still heard nothing save a faint noise from somewhere on down the passage. "What it means is more to the point though."

Ferret shrugged. "Means we'll be coming to the place this sewer empties into—all the drains of Torenegro from the sound of it. Must be their public fountains and a lot of other liquid running into a nexus not far ahead."

"Oh, sure," Raker responded sagely. He hadn't any idea what his friend meant, but he would soon find out. In a hundred yards or so they detected a faint luminosity ahead, and the sound Ferret had heard some time ago became discernable to Raker's ears. "Daylight there!"

"Don't count on it, chum," Ferret warned. "I hear there are other sources of light underground which give that impression from a distance."

Further progress finally brought them to the source of the dim light. It was the place where the sound came from. They saw a big opening of natural rock resembling a massive sinkhole. It was in the center of a low-domed cavern, partly natural, partly constructed of hewn rock and stone blocks. The radiance came from some sort of fungi growing on the roof of the cavern.

The floor of the place was likewise a combination of nature and artifice. Their tunnel opened into the cavern, its flow of waste running more rapidly as it wended along an ever-steeper incline to where the channel ended at the brink of the hole. A half-dozen similar openings could be seen around the roughly circular wall of the big cave, all emptying their effluvia to fall into the depths accessed by the sinkhole. Two of the tunnels discharged considerable amounts, one a near-torrent. They walked along the relatively dry and level areas to a point where they could see into the pit.

"GRAND TERMINUS OF THE SEWER!" Ferret shouted over the noise. "IT ALL GOES INTO THE SUBTERRANEAN REALMS VIA THIS SHAFT!"

Raker had enough of the view, and he tugged on Ferret's arm, drawing his companion back away from the place where the roar of the cascading water was less deafening. "Better," he breathed. "Which of those other tunnels do you think is our best bet to escape from here?"

"None of 'em," Ferret told his friend. "Think of that thing which came after us back there. If there's that sort of beast roaming around down here, every sewer line is going to be pretty carefully guarded. Besides, Neva might be trying to keep tabs on us, too."

"So what does that mean? You think we should take a long plunge like those streams of piss?"

Ferret scoffed. "That's mostly waste water, and from the size of that outflow there, I think springs discharge here, too—but no. The critter that attacked us had to come from down there," and he waved toward the sinkhole.

"Critter? Monster, you mean. Maybe it did, but I can't believe that even the subterranean realms produce things like *that* naturally."

"Call it what you like, chum. It had to come from there, and got up here somehow in quick time too—that you can be sure of. Come on! Shine the light down along the rim. There's bound to be a path."

Without hesitation Raker moved to the edge of the gaping hole and played the harsh light from his now-doubly-enchanted stone inside the opening. The beam spread so that after a few rods the illumination was vague, but it allowed them to see clearly enough. The bottom was at least a bowshot below. He leaned close to his comrade, speaking nearly into Ferret's ear. "Two hundred feet is a long way down, and—" Raker didn't finish because there was a sudden, violent roiling in the dark and churning water of the pool upon which he was directing the light. "Did you see that?!"

"Yeah. Whatever lives in the water down there doesn't like light, I'd say."

"And you want to go down there? It was bigger than a hippo!"

Ferret took hold of the balking man's arm and moved it so that the beam of radiance illuminated the wall at their feet, moving the light from side to side in a gradual arc. "We don't have to go all the way to the bottom. There should be—look there!"

Raker looked. The violet-white light showed a black opening in the side about half-way down and to their left about twenty paces. "Okay. I see it. Those shadows there look like stepped ledges."

"Think you're right, Rake. Now let's find where the path starts up here."

Each man moved off a little, peering at the lip of the pit, Raker keeping the beam moving to occasionally assist the lanky adventurer in his examination. He was the one to discover what they sought, though. "BACK HERE, FERRET," he called. "THIS HAS TO BE THE WAY." His companion heard sound but wasn't quite sure. He peered inquiringly at Raker, and the blond man gestured for him to come to where he now crouched on hands and knees.

"Quite a bit of traffic here," Ferret commented when he joined his friend. "It looks like a pretty easy descent too."

Raker was an adept mountain climber, and his comrade oft times made his living as a cat burglar, so he couldn't disagree with Ferret's assessment. The rock was damp and undoubtedly slippery, but the path leading below was plain, its footholds generally wide and level with few breaks in the route. "I'd better go first. As soon as I get to a good place I'll shine the light back for you."

"Better hurry up. The casting I laid on it won't last much longer, and then we'll be back to the usual dull red beam... I hope."

"You hope? You mean you want that or...?"

Ferret didn't meet his comrade's eyes as he said, "Well, I'm not sure if I managed to add energy to cause the shift upward in the spectrum and the more intense beam."

"If you didn't add heka, what then?"

"Then the enchantment is using up its store of power at ten times its normal rate, and when it's gone the stone won't shed any light."

Raker turned away in disgust, then looked back with a glare. "Swell, Ferret, just great! The thing'll burn out in a little while, is that it?"

"Calm down, chum! We don't know that for sure. Even if I did mess up the casting, the thing might take days to use up all of its heka energy." He smiled feebly at Raker and pointed at their path downwards. "No telling—or use in fretting, right? Better get moving."

Chapter Sixteen

THE VIEW FROM above had been misleading. The path leading deeper into the subterranean realms was far more difficult and precarious than it had initially appeared. After a couple of particularly harrowing slips, Ferret was wishing for pitons and such and said as much when Raker closed to join him on a little shelf of rock. "My climbing gear would be handy now. This is a nasty descent!"

"I'd settle for a rope," Ferret told him. "No wonder that thing was what came up out of here to see about us as a meal. Fucker had six legs, claws, and suction cups to make the climb. At least the light's holding, and we have only twenty of thirty yards to go."

Raker surveyed the route ahead. He and his comrade had worked their way some sixty feet down and were now a third that distance from their starting place on the rim above. They had to go down another fifty feet, laterally about twenty, passing under the fall of spray from one of the streams high above them. Fortunately, the side of the sinkhole was dished in in this place, so the fall was like a curtain some little distance from the rock face. "It's going to be very slick, pal, and the stone's smooth. Watch it!" With that caution, Raker begin to work his way down again. It took him a full half hour to make their goal, for he had to pause regularly and light the path for Ferret to come after him. The phosphorescent fungi high above them sent little of its glow down into the pit. When at last he crouched in the mouth of the opening on the side of the sinkhole they had selected as their best bet to escape, Raker breathed a sigh of relief. He waved the light to show he'd made it, then shown the beam at his friend's feet.

"Crap, that was close!" Ferret whooshed out as he hopped down beside Raker a couple of minutes later. "I almost lost my balance on that upthrust spur."

What the lean man said was all too true. For a second Ferret had teetered and almost lost his balance. If the fall hadn't killed him, whatever lurked at the bottom would have. His comrade was angry. "Godsdamnit, Ferret, sometimes you act like a fool! You took that way too fast. Janus and Jupiter! You were hopping!"

Ferret grinned, but surreptitiously wiped the sweat from his palms onto his leather trousers. "Didn't want to keep you waiting, old man. We haven't all the time in the world now, do we? Besides, I'm adept at such stuff—famed for such feats, in fact, right?"

"Horseshit. You risked your life unnecessarily, and that risks mine. Don't do that again!" Raker spoke harshly and selfishly to hide his true feelings. Ferret was best friend, brother, and father all rolled into one as far as he was concerned. "Let's see if this is a dead end or a passage leading somewhere." So saying, Raker turned the light into the low tunnel at whose entrance they stooped.

"Wait a mo', chum. Let's have a last look down before we enter."

Raker was as curious as his companion, so he lay prone, worked his upper body over the ledge, and with arm extended pointed the violet-white beam of the witchlight below. The light shown first upon the pool. A pair of bloated shapes near the churning surface dived to hide beneath the water as the ray illuminated their habitat. "Take that!" the blond man laughed as if he were a child throwing stones to make cattle shy. It was fun to cause the monstrous things down there to surge down; it gave him a feeling of power.

"What surrounds the pool?" Ferret nudged his friend to make him quit annoying the horrid denizens of the watery muck in order to show more of this verge of the underground maze. The harsh light glittered on wet rocks, showed the space below to be shaped something akin to a globular bottle in all probability. The water collected in the concave bottom, lapped a rising shore. Where it flowed away, the lower cavern was much distended. "Hold steady!"

There was weird vegetation growing near the collection basin and along the outlet's banks. This growth was considerable further from the pool. Raker saw what made his comrade excited. Some of those things were moving. "Does that stick-like bush fish in the stream?"

"Beats me. That toadstool seems to be ambling along, though. Hey, look. There's some sort of bumpy creature trying to catch it, but its damned slow, too." The fungoid teetered, fell, and the slow motion chase came to an end a minute later as the pursuer devoured it. There was still a lot of movement, but suddenly it all ceased. Raker swung the beam around to see what had caused this to occur. "Uh-oh. Let's get the hells out of here!"

There were at least three other exits from the place below in addition to the tunnel made by the outflowing of the pool. From the largest of the former came a gigantic centipede. Ferret recognized this subterranean killer. "You said it, my friend! That's a steelback. Its fast, can climb, and is as poisonous as any cobra!"

Raker was already heading into the passage behind, so Ferret had to catch up. "Will it follow us?" he asked urgently when he heard his comrade come shuffling near.

"Not very likely," Ferret said as he hastened along in ape-like posture. Their tunnel was low, uneven too, so that every so often the two had to crawl on hands and knees, while in places they could relieve their aching backs by moving fully upright for awhile. "With all the goodies to eat down in that place, why come way up here for scraps?"

"What if light attracts it?"

"Then we're screwed."

The blond swordsman picked up the pace to a near run. "Well, let's try to make sure we aren't easy to catch." After a couple of turns and a very narrow place, the passage widened into a cave. The light showed that there was a tunnel high up on the far end wall, a larger exit over to the left, and a hole in the floor nearby which slanted down at a gradual angle. "Up? That's surely the best bet, isn't it?"

"If we can get up there quickly."

"Why quickly?"

"'Cause that godsdamned steelback's comin' up out of the hole, Rake!"

Both men made a frantic dash for the far end of the cave. Ferret's longer legs and fleetness of foot put him in the lead by six strides. When he reached the wall he turned, cupped his hands, and braced his back against it. Raker needed no coaching. He leaped to put his right foot in his friend's ready step, and then uncoiled his bunched muscles as Ferret hoisted him upward with a heave.

Raker shot high, and his hands caught the rough rock of the lower lip of the opening. He wasn't quite high enough, though, and his hold was poor. He tried to use thrashing feet and right hand to get a purchase, but instead his left hand slipped, and he started to fall back. Then something sinewy clamped around his wrist and hauled him up.

Below, Ferret stared a second in horror. What little light there was danced and swayed wildly, but it was sufficient to show him the ugly mandibles and head of the steelback as the monster came up into the cave. The hole's exit was a tight fit for it, but the myriapod was forcing its hard body through it all too quickly. Each segment through gave it two more legs with which to haul the rest of it out to get at its prey. "Oh, crap! Now what?" Ferret cursed as he turned to look for a really fast means of getting up to the passage he wasn't sure would save them from the hunting giant centipede. At that moment a braided leather rope dropped in front of him. Ferret needed no urging, and he swarmed up hand-over-hand. "Where'd you get the rope, Ra—"

His jaw fell slack as he saw the welcoming committee awaiting him. One of that number jerked him all the way inside, pulled him out of the way, as two others rolled a rounded boulder to the brink of the tunnel. "—ker?

His companion was as shocked as Ferret. Raker gave his head a slight shake as if to say, "I haven't the slightest notion," and then stared at the two lithe forms which were just in the process of shoving the big stone over the edge. They heard a thump and a sharp crack followed by scrabbling noises which slowly died away.

"Gottum!" One of the creatures who had sent the boulder down chittered in something which sounded vaguely like human speech as it turned and showed a mouthful of sharp fangs to the two men.

"That's trade talk," Raker murmured, referring to the pidgin Phonecian commonly used throughout much of Ærth to conduct business.

"And that's a... a... man-sized stoat," Ferret breathed.

"Sure, talk pretty fine with hewmuns allatime now and then, but no Stoatie. Nonono. Thurr we are—Ferretfolk you name we, us say *Thurr.*" The creature trilled the *r*'s as it pronounced the name of its folk. "See dead manyfoot?"

The creature talked as fast as it moved. Ferret couldn't believe this. They did look like huge, slender ferrets, down to their buff fur and black "masks." He gaped, then asked rather stupidly, "Real ferretfolk?" He had heard of them but never believed they existed. "I am called Ferret."

The one who had hauled him to safety ignored the question. "Come. See it broken. Good."

Both men went to where the creature proudly pointed with its nose, stared down to see the steelback below, forepart a gory ruin under the boulder. "You sure squashed the shit out of that head!" Raker said with enthusiasm.

"Bad thing, manyfoot. Kill hewmuns, kill you, kill Thurr, too, so we allatime kill 'em first. Pretty good, sure?" And as it rattled that off the creature showed its teeth again in what was surely meant to be an imitation of a human smile.

"Good thing, yes," Raker agreed, showing his own teeth broadly in a grin.

His comrade was meanwhile shifting his gaze around to take in the other pair of so-called ferretfolk who had rescued him and Raker. Each of them was taller than he was, weasel-bodied, but bipedal and standing upright. Ferret supposed that when these creatures really wanted to move they'd drop to all fours and become thus as nimble as their normal-sized little cousins, and fast!

One of the three noticed his stare. "Not saw before Thurr, yes?" When Ferret shook his head, the creature was puzzled. "No? Have Thurr you met then?"

"No meant yes," he corrected. "This is my first introduction to your kind. I do not mean to stare, but as I said, I am called Ferret, for I am lean, fast, and—"

"Suresure. See that, I. Thinks you a good hunter too. Proud of name?"

"Well... yes."

The creature showed its teeth, pointed its nose, moved it forward, then back to indicate Raker. "He bigtime hunter to be brother of, eh?"

Ferret didn't understand what was being alluded to, but he nodded his head agreeably. "Yes. How did you know that?"

"See tongue of zoffle, easyeasy know. Can smell too. Fresh kill!"

"Raker, show these fine fellows—er, Thurr—the tongue of that monstrosity you killed."

The blond man reached down and dragged it free from his belt, holding it forth uncertainly. "Why do they want to see this thing?"

All three of the ferretfolk clustered close to admire the two-foot section of tongue, and their enthusiasm answered Raker's query as they jabbered excitedly:

"Big buck zoffle that belong!"

"No hurt even small killing either."

"You do it how, hewmun?" the largest of the trio asked. "Use awfulbright light thing you hold?"

Raker patted his rapier's hilt, waved a hand depreciatingly at the garnet enspelled to produce the now violet-white blaze of witchlight.

"Just weapon? Impressed we am!"

That made the gray-eyed swordsman preen a bit. "Thank you, good Thurrs!"

"Don't lisp," his comrade drawled.

"I am called Raker, and as always, I slew with my sword."

The biggest of the three creatures chittered in rapid fire to its fellows, and they both answered back in kind. Then it spoke again in its strange trade Phonecian: "Names Chit-tzick I, he Ur-rrki, that one Gurr-ajur. Hewmun Rakker, to we show sorrd."

"Of course," Raker replied happily, and drew the rapier with a little flourish.

"Pretend kill now," the ferretfolk leader, Chit-tzick, urged.

Raker posed, stamped as he made a lunge at an imaginary monster, shouted "Hah!" Then he recovered, saluted the three, and said "That's how I did it. My friend here, Ferret," and he nodded to the lanky adventurer to show his generosity in allowing a small share of credit to him, "assisted a bit by getting astride the… zoffle?… and slowing it."

There was again rapid churrings and chitterings between the three. The spokesthurr then shook his head. "Hewmun after little kin we named rides zoffle while you with short weapon sorrd stick it? Both very brave or very crazy, which?"

Raker and Ferret looked at eachother, then turned to the strange creature who asked them such a question. Neither spoke, but both shook their heads.

"No? Thought you crazy not. Too old—crazy dead soonsoon." He rattled off something in their own language to the others, and all three gathered around the men. "Now we take you to our den-safe. Honor great for all. Come with Chit-tzick, Urrrki, Gurr-ajur."

Ferret spoke without thinking. "Where is your home… den?"

"Lower. Farness modest—one meal journey. Lottsa meat on manyfoot. Come get food now and gogogo."

Raker started to protest but Ferret cleared his throat loudly to drown him out, smiled, saying, "Actually, kind thurrs, we had been seeking a way up!"

"Bark understood, Ferret-hewman. Quiets brother. Why above? Pretty bad there, no?"

"Not for us... exactly. Well, you see," he added hastily, "We have more hunting to do—something worse than the zoffle."

All three ferretfolk whistled. "True?"

"True."

"I'll give you this trophy as a token of our esteem," Raker interjected, "if you three stout thurrs would show us a way up."

Again there was more chittered conversation between them. At a break Gurr-ajur said, "Hard to believe such great hunters lost," and then resumed rapid chittering to its fellows.

At last the big one, Chit-tzick, silenced the other two. "No. If braves hewmuns must hunt above, we help. We go soon as eat some manyfoot." He went to where the three creatures had dumped their gear off in order to save Ferret and roll the boulder down on top of the giant centipede. Both men noted that the thurr employed equipment very much like that of more primitive humans. Each of the ferretfolk had a braided leather rope which they so wrapped as to form a sort of harness and belt, beginning the process with the latter. That is, the rope was fashioned into a lasso, and with that around their midsection as a base, the thurr then used a complex series of loops and ties to make the rest of the harness, with a last knot to prevent the lasso part from tightening due to weight on the cross-parts. Each also had a small hide shield with four big darts stored along its back side. When the leader noted Raker's curiosity, he showed his teeth, pointed with his black nose. "Poison on'em. Veryvery bad for enemy."

"Your spears, too?" Raker asked as the three picked up their long weapons. Each spear consisted of a stout wooden shaft almost six feet long at whose butt was a finger-long metal spike. An iron head brought the overall length to over seven feet. The blade was barbed where it broadened at the base to about a palm's width, and below that was a straight crosspiece.

"Not," the thurr said. "Tootoo risky for us—yousee?"

Raker nodded. The darts were in pockets built into the shields, so their envenomed points weren't a hazard. A poisoned spear blade carried exposed, especially when the subterranean passages often required single-file going, would be dangerous to these creatures traveling in company thus. "So you use them to slay zoffles?"

"First darts to make zoffle slower, then several thurr stick with spears. Only lose few hunters so." Chit-tzick used his spear to point back into the tunnel. "Nice chitchat alldone. Hurryhurry time now. Lost hewmuns go there. We thurr catch up soon-soon."

Ferret grinned and nodded at those giants of his namesake animal. "Best news I've heard all day. Come on, Rake, let's move out!"

Chapter Seventeen

THE TRIO OF thurr had caught up with Ferret and Raker in a few minutes. The men learned that the creatures had eaten some of the dead steelback, probably as much in ritual as hunger, and also checked to see if any of the monstrous centipede's poison remained intact in its gland sacks. In fact, one had been salvaged, which made the ferretfolk satisfied indeed.

Neither of the adventurers could recall exactly what route their guides took them on through the Shallowshadow verges of the subterranean realms. The way consisted of a lot of changing passages and one rough climb, but in less than an hour Chit-tzick, Urrrki, and Gurr-ajur brought them to a place where a wall of ashlar blocks made it clear masons had been at work. The leader of the ferretfolk hunters said, "Hewmuns' wall. Passage just otherside."

"Ah... how do we get through the wall?" Ferret asked hesitantly

"Suresure. Sorry. Forgot you know not this place," Chit-tzick rattled. The creature tapped a low block with his spear. "Way." Then he chattered to his fellows, and all three began to return from whence they had come. "Anytime back in thurr place, come visit den-safe. Just ask for Chit-tzick."

"Thank you," Ferret and Raker chimed with real sincerity. "We are honored to have such clever war—" Raker added, then stopped short as the three ferretfolk disappeared from view.

"Guess they're not much for goodbyes... or flowery speeches, old man."

Raker looked miffed at being ignored thus. "Come on and lend a hand. I want to get the hells out of this underground deathtrap!"

"There I couldn't agree more, mate! Looks like there's no mortar holding it, so all we should have to do is prise it free from below."

"Use one of those dags of yours to probe the place, Ferret. I've no wish to have some lurking little horror sting or bite me at this juncture."

Ferret used both of his long-bladed daggers to make certain the small niche below the stone block was free of inhabitants. "All clear," he murmured, and as he held the witchlight for his comrade, Raker reached in with both hands.

"A shallow groove! Uff! Aaah..." There was a scraping sound following the grunt of effort and the sigh of satisfaction. The block of granite was sliding back toward them as Raker pulled. "See what's beyond," he told Ferret urgently.

The lean adventurer lay flat, shined their light into the hole where the stone had been, peered and saw nothing threatening. Then Ferret inserted his arm and followed it gingerly with his head. "*Mumblemumble*—sage."

Raker tugged at his comrade's free arm irritably. "Come out of there so I can understand what you're saying, Ferret!"

Wriggling backward, Ferret backed to get clear. "I said, sport, that there's only a dusty little passage beyond. Looks like it hasn't been used in some time. Haven't the faintest notion of where it leads."

"At this point I hardly care, as long as it will get us above! Listen, chum, I'll go through first. I expect it'll be a bit rough because of my broad shoulders, so shove against the soles of my boots when I tell you, right?"

"Fat head, you say?"

"And when you follow, weasel, come feet first and hold fast the block. I'll haul you through—you pull it along after. I want to try to close up this hole so no chance tracker will be able to slither through freely."

Ferret had thought of the same thing, so he gave his companion no additional difficulty, verbally or otherwise. Raker had to strip off his upper body armor before going through the narrow space, but with a couple of solid assists from behind, he was inside the further passage. Then Ferret accepted the witchlight, pushed the pieces of armor through, and readied his own exit from the subterranean realms. First he turned the stone block halfway around. That put the slightly hollow edge with the hand grip on the inside. Then he belly-backed, and when he felt Raker's hands grab firmly onto his boots, Ferret hooked his fingers into the lower place on the stone and shouted, "Pull away!"

In a few minutes the block was so set that only close inspection would reveal it could and had been moved. "Shuts the other side more securely than before," Ferret noted. "The owner of this wee passageway should be pleased!"

"Remains to be seen," his companion said sourly. "Which brings another possible problem to mind. What if the bitch still scries to know our whereabouts and doings?"

"I'm no master of magicks, as you have been so kind as to remind me of frequently, Raker, but it's not a very likely prospect. There's a lot of stone down here full of energy—heka energy."

"Sure. That's why they call that kind of rock hekalite."

Ferret sneered, "Smart ass. So anyway, she'd have lost us when we went down into the sinkhole. By now she'll figure we're hopelessly lost in the mazes there or else dead. Neva must have a lot of more important things to worry about.... "

"Got you, old boy. Sorry I'm not good company. I'm tired and nervous, too. All I want to do is get up and out. What we know should fetch that reward we were promised, and Dertosal can't be much more distant, right?"

"Agreed, we should come up somewhere near Torenegro, so the colonel and his spiritual advisor are a couple of days' ride away at worst, but..."

Raker glanced apprehensively at his comrade. "I hate it when you say that!"

"Never mind. Let's just see where this way leads; then we'll determine what follows."

Sometime later they found a very narrow and long flight of steps which they followed up to a concealed exit from the passage. Beyond that portal was a bare and unoccupied little room. Pale light came into the semicircular chamber from a pair of narrow windows. There was a small, iron-bound door on one of the two straight walls.

Raker went over to the nearest arrow slit and looked out. Ferret tried the door.

"I see hills which look a whole lot like those north of Torenegro, Ferret," the blond swordsman hissed.

Ferret eased the door shut in a hurry. "And I see what looks a lot like the interior of the great hall building of the castle, chum. We're back in the godsdamned grandee's fortress!"

The two looked at each other, wanting to curse but near to guffaws of mirth at the same time. It took almost a minute before they could speak. "What a hell of a detour, Ferret!" Raker managed to exclaim as he choked back laughter.

"No charge for the trip, either" Ferret replied. "And now comes the really good part. We're going to go out there, find something to eat, and then locate a place to stow away and get a little sleep."

"Have you gone daft?"

Ferret shrugged. "Stay put if you like. It's just dawn, so if we hurry, we can get away with it. Come dark again, we'll have a much better chance to escape. After all, there's no hunt in here for us now, is there?"

"I bow to your wisdom, master burgular. I'm almost hungry enough to eat giant centipede, thirsty too, and crave sleep more than a buxom lass. Provide me with the first three, and I'll treat us both to the latter when we are shed of the grandee's dust."

The hallway outside was still and deserted. They had been in a corner tower room set into an angle of the building's back wall, and this passage went this way and that along the length of the fourth story of the huge hall. Ferret followed his nose, located a staircase, and the two went boldly down, knowing it to be a servants' way. It brought them to the ground floor and the kitchens. There frantic bakers, cooks, and scullions were emptying ovens, preparing great cauldrons of stuff, and otherwise doing such things as were necessary for the castle's morning meal.

Ferret saw a large basket and grabbed it. "Here, my man, put a half-dozen of those little loaves in. Look smart now." Raker hurriedly picked up the still steaming bread and dropped it into the basket. He led on into a smaller room.

"Smells even better this morning than usual, my dear cook," Ferret told a young assistant there. She dimpled.

"Can I help you?"

"We're in a great hurry. Just cheese and sausage for a patrol of six—and wine of course!"

She took a long line of linked sausages, cut off the number required, and put in a small wheel of cheese. "Wine is just through there with the junior butler... you do mean usual stuff for soldiers, don't you?"

"That I do, my love," Ferret beamed. "A nice full demijohn of two gallons would be nice. Say, would you mind fetching it for me? That porridge you're cooking tempts me to tase it, but time presses. Here is a duro for your help, eh?"

She was quick to accept the copper coin and slip it into her bodice. "There are bowls there, spoons here. Help yourselves. I'll be back in a little while."

As soon as she was gone Raker queried uneasily, "Isn't that risky?"

Ferret was already spooning the gruel into a wooden bowl, salting and buttering it. "No more that going ourselves—less risky in fact."

"But..."

"You... want... wine... don't you?" Ferret asked slowly between hurried mouthfuls. "Hot!"

The blond swordsman gave up and likewise helped himself to the porridge. "Great," he murmured, devouring it faster even than his lanky comrade.

They had just finished and were considering seconds when the young cook's assistant returned. "Pedro knew nothing about wine for the patrol, and he has orders not to hand it out, so I had to give him the duro," she said sulkily as she set down the straw-wrapped jug. "Even so he gave me but a one-gallon bottle."

Raker handed her a pair of duros, patted her plump bottom. "You are as clever as you are lovely. If I marry you, will you promise to cook?"

"Get out of here you two, I have work to do!"

They left her as she sang happily at her work. Ferret led the way back up the stairs, and back to their point of entry. Because there was nobody up there he stopped and peered into several rooms along the way. In one used for storage they found old draperies and other material, and some of these he folded up and carried along.

Raker set the basket down inside their hideaway, secured the latch so nobody could walk in unannounced. "Let's have something solid now," he said with enthusiasm as he eyed the contents of the container."

"Good plan, old friend. You make compilations of meat, cheese, and bread for us both while I arrange our couches, right?" Ferret was laying the thick draperies on the floor so as to make pads upon which they could sleep. "A trifle dusty, but better than the boards. Now methinks we should have the secret door ajar—just in case we need to make a hasty exit."

Soon both had eaten to surfeit. "Enough for supper, too," Ferret observed after consuming enough for two brawny laborers.

"Do we need a watch?" queried his companion.

"Yes, but what the hells, let's skip it. We've both had about all we can take. I'll sleep with one eye open."

Raker grunted, lay down, and was asleep almost immediately, for he knew that his companion wasn't jesting. Ferret's keen senses did enable him to get rest and still spring instantly alert from sleep at the sound of a soft footfall a dozen paces distant behind a door. Besides, the gray-eyed adventurer was happy to be so high up, with sunlight spilling in and blue sky visible through the tall, thin slits nearby. When he snored it was a sound so soft even Ferret hardly heard it.

It was hot when they awoke, the hour being just that before sundown. No prowling inhabitant of the fortress had come to their hiding place, and it seemed unlikely that they would be disturbed now. Neither was disappointed.

"Now I wish we had picked up a jug of water too," Raker grumbled, rinsing his mouth with wine and spitting it out.

"Can't think of everything under these circumstances," Ferret said without apology. "Make do, Rake. In a bit we'll be gone, and there's plenty of water in that stream a few miles from here."

The blond man sipped a little more wine from the demijohn, swallowing this time. "Miles, bah! I want a wash now. Oh well, what's the plan?"

"Sit here until dusk, then work our way down and slip out with the mercenaries going into town for some fun. Should be easy. Hungry?" Ferret was already busy with his dagger, slicing off a piece of sausage and eyeing the cheese.

"No. If I ate as much as you do I'd be as fat as you are lean. Besides, I'm too nervous to think about food."

His friend chuckled. "Just because they'll kill us in some unspeakable fashion if we're caught? Usual stuff, I'd say." He began munching, and Raker got up and paced. "Seeing as how you seem to need something to do, take a look at the old garments I rolled up to make pillows for us."

Raker stopped moving back and forth and did as his friend suggested. "Pretty useless," he said unenthusiastically.

"How about those smocks? I thought maybe we could use them to get outside, sort of hide our armor that way."

"Hmmm. I suppose so, especially if we carry stuff, too—like the basket and those old draperies. We'll look like a couple of varlets stepping and fetching." Raker followed his line of reasoning further. "Yes, not bad at all, old chum! We tote the stuff down to the outer bailey area. Nobody pays attention to workers. Wherever we dump it, and that's no problem in a citadel this size, we shuck off the smocks and voila! Soldiers off to sport in Torenegro's taverns."

"I'll buy that," Ferret agreed as he washed down bread with a swig from the big bottle of wine. "What say we get into costume now while there's still light enough to see ourselves. We might have to hunt up more props."

Not long thereafter a pair of nondescript men made their way down through the main building of the great castle, each with some burden carried before him. They made it all the way back to the ground floor without incident, but as they were about to exit through the scullery a guard brought them up short. "Hold on there, you two! Nobody passes this way—you know the order."

"But the chamberlain—" Ferret began hastily.

"Don't hand me that crap. I don't care of the seneschal hisself tol' you—which ain't likely. Nobody passes in or out of this here hall after dark 'cept through the front or the upper bridgeways."

"But—"

The fellow was impatient. "One more word an' I'm havin' you hauled before the serjeant at arms. Get your lazy asses outta here. Just 'cause you can't use the front don't mean you can take a shortcut this way! Now go on up and around through the way yer supposed to. I don't care if it's a godsdamned mile up an' down stairs that way, its *orders*!"

Ferret and Raker beat a hasty retreat, with the guardsman's grumbling coming after them. "What now?" asked Raker.

"We have to find someplace we can climb outside and down," Ferret whispered as they made for the secluded servants' stair they had now become all too familiar with. "Security's been tightened since we slipped in yesterday."

"Hey, no shit?" Raker snapped back sarcastically. "Wasn't it then you said we couldn't go up to escape?"

"That was yesterday," the lanky adventurer responded blandly as if oblivious to his companion's doubts. "Remember there was a hue and cry then? Now we can take our time and find a safe route." Ferret kept his own uncertainties to himself. His worry was how they would manage avoiding suspicion as they prowled around above, but Raker was already tense, and if he had any inkling that Ferret was likewise, then their chances were slim indeed.

The first floor was humming with activity, so they went on up quickly. Because they needed to get out and climb down, the obvious choice was then the next story above the high hall's floor, even if it happened to be the one on which the lord and officials of the fortress were quartered. Ferret led the way, stepping boldly into the main corridor, marching along as if knowing exactly where he was to go. Raker stayed just a half-step behind, trying to look as if he too belonged where they were, but he couldn't help letting out a little "whew!" of relief as his comrade turned off into a narrower, dim passage.

They had gone only a few paces along that way, though, when they heard the sound of marching feet, the clatter and clang of metal on metal, which could mean only that a squad of guardsmen was coming. In a moment the soldiers would be right at the intersection of their corridor, maybe turn down it, too. Ferret fairly flew ahead, grabbed the handle of the nearest door, and leaped inside. Raker was hot on his heels.

"How dare you enter my chambers?!" The challenge came in a melodious but sharp female voice.

The speaker was Neva.

Chapter Eighteen

BECAUSE FERRET WAS nearly on top of her where Neva stood scowling, he reacted instinctively. One shriek from her and they were done. He dumped his armload of material atop her, following with his whole body. Head swathed in dusty drapery, mouth stifled by the thick stuff, Neva was knocked over backwards. Ferret fell atop her, driving any breath she had from her lungs. The noise was minimal, as the floor was thickly carpeted.

Raker managed to shut the door behind him just as Ferret acted. He stared in shock at the scene, then stepped toward the two forms sprawled there before him. Just as he was about to speak, though, a voice from an adjoining room silenced him.

"Is everything all right, Donna Neva?"

Lupe! Raker would never forget that voice, no more than he would Neva's beautiful face. Moving as fast as he dared, the blond swordsman headed further inside, meaning to ambush Neva's unnatural maidservant when Lupe came to discover why her mistress didn't reply. He had gotten almost as far as the interconnecting door when the weretherion "woman" darted through it, eyes fixed on Ferret and the cloth-wrapped Neva where they silently struggled on the floor.

Fast as she was, her attention riveted there enabled Raker to emulate his friend's attack. *Whoosh, whump!* Hangings and heavy basket arced and came to a sudden stop as they struck the weretherion in human form. Having been brought up an aristocrat and a cavalier, Raker might have hesitated at doing what he did next, save that he had seen Lupe in her wolf form. With his hands free of the loaded basket, the muscular swordsman brought his left fist down atop the bottom of that container as hard as he could where it teetered on Lupe's head. Then with his right he struck an uppercut squarely into her midsection. Raker packed a terrific punch....

No doubt in her true form she could have taken such punishment and been unharmed. As "Lupe," though, it was an altogether different thing. With a grunt of pain and a sharp discharge of air, she crumpled in a heap. Not sure, Raker did the only thing he could think of. He jumped up on top of the big wicker container under which Lupe had collapsed, trying madly to recover his rapier from where it was concealed under his voluminous smock as he pranced atop the basket.

"Practicing your flamenco steps?"

"Shut up, the guards will hear you!"

Ferret had one of his poniards so thrust that its point touched the tender flesh of the one he held enwrapped in old draperies. Thus Neva had become both still and silent, and he was able to kneel beside her and observe his comrade's frantic activity. "Whatever can you mean, old chum? The racket you're making sounds like the bed-creakings from a dozen lusty fornicators. It's you who should quiet down. Besides, the squad went past a minute ago."

Sword finally freed, Raker stopped his mad tromping, placed the tip of the rapier into an opening of the wickerwork basket bottom, and pushed it down. "Now, by the gods, that bitch woman-wolf is going to die," he cursed.

"Gently, Raker, gently!" Ferret called as he saw his friend begin to lean upon the weapon so as to sink it into his entrapped adversary. "Hold a mortal stroke—we might need her."

"You have the witch, why worry about this ... thing?!"

"*Unnnf el oo,*" came faintly from the bundle of cloth Ferret guarded.

"Just hold short of spilling Lupe's blood for a moment. I think Neva has something to tell us."

Raker hesitated, uncertain. "Be careful with her. She's worse than this shape-shifter."

"Don't worry, I know that." Ferret directed his attention to the now-moving form within the cloth swathing. "Stay still, damn you! You heard what we just said—at least clearly enough to know that we mean business. One word, and Raker will skewer your wolf-woman. I'll not hesitate to use my own blade on you either. Remember, Neva, I am also able to employ heka. No tricks, and that means trying to sneak in some evil glance bringing woe, too. I know about eyebiting."

When the bundle moved and "*Ahreeg*" came forth from the muffling folds, Ferret used his free hand to begin pulling the stuff away from his prisoner. He didn't bother to check on Raker, knowing his companion was quite capable of managing the matter of keeping Lupe in any form from causing trouble. The lean adventurer did watch Neva closely, kept his dagger at a place where one push would kill. When her face finally showed, he quickly drew his second long dirk, aimed that at her as well.

"The vaunted Ferret—what a brave fellow you are," Neva said scornfully. She ignored the threats as she straightened her gown, patted her hair into place. Even in her present state she was a gorgeous woman. Her perfect complexion, doll-like face, and huge eyes made Neva look almost childlike; an illusion belied by her very evident breasts and shapeliness of arm, leg, buttocks—not to mention lips, smile, and glance. Of course she wasn't being seductive now. Her voice was hard and her expression hinted at some inner quality far from grace and beauty. Her next words underscored that. "What the fuck are you two assholes after? Surely not trying to settle that old score, are you?"

"What about yesterday's little number? Didn't you do your best to have us torn to bits in that godsdamned sewer?" Raker shot back from his perch atop the upturned basket. "For that you should—"

Neva laughed derisively, cutting him off. "Get real. I wouldn't have been able to try and have you flushed down if you hadn't been here already. Did I drag you into the castle, order you to get caught spying and try to run away down the sewer tunnels? I repeat: what are you after?"

"Okay, Neva. Here's what we want," Ferret said with soft menace. "The jewels you stole from Chasal Mer-al."

Again Neva laughed, and this time the sound of it bore an even greater mockery than before. "Better stick that dagger into me now then, you dumb shit. I don't have the stuff, and I never will."

"You're a liar."

"Of course I am, Raker, but I'm not lying now. It's true."

"Kill her," urged Raker, beginning to press down on the rapier's hilt.

"Good idea," Ferret concurred, and his arm moved so that a crimson bead showed on Neva's skin where the point of his dagger pressed it inward.

She flinched away. "For Ishtar's sake, don't be so hasty! You need me."

"Like a boil on my butt," Raker said, but he stopped his move to drive the sword's long blade through Lupe. "I say show her the same tender mercy she gave to me, Ferret."

His comrade shot him a meaningful glance. "Got you, chum. Sorry, Neva, but..."

"I can get you out of here—right now, too! There are three thousand soldiers who stand between you and freedom otherwise."

"Bullshit. We'll take our chance with that bunch of clods," Raker retorted. "They don't even know to look for us, and we'll be well away from here before they discover your body."

Ferret waved a dagger toward him. "Maybe she can sweeten up the offer, make us interested." He nodded to her saying, "So thanks to you we walk out of here nice and peaceful, nobody knows it, and you do what else?"

"I give you ten thousand each." The dagger started to press again, and Neva hastily added, "Easy there! That's not ten thousand reals, that's duros—ouch! All right, Ferret, godsdamnit, platas!"

He eased off. "What say, Rake? She's saying her life is worth a quarter million apiece."

"What about the wolf woman?" Raker asked Neva.

"Her you can kill," Neva said unemotionally. "I'm not paying for Lupe's life, only my own."

"You are a piece of work," murmured Ferret in a tone which conveyed both wonderment and revulsion. "Why the gods chose to make someone as beautiful and as vile I'll never understand."

Neva looked disdainfully at him. "You understand so little it is no matter at all. Do we have a deal or not?"

"No deal, Neva. I know damn well the stuff you took out of the goldsmith's place was worth ten times more than you're offering us."

"Ten times," she shot back, "is a laugh. What I took from that stupid old fool was worth more than a hundred times that amount—only the stuff was never mine."

Ferret looked interested. "Whose was it, then?"

"Let's just say it's the property of a consortium."

"And the combine didn't want to have to pay Mer-al's bill, right?"

Neva shrugged, careful to avoid the dirk as she did so. "He demanded too much for his services." Her face showed there was more. The dead goldsmith could not boast of his work.

Ferret noted that, chose to ignore what was unsaid. "Well, so do we demand high payment, but our service is refraining from killing you, and we aren't a mark like the gemner was. Let's see the stuff you took!"

"I could try to cozen you into believing that I could take you to it," Neva said after a brief pause to consider, "but I don't think I could manage to get you two dead before you got me. I'm playing this straight, because I want to live, understand?" She looked at Ferret, then Raker, getting a slight nod from each before continuing. "The grandee has the… jewels. They're locked up in his vault, and there is no possible way for me to take you there—or for me to get them."

Ferret leaned back without diminishing the immanent threat of his blade. "So let's say that's true. Describe the stuff, and tell us exactly why its worth more than fifty million reals."

"Diamonds, sapphires, corundum, and emeralds set in gold and oricalcum by a master jewler." Neva sounded confident and her look was assured as she answered.

Of course that made the lanky adventurer suspicious. He knew she wasn't lying now, but at the same time Ferret could sense she was holding back a whole lot of important facts. He made some quick calculations. "As a professional jewel thief, Neva, I am well aware of the value of stones such as you mention. Tell me the whole story. I can't see why the marquis would want a chestful of jewelry when coin is more useful in fomenting a rebellion."

"So you know about—" Neva clipped the rest of what she had been about to say short as she realized his trick. "All right, I'll admit I'm a part of the plot, Ferret. You know, you are rather like your namesake in tracking things down."

"Save the flattery. Get to the jewelry."

"It's the grandee's vanity. Lord Armando del Vargos is vain, and he demanded special regalia for his coming coronation as king."

Ferret wasn't buying that. "King? Emperor? Who cares what he claims to be? What do you think I am, a chump? If he seriously connives to become monarch of some or all of Iberia, I know damned well his begemmed goodies have to be loaded with special enchantments and have heka ready to pour out in torrents. I think we'd better cut this little conversation short."

"Don't jab me with that blade again, you son of a bitch! I'm getting to that." Her pretty, pouting mouth spoke the lie easily despite the circumstances. "Of course the coronation pieces are enspelled. I helped, and that's why I'm in the affair at all."

Raker couldn't remain a silent listener any longer. "Witchery to bind into such regalia? That's a joke."

"Witchcræft isn't my forte, you dolt. I am a sorceress and demonurge!"

"No doubt an able one, too," drawled Ferret. "So just what's worth so much cash, dweomers and devilshine aside? Phæree gems or elemental stones to contain such magicks and energies?"

Neva paused, then looked the lanky man squarely in the eyes, her innocent blue orbs defying his dark ones to find the least hint of prevarication as she responded: "There are mahydrols set in the major pieces—four of them. If the set were broken up and fenced, there's not a lock in Æropa who wouldn't pay fifty million for the mahydrols and the other stones. If the jewelry was sold at market price, Ferret, the grandee's regalia would fetch five hundred million reals!"

That brought a low whistle from Raker. "Zow! Sounds great to me. We'll take a tithe of your share, Neva—five mil'?"

"You must be cr—"

Ferret's gesture made her chop off her insult. "How about both of you shutting up? Raker, just make certain the weretherion bitch doesn't get free. Listen, but don't interrupt until I'm finished; then you can have your turn."

"Yah, sure," Raker grumbled.

"If you think I'll just sit here to be..."

Ferret's cold stare made Neva stop speaking once again. "You are really pressing it, dearie," he growled. "And when you do speak, keep your voice down. Let me get this straight. You are a part of the cabal around the grandee. He aims at becoming a monarch, and you're involved in supplying the heka power and castings for the coming uprising. That includes charging up his crown and the rest to make him a for-real sovereign. Right so far?"

Neva nodded, and gave a little shrug thereafter.

"So your group sets up this Chasal Mer-al to make the soon-to-be crown jewels for old Grandee Alphonso, and when he delivers to your specifications, you get rid of the goldsmith—too big a security risk, too much payment demanded. Who did for him, you?"

"Yes."

"I'm surprised—such a lovely little girl. Then you bring the regalia back here to Torenegro, and just in case somebody's clever enough to track you, you set Lupe and her two pals on the back-trail."

"Not a perfect grasp, but close enough," Neva agreed.

Ferret seemed satisfied. "When the marquis is crowned, you'll become important.

"I am right now," she countered. His suggestion that she wasn't a key figure in the plot stung Neva.

"That you are," the lean adventurer snapped. "How will you come up with your ransom, and I mean now!"

"Well… I have a half million in gold… readily available."

With a quick wink shot to his comrade, Ferret laughed. "I don't doubt it a bit, and it's here in your room. We'll take the rest of your payment in less readily exchanged stuff, Neva, such as your jewelry."

Her face flushed with rage, and Neva's mouth writhed as she spat, "You stinking pig's ass, I'll—"

"You'll stop playing the fishwife and go over there," he waved to the boudoir, "and fetch the money and trinkets for us. Otherwise, *I'll* put paid to you."

Neva sprang up as might a leopardess, but Ferret was with her, daggers still poised to strike. Pale but trembling a little, she held her composure, stalked to the bed chamber. "I'll have to use a charm to disarm the wards on this," she told him as she reached for a beaten brass coffer standing on a vanity.

"Not on your life. Don't so much as *think* of heka." Ferret sheathed one of his daggers, and used his now-free left hand to search inside his coat. Finally locating what he sought, the lean man used his long fingers to delicately extract and unfold a square of papyrus. It bore an inscription in green ink, something resembling a thaumaturgic triangle, only the double circles sandwiching magicked hieroglyphs surrounded a figure depicting a four-sided pyramid whose apex was key-like. Each corner of the square had a different elemental symbol in it—fire, ærth, air, water—with a like number of cat figures distributed between them.

Neva sneered when she got a glimpse of it. "What do you think that charm will do?"

"I know what this talisman will do," Ferret said to her as he held it over the casket, then let it flutter down. She jumped when there was a dark green flash of energy released as the papyrus touched the brass coffer. They felt rather than heard the force of the discharge. "So much for your magickal guards, Neva. Shall we see what's inside?"

"How did you manage to do that? Keep your hands off my jewel box, you turd!"

Ferret laughed as he used his redrawn left-hand dagger to flip open the lid of her strongbox. "Such foul talk from so pretty a mouth. Do you kiss your mommy with the same lips? I told you I knew a bit about heka-bending, didn't I? That little trick is something I picked up in Ægypt. I love it."

"Fuck you."

"But that last part was good advice. Thank you! I see you had a nasty little array of 'cobra fangs' to prick unwary fingers," he said noting the sharp hooks of metal which curled out along the upper edge of the coffer's top as it came open. "Nasty poison on them too, I'll bet."

She became philosophical. "Too bad you didn't discover just how potent, but one can't always prevail. The coins and my jewels are there. Help yourself." Neva watched as Ferret carefully stirred the contents with the blade of his weapon before actually taking any of the things there.

"More like sixty doubloons here than fifty, but who can bother counting at a time like this, right? So I will rely on your word and take the lot—but not the jewelry."

"No? I thank you."

The long fingers moved aside the pearl strands from the middle compartment, pressed and pried, lifted the velvet bottom. "You're welcome… but what have we here! Why, it's a jeweled egg," and he paused to give it a little shake.

Neva tried to grab it. "Give me that, Ferret, or you're a dead man," she hissed in frustration when he kept if from her, held her at bay with the poniard.

"Quite the contrary, Neva. I'm taking this as the balance of your ransom, and you are dead if you object further. But enough of this play, says I. Lead us on to a safe departure from this castle, my dear sorceress."

He tucked the little ovoid away, and again armed with two blades prodded her back to where Raker stood perched. "Let Lupe out of that cage, my friend. She'll accompany us."

"Are you crazed?"

The words came simultaneously from the blond swordsman and Neva. Both then gaped at the other, looked away in disgust. "Peas in a pod," Ferret said in droll tone. "Do as I ask, Rake, and you'll soon see my reasoning." As soon as his comrade raised his rapier and leaped nimbly down from the basket, the container flipped over and the weretherion woman arose from the draperies that had ensnared her. "Lupe, you heard all that went on here?"

"I heard all," she said in a flat voice. Neva looked away.

"So, my companion and I choose to spare your life providing you give us your oath that you will aid us in escaping from here."

The wolf woman inclined her head. "You have my pledge—naught will follow you outside. We are square, no feud exists between us."

"As I thought, Lupe. Now, I want you to assist Neva in making herself presentable, for we must soon venture downstairs. Nobody must see the slightest thing wrong in her dress or manner. Then you will go with us."

Neva and Lupe went slowly into the adjoining bed chamber, with both men at their heels, blades ready. "What about our charge to bring back... you know...?" Raker murmured in Ferret's ear.

"In due course that will be addressed. For now, let's see that their 'ladyships' are dressed."

Chapter Nineteen

IT TOOK NEVA almost an hour to get ready. Both men were growing extremely nervous near the end of that time, even though the delicate beauty assured them that she was not subject to demands and no unwanted callers dared to disturb her here. Ferret marked her words as significant. He asked, "What is going on with the grandee this night that you aren't required?"

"Lord Armando marks the end of his planning and preparation. He now entertains his noble supporters and military men in a sort of pre-victory celebration."

Neva's blunt statement puzzled him. "You mean that he makes his move soon? If so, why aren't you there to show the loyal followers the might of your heka prowess?"

She waved a finger in a depreciatory gesture. It was for Ferret's questions, not her role. "You are mistaken on both counts, sneak-thief Ferret. Tomorrow his liegemen go back to gather their forces. It will be... sometime later that they combine and march. As to my presence," Neva said with a haughty sniff, "it is not necessary. They have seen a demonstration or two already and are convinced. I am neither leman armpiece nor fawning follower, and both Alphonso and those who are his servants must needs know that."

Ferret was secretly impressed by her last statement. She was indeed a power in the marquis's band of plotters, one more potent than he had given credit, and that made him uneasy. How to control such a practitioner of the heka arts in different surroundings posed a problem.

Raker, though, had other things on his mind. "What did you do to get rid of the goldsmith? Nobody can figure it out."

"How do you know nobody can?" Neva countered.

That made the muscular swordsman scowl. "Oh, come on! You damned well threw us to those dogs there in Dertosal, so of course we heard all about it."

She looked at Raker in the mirror, and Neva's lack of comprehension was clear. Not even so accomplished a dissembler as was she could manage such an expression and timbre as she asked, "What do you mean, Raker? I didn't even know you and your friend were in that city, let alone tell the authorities about you. You were blamed for the business at Mer-al's? That is quite unacceptable. Credit is mine, and in a short time I want all to know that it was me who did the work—a demonstration of my power, if you will. They must fear to cross me."

"Who do you mean by 'they'?" Ferret interjected.

Neva didn't even glance at him as she responded, "Every one of Alphonso's subjects and foes not already aware of what I can work."

"Just what 'work' did you do on Mer-al?" Raker again queried.

Her face showed an angelic look as she replied, "Why, I merely allowed his own greed to condemn him, silly boy. He lusted for riches... and got burned."

"Literally?"

"Of course. I used a special something, and the old fool's own words entrapped him. His material form was consumed, and his mind and spirit taken away from this sphere to another, less pleasant one."

Raker recoiled. "That's horrible!"

"No more than he asked for." Neva was sincere and not unemotional as she went on, "Such ones as he must always end thus. I merely hastened the process. Don't judge me for *that*. And don't accuse me of trying to blame it on you, either. I did no such thing."

"Not judge you? That's ironic from she who tried to slay me. If you are so guiltless, Neva, why did you stab me?" he finally demanded.

"Because you had learned too much about me, and your knowledge posed a danger. Then, too, how else was I to get *all* of the money?" She paused, considered a moment, then added with a touch of wistfulness, "Maybe the real reason was because I found myself liking you. What does it matter?"

"It doesn't," Raker said with a hoarse voice and forced gruffness.

"Be careful, son," his comrade cautioned, knowing the gray-eyed man's weaknesses all too well. "She is single-minded and as unscrupulous as she is beautiful."

Neva smiled sweetly. "I love to be talked about like that, you weasel. Am I an animal on display?"

"No," Ferret said without heat, "you are more like a deadly spider caught in its own web. But I'll refrain from personal remarks if you will." Ferret turned, set aside one dagger, and again fumbled inside his jack. "Speaking of deadly, do you know what this is?" He held a lustrous, gray rhomboid in his leather-gloved palm. It was about the size of a dove's egg.

The blue eyes were veiled by the thick, sweeping lashes above them as Neva looked down to view the little globe. "I haven't the slightest idea," she said turning back to her mirror.

"Well, I owe my having it to you, Neva. I found it down below when you and your friends sort of packed us off to enjoy the tender mercies of the underground realms, so to speak. I've only seen its like once before. This is an egg. Have you heard of the arrowsnake?"

She turned to stare. "A what?"

Ferret wasn't buying that. "You heard me, and I'm damned sure you know just what it is, don't you." He was not asking her anything, he was stating a fact. "Look at it close to the lamp. You can see the little devil inside. It's near hatching. Now here's what I'm going to do: Seeing as how it would be quite impossible for us to strut around down there with our blades at your throats, this little egg is going inside your gown—right next to your heart, in fact. One false move, and I'll simply strike you there with my open hand. That will crack the shell, and the hatchling will do the rest."

"You *are* mad! The warmth of my body could cause it to hatch. Arrowsnakes strike at any living thing!"

His companion was as shocked as was Neva. "Hold on, Ferret, you can't do that! She's right—and what if it hatches before Neva's managed to get us outside the castle?"

"Do you trust me, Raker?"

"Of course. You know that I do."

Ferret nodded. "Then let me handle this, my friend. I'm not going to risk our own skins, nor is my little surety a hazard to Neva's life, for that would jeopardize ours in the process. Only if she tries to betray us will she die by the poison of the hatchling arrowsnake—for then assuredly I'll crack it!"

All three started when Lupe spoke. "All of you waste time."

Only Raker laughed at the break in the tension that had been spiraling upward without any of them meaning to cause it to do so. "Wisdom from a bitch wolf," he chuckled. "Right she is, too. We have danger enough to face and have no need for added turmoil. Give me that godsdamned egg, and I'll see that this murderous witch is leashed thus."

"No, chum. I'm the one who'll do that. You're too involved." Ferret looked at his friend, smiled. "It needs be secure, no slippage. Exacting work. Besides, you might be tempted to crack its case and even the score between you two." He took the egg and stood over the seated Neva. "Hold still. I take no pleasure from this intimacy," he added as he gently thrust hand and egg into the bodice of her gown.

"Better the snake that you, Ferret," Neva hissed between clenched teeth, but she made no resistance to his intrusion. "Hurry up. Let's get this over with."

In a few minutes they were heading along a side corridor which Neva assured them was the fastest and safest route for their escape. Ferret walked on Neva's left, Lupe was behind her mistress, and Raker a half-step behind the wolf-woman. Various servitors and a pair of armed guardsmen passed them, but nobody paid any attention, save to acknowledge Neva with a bowed head and a shrinking toward the wall furthest from her. Just as they neared a staircase, Ferret halted progress.

"Hold a moment, Neva. I have second thoughts. Take us to where the grandee keeps his regalia."

"No! That is too dangerous."

"How so? You said he is feting his loyal followers. Surely Armando doesn't cache his jewels in the high hall—or any other public place." When she seemed still intractable, the lean adventurer whispered, "Danger to you, dear sorceress, is making me cross enough to smash the little burden snuggled at your breast. Besides, if you cooperate, I'll return that which you hold most dear."

Neva's smooth brow showed a little wrinkle. "What do you mean?"

Ferret murmured in her ear, "Why I mean the empyrium you keep in the egg I have in my bosom, Neva."

"How did you know?" Neva blurted out.

With a finger to his lips and a secret smile, Ferret began walking very slowly again toward the steps. "Deduced it from what you said about the goldsmith, other things you have said and done. If you can produce mahydrols for someone like the grandee, you can surely have an *infernium* for yourself, sorceress." He stressed the less common name for the stone of elemental fire, empyrium. "Isn't it a boon to those who deal with such practice as yours?"

"You will steal the jewels and ruin me!"

"Not at all. I fear possessing them would be a death warrant."

She stopped, stared at the lean face, trying to read what his dark eyes held. "You speak the truth when you say that, Ferret. If you took so much as a single piece of that regalia, you would not live for many days thereafter."

"And I have no intention of being so greedy. Mark it up to a need to learn if you must. I will see the jewels, and when I have done so, the gem that is your special one will be left here."

Neva couldn't believe him. "It is too high a price to pay for a mere look. You lie!"

"It is too traceable a stone, one most difficult to dispose of in secret. I am merely being practical. If I don't leave it here, I'll toss it into the sea so as to be free of scrying and sendings keyed to the empyrium."

"Very well, I'll show you. Hurry."

The exchange had been in hushed tones, but both Lupe and Raker had heard every word, of course. The weretherion showed not the least interest, but Raker was baffled and said so. "I thought you couldn't open the marquis's vault—you swore that."

"Don't be so trusting, Rake," Ferret said in a jovial voice. "If she ensorcelled the damned things she's certainly able to get at them whenever she wishes.

"Is that so?" he asked her.

Neva didn't turn as she hissed, "Certainly, you ass."

"Then the grandee is a fool, for she can't be trusted."

Ferret's voice was harsh as he told his friend, "The dilemmas of crowned heads are ever thus. Trust? He trusts no one! Nor can he. He uses, bribes, threats, promises—and sets his followers against each other. Rest assured of that. What little counters has he put to make sure you don't abscond with his regalia, Neva?"

"Negligible ones. Besides, I have no use for the jewels."

Raker's voice was scornful as he corrected, "You mean you can't make use of them personally because you can't pretend to royal status, so you'll manipulate the monarch wearing them."

"Whatever. In any event, it isn't your affair. It is time to stop this useless conversation, though, for we might be overheard." She had brought them through a little archway off a landing, and the four now moved at a normal walking pace along a narrow hallway. After passing through several rooms, and down another crooked flight of stairs, they came to a cluttered storage chamber. "The vault is beyond there," she said, pointing to the corner of the room.

"How do we enter?" queried Ferret.

She couldn't resist giving a small smile of pride. "I located a secret entrance built centuries ago. Not even Armando has any idea it exists. Here, I'll show you."

Before she could act, Ferret was close beside her. "I trust you with my life, Neva, but just in case..."

Neva actually spat and cursed, "Godsdamn you!"

"Tut, tut! Have I done something wrong? You weren't thinking of giving us the slip now, were you? Don't answer, just work the panel."

"Satisfied?" Neva said as she depressed a piece of molding. There was a soft click, and a slight crack appeared. "The place where the wall panels meet here in the corner turns. Push, and you can step through."

Ferret saw clearly. The section was V-shaped, and but one person at a time could pass beyond thus. "How interesting a problem." He motioned to Lupe. "Please go first." The wolf-woman didn't hesitate in obeying. "Now Raker, you enter." His comrade was quick to follow, although he drew his sword before going after Lupe.

"Are you two safe there?" Ferret called softly through the crack.

"Aye," answered Raker. "Lupe is being most docile and cooperative."

The lanky man grinned at Neva, then said to Raker, "I suspected she would be. Stand ready to receive our guide. Go through Neva."

"Bastard," she muttered under her breath as she used the turning panels to disappear from the storeroom.

It was only a few heartbeats between her exit and Ferret's own. A glance showed Raker watching both carefully. They were in a small space whose far wall was of solid ashlar blocks. A dim illumination came from some magickally engendered source above. "Your work, Neva?"

She nodded. "Of course. It is keyed to activate in my presence."

"Clever. I'll have to remember that trick," Ferret said with a hint of admiration. He slipped the catch back into place so that the panel was locked again, and none would note its presence. "The vault is beyond the stone wall, I take it."

"Where else? There's another secret door in the blocks. Some old mason built a pivoting section which is beautifully balanced." So stating, Neva moved to a place near the wall in question. There she kneeled, pushed a small pave sideways, then stood up and stepped on it with all her weight.

Ferret's keen ears heard the muffled sound of the stone working a metal rocker arm, drawing up one end of another at right angles to it. A pin in that second arm dropped free of its stone housing, and a slight pressure from Neva's little hand caused the granite blocks there to move inwards. "Your witchlight, Rake. It's dark in the vault."

The blond swordsman quickly brought forth the little case, opened it one-handed, and shined the still-intense violet-white beam inside. "Diana's dimpled derriere!" he exclaimed.

His surprise and amazement could be shared. All three could see a fantastic play of blue and green rays from where they stood as the harsh witchlight struck the mahydrols and was turned into reflections of watery wonder. Neva and Lupe had probably seen this effect before, of course, for they displayed no awe. Not so Ferret, who goggled at the play of lights, then took a quick look inside. "Better that that!" he said as he hastily withdrew his head so as to keep an eye on the sorceress and wolf woman, "Go on in, Raker—and you two follow him. I want to get a close look."

"All right," Neva agreed reluctantly, "But we can't stay long. Someone could enter the vault anytime."

With left arm placed carefully around the dainty woman's shoulders, Ferret bent low to examine the pieces of bejeweled regalia where they rested in their open cases atop a long gilt table placed in the treasure repository. "This workmanship is incredible. These look like the most ancient of masterpieces, not like some newly wrought stuff."

"The grandee is of ancient lineage, no upstart pretender. He had old drawings from which the goldsmith worked. Mer-al was a copyist, not a creator," Neva asserted almost defensively.

"I can't say, not having seen the drawings. The pieces do call to mind some like ones of famous sort—which, Neva?"

She shook her head. "I promised you a look, not a lecture. You've had your chance to gawk, so keep your word. The bargain is now complete. Give me my empyrium or be damned!"

"Neither," Ferret said as he moved as fast as his namesake. His hand held flat, he struck Neva's chest where the egg lay beneath her gown.

With a horrified gasp, the woman fainted.

"You promised her..." Raker managed, shocked by his friend's act.

"Neva isn't the only one able to lie," Ferret responded grimly.

Lupe was laughing silently during that exchange.

Chapter Twenty

As the other two stood watching, the lean adventurer busily took the jeweled gold case from where he kept it, opened the box, and withdrew a gleaming stone of fiery hues. "I said I wouldn't carry this empyrium away, and there I spoke true. Rake, old chum of mine, have you that pair of magnets on you?"

Raker didn't want to assist his comrade, not after what he had just seen. Yes, Neva had tried to kill him once, but she was so lovely, so desirable! Besides, such a treacherous act was absolutely anathema to Raker, and it was his character, not merely chivalric training, which made it go against his grain. "I'm not aiding you in anything, Ferret—not after murdering Neva in such foul fashion!"

"Oh, do stop being such a blockhead. She's not dead."

"Bullshit."

Lupe couldn't remain silent. "Your packmate tells you truth. I can see her breathing, hear it, smell her exhalations. My 'mistress' swooned from fright, for the act Ferret performed is something she herself would have done."

"I don't understand," Raker said angrily to Ferret. "Why are you screwing around with my head?!"

His comrade spoke hurriedly. "I'm not, but I haven't time to explain and plead. Hurry, man! I need those magnets. Neva's just fainted, as Lupe told you. The so-called arrowsnake egg was naught but a pigeon's. I found in a nest on the ledge of one of the loopholes in that tower room. Aren't you glad I picked it up and took it along on a whim?"

"Whim?" Raker said as brought forth his little magnets and handed them to Ferret. "You seldom act on capricious notions, Ferret. I'll expect to hear your full accounting as soon as we get out of here. What are you doing?"

"About the same thing you use them for—sympathetic magick, but a bit more complex than that you employ. Instead of using them as attractants, I plan to make them a part of an antipathetic casting." As he spoke, Ferret was already at work. First he found which ends of the little iron bars were polarized so as to draw each other away or repel, then he set one aside, careful to note the alignment. He used the one he held to stroke the huge mahydrol in the crown, repeating some formula as he worked. After some time he was satisfied, set the magnet aside.

"Now for the empyrium." With that jewel in hand, he took up the second little iron bar, worked it along the flame-gem as he again spoke the words to invoke a specific quality borne by the magnet upon the stone. "There, I think that this will suffice. I've adapted one of the old enchantments of the master purloiners to a special use—as you'll soon see, Raker. Are you with me?"

"Of course! What must I do then?"

Ferret grinned. "Sheath that blade of yours, and hold the magnets so that you feel their opposition."

"That's all? But Lupe..."

"Lupe will carry Neva, right Lupe?"

The weretherion stepped over to where the fragile-looking woman lay, picked her up, and only then said, "You may concentrate on what your brother asks of you, man. I will not interfere nor cause you harm." She addressed Raker, not Ferret, for she knew the lean man's reasoning.

"I'll be boiled in batshit," Raker exclaimed as he accepted the pair of magnets and held them as he had been told. "Why does that feral bitch now act so docilely?"

"Hush! Hold those bars steady," Ferret told his comrade in a tense voice as he held the empyrium directly above the crown. He was centering the fiery gem above the watery jewel, moving the former this way and that, up and down. "There... I *think* that's got it," he breathed as he relaxed the two fingers which held the blazing stone. "Yes!"

With the empyrium floating a half-foot above the huge mahydrol, swaying ever so slightly, Ferret stepped back softly, waved the others to the secret way standing open. "Back now, and hurry!"

Lupe was strong. She carried Neva as a child would bear a doll, easily and without strain. She slipped out of the vault, Raker at her heels, and Ferret brought up the rear. As he passed through he pivoted the stones, and the opening became solid blocks of ashlar once more. After making sure the vault was locked, and returning the flagstone to its original position, he breathed a sigh of relief.

"So far so good. Will you guide us from the fortress, Lupe?"

She smiled at him, and the look was appropriately wolfish. "As you knew, Ferret, I will be most pleased to—but *she* will come with us!"

Ferret shook his head. "No. Neva will remain here in the castle. Getting her out is too difficult, puts us at too great a risk, Lupe. You can leave her here, though."

"Why should that satisfy me?"

"You know my opinion of her," Ferret said levelly. "I do her no favors, especially if she is discovered near the vault."

Lupe was willing to go along with what the lanky adventurer said. "I'm not sure what you plan, but surely it is fitting. You are worthy of bearing an animal name, man."

"Call me Ferret," he said sweetly as he watcher Lupe place her former mistress gently on the floor of the little hidden room.

Raker looked from one to the other, an expression of slow understanding coming to his face as he thought. "Bouff! Now I catch on. She was ready to sacrifice you, wouldn't pay a sou to save you," he said looking up from the unconscious Neva to the wolf woman. Lupe met his gaze, nodded curtly, then went to the panel. "If I am to lead you two from this pile, I must go first. Follow me exactly. I may move very quickly, and then so must you—and make no more noise than clumsy humans must."

"Be kind, Lupe," Ferret admonished in jest. "In any case I am sure that you'll find both Rake here and myself a bit above the average when it comes to men."

"Had I thought otherwise, I'd have taken my chances alone," the weretherion countered as she eased open the secret panel.

Lupe took an entirely different route. They were soon down to the level below the ground, that portion in which the common folk worked and dwelled. The wolf woman seemed to have familiarized herself with the warren of ways in the basements and cellars of the castle complex. With her hyper-keen senses, she avoided the numerous others they would have otherwise encountered. That there were frequent patrols of armed guards couldn't be doubted, and they glimpsed several, were nearly cornered by one squad whose officer inadvertently led them down a wrong corridor. The serjeant managed to call attention to the error just before it was too late for all concerned.

"Why not patrol here?" whispered Ferret as the armored backs of the last two soldiers disappeared around the corner.

"This is the route to the prison-place below. Only the dungeon gaol-men are supposed to go here."

"Makes sense," Raker observed. "Don't want just anyone to know who's held down there, or how they're treated, do we?"

They continued their circuitous route, alternately traveling and lurking in hiding, for almost half of an hour. At last Lupe pointed to a spiral stairway. "This leads up to a tower flanking the little door at the back of the side of this place."

"The postern gate?" Raker asked.

"I think that is what it is called. It opens to the countryside, not the town. There are guards up there, so we must fight. Be ready."

Ferret put his hand on her arm. "Hold a bit, Lupe. We thank you for this aid—later there won't be time."

"It is nothing. Don't delay."

"But I must. Before we confront the guards there is something I need to do. What's at the head of those stairs?"

She thought a moment. "A round room, a door to a little yard before the gate. At night there are four soldiers there with big axes, two more above with crossbows."

"You are a nonesuch, Lupe. I think Raker and I own you a debt." He looked up the steps, considered, then turned to the wolf woman again. "When we get to the room up there, have the door ready to open, but wait until I say 'open'—and that means no matter what else happens, got it?"

Lupe looked blankly at him. "What is to get? I will do as you say."

"More women should be like you in some ways, Lupe!"

"I am a weretherion bitch, not a human woman."

"My statement stands," Ferret said with a grin. "Let's go!"

Lupe wound her way up the stone stairs first, then came Raker, and Ferret brought up the rear. A single, dirty-brown witchlight cast its glow into the tower, and by staying close to the wall the three were almost invisible in the near gloom. As soon as Lupe was stationed at the door she looked at the two men and waited expectantly.

"Tired of holding those magnets at their opposition point, chum?"

Raker wasn't jesting when he replied, "My fingers tremble and arms ache from the strain, Ferret. Can I stop now?"

"No! What I want you to do it reverse one as quickly as you can, and then bring the two smoothly together so that they cling to eachother."

"Easy," the blond swordsman said, and with a little twist of his lower hand to initiate the move, he had the two little bars of metal locked together in mutual embrace. "So?"

"Just so!" Ferret had hardly gotten that out when a silent shock wave struck the castle. It was followed by a flash of fiery turquoise light, and then a whooshing and hissing and roaring and crashing sound that seemed to come from everywhere. The whole lasted only a few seconds, then all was normal, save the sounds of uproar.

The wolf woman stared at Ferret. "Are you a sorcerer too?"

"Relax, Lupe. My friend is but a hedge-magician—but he does cobble us some great bits of magick from time to time," Raker added with enthusiasm as he punched Ferret's arm without too much force. "Great going, old boy!" He understood now exactly what his comrade had done. "That puts little Neva into the cesspool head first," he gloated. Then remorse overtook him. "Oh, no! What about the jewels?!"

At the same time, Lupe, recalling the lean adventurer's magickal work the night she lost her two fellows, was not so pleased. It was sufficient for her, though, that Ferret was not like Neva. "Now?" she asked.

Ferret waved away Raker's concern. "Your rapier, man!" Raker forgot the lost wealth, recalling the guardsmen outside and their need to escape. The sword was out of its scabbard in a trice. "Open, Lupe," Ferret barked as he drew his own blades.

She easily yanked the heavy door aside, keeping clear to enable the two armed men to exit into the postern yard.

Ferret came out in a low crouch. His head swiveled to take in the whole scene at once, then he scuttled sideways to give his companion room. All four of the guards were standing in a row with their backs partially turned, staring at the main hall building off to the right. The one on the far end never knew what hit him as Ferret's daggers struck.

Raker came forth as soon as he saw Ferret move away, and without hesitation he advanced at a near-run, lunged, and the soldier on the opposite end of the line gasped and clawed frantically at the foot of steel protruding from the front of his neck.

As if on cue, the two surviving guardsmen turned in opposite directions to see what had happened to their neighbors, trying at the same time to bring their unwieldly voulge-forks to bear. There was a clangor as metal-clad bodies struck stone. Ferret was already inside his foeman's reach, so the contest was uneven indeed.

The gray-eyed man with the long rapier, however, had to free his weapon, recover, and by then the soldier had managed to assess the situation, level his polearm, and defend himself. Knowing he had little hope he still did his best, and as he fought he shouted, "ENEMY AT THE POSTERN GATE!" He called nothing further, because by then Raker had deflected the stabbing lunge he made with the weapon, spun along the shaft, and driven the sword into his body. The guardsman groaned, fell with a clatter. "Four down," Raker said to his still-crouching friend.

"Get over and help Lupe unbar the gate," Ferret said in a hoarse whisper. "I'll stay here to keep anyone else who shows up busy—and take care of the arbalesters above." As he spoke the lean man slipped back to a shadowy place where he could look at the rampart above and watch the two ways leading into the little bailey. His dirks were gone, and in his hands he held steel throwing knives.

Raker ran to assist the wolf woman, knowing that besides the heavy bar and the numerous bolts to draw, an entry point of this sort would be locked, chained, and padlocked, too. "Damn that noisy fellow," he muttered as he came to the gateway and attacked the big lock he saw set in the oak there.

Of course the guardsman's cry for help brought the two crossbowmen, albeit tardily. They had been dicing in a turret above, so they arrived far too late to succor their fellows. "Tlokhala!" the first to peer down into the yard exclaimed, naming the Atlantlan goddess of vengeance and destruction as he saw his dead comrades sprawled there. Then he looked towards the gate, raised his arbalest, and said, "They're at the postern, and I've got one—yaagh!"

A steel point had sliced across his forehead, passing just below his helmet, a bit above his eyes. An inch closer, and the blade would have pierced his skull, a bit lower and it would have taken his eyes. As it was he was not seriously harmed, merely blinded by the gush of blood streaming down into his eyes. He dropped the crossbow, pawing at his face.

Next to him the other archer tried to bring his arbalest to bear on whomever had sent that missile to bring down his companion, ducked back quickly as another steel blade sent sparks flying from the granite next to him as it whizzed past.

"Hurry!" Ferret urged unnecessarily, for Raker was working at his best speed, and Lupe could do nothing more save await his opening of the two locks still preventing their opening of the rear gate. His voice did bring a response from the crossbowman above, who sent his quarrel flying toward the sound.

The commotion in the great hall aside, there were still plenty of men to heed the call at the postern. Running feet could be heard on the parapets above, more coming from the place which led to the long building flanking the hall. Raker cried, "Got one!" as he turned the main lock open. There was still the padlock securing the chain to go. It would take a full minute for him to work that mechanism. Too long. The blond swordsman dashed back into the open, diving to grab up one of the heavy voulges there on the pavement.

Ferret saw him, winced as several bolts clacked and thunked dangerously near Raker, went skittering off in ricochet or shattered from square impact on the granite. He moved, threw, sending all of his remaining points upward to where a full dozen arbalesters were ranked. A bolt passed through his sleeve, another brushed his cheek and left a little gash, but no worse occurred. In return, Ferret was rewarded by the sound of several cries and groans, and the sight of disappearing upper bodies as the guardsmen ducked to avoid his deadly missiles.

Clang-THUD. The noise came as Raker used his full power and weight to complete a massive swing of the polearm. He spun as he brought it up and around, extending his arms to their fullest as might a hammer thrower. The thick iron links of the chain took the full force of the blow. The sharp steel of the voulge's cleaver-like head, with incredible weight and momentum driving it on, struck those links squarely. The oak behind them was unyielding, so the iron loops were cut through, the chain sundered. As the voulge continued on to bury itself deep in the wood, the long broken chain rattled against the stone, the still-fast padlock ringing upon the paves. "Come on, Ferret!"

He had heard the noise, knew what it meant, and was already sprinting towards them as Raker and Lupe hauled the thick planks of the postern gate inwards. Ferret shot through the opening first, for this was no time to hesitate.

"DRO—uff!"

Raker was shoving Lupe through the partially opened gate, pressing her on even as his comrade vanished. That sound which came was just sufficient for him to react, so as his feet found nothingness, Raker managed to relax, take the fall, and roll, even as he retained his grip on the sword. He saw Ferret nearby in the darkness, half kneeling, feeling himself. "You okay?"

"I think so, but I'll have a few nasty bruises to show for my haste, chum. Let's haul ass out of here!"

Without hesitation Raker moved ahead in a loping run, not going full speed because Ferret was limping a little. After a couple of dozen strides, though, the lanky man was going along at a near-normal clip, so his friend was having to exert himself to keep up. They had covered nearly a half-mile when Lupe suddenly came running up to join them.

"This way," she said without any sign of pant or strain. "I know where there are horses for you to ride."

Chapter Twenty-One

"CHAR-RUP! MOVE YOU slug, *move*!" Raker's mount responded by going from an ambling walk to what might have passed for a canter. "Horses, she said. Damned bitch!"

Ferret, nearby, laughed. "What wolf wouldn't want such steeds as ours? Meat on the table. Heh, heh, heh!"

In fact the weretherion had led them to a small cluster of dwellings about a league distant from Torenegro. There the two had managed to steal their mounts, a pair of worn dray horses. Lupe pointed out their path, then vanished into the night. It was now midmorning, and the two fugitives were somewhere in the midst of the wildest portion of the Penumbratos. So far they could detect no pursuit. Both were skilled in evasion, and they had taken pains to hide their trail.

"To have lost those steeds we left in the town is a crime, Ferret," his companion lamented as his plug slowed down to its ambling walk again.

The lean adventurer agreed, to a point. "If there were anyone hot on our trail, I would have to concur. As it is, these bags of bones will make our return to Dertosal a longer proposition—but it beats walking, no?"

"Not by much."

"Let's look on the bright side, what say?"

Raker glanced blackly at his comrade. "Is there one? Without Neva in tow, I don't even know why we're bothering to go back to see the colonel and his pet priest. It's crazy!"

"Well, you and I aren't walking; that's a plus."

"The genets we once owned are lost and gone forever."

Ferret ignored the counter. "They haven't managed to find our tracks yet. That means our amulets are working, which in turn means that the grandee hasn't managed to get a big-time hekabender onto us. Aren't you glad that Neva is in... disfavor, shall we say?"

"You mean dead."

"Not bloody likely, chum! She fainted and bumped her head in the fall—it wasn't as if she were drugged, bound, and gagged. Hells, Rake, she had plenty of time to recover and get clear before my little diversion was activated."

The blond swordsman wasn't buying that. "You're telling me that you left her there safe and sound? No way. If she'd have come to, Neva would have gone back into the vault and mucked up your casting. Hey, what did you do there with those elemental gems?"

"Neva couldn't get back through the pivoting stones, my friend," Ferret said with a chortle. "I'm not *that* stupid! When I re-set the pin which locked the stones in place, I bent the bar so that it couldn't operate again—at least not until someone came and fixed the mechanism, and that would take hours. I can see it now. Neva wakes up, tries to check on the goodies in the marquis's vault, and then beats a hasty retreat when she discovers the secret door is inoperable."

"Uh-uh. She'd run and tell Lord Armando. They'd have gone in the front entrance and messed up things that way. So what *did* you do there?"

"Time to give these nags a rest, don't you think?" Ferret said unresponsively. "We'd better keep moving, though. Let dismount and walk 'em."

Raker was the more knowledgeable horseman by far, and he swore at his comrade as he dismounted and began to trudge up the long slope, "By the gods, Ferret, you've got me enmeshed in your damned yarn-spinning and not paying attention to important matters! Will you stop spinning this out and give plain answers?"

"Sorry, Rake. I'll try. Neva couldn't ask for anyone's help because what she had done was treason. She certainly got away and went back posthaste to her own chambers. She's now out of favor because she's the one that was supposed to wield heka to, amongst other things, prevent what happened from happening."

"Which was?"

The long face of his companion broadened in a grin as Ferret told Raker, "I used fire to fight water."

Raker sneered. "Very amusing. Pray tell me how?"

"But you said I was an inept practitioner...."

"'Piss-poor' is possibly preferable to 'inept,' but so what?"

Ferret laughed again. "How you hate to give me credit. I think you'll soon be studying one or another of the casting arts so as to surpass mine own considerable skills and talents. Ah well," the lean man sighed with mock resignation, "the great are forever being chased after by those wishing to displace them."

"Now I mean it, weasel—cut the crap and tell me straight!"

"All right, all right! No need to get huffy, chum. Because the mahydrol in the crown and Neva's big empyrium were heavily charged with castings, it was easy for me to add a little something on top—a short-term enchantment to make the two repel each other. The magnets were the tool, the key. By reversing their polarity fields, you brought the two gems into sudden, sharp contact."

Raker's eyebrows shot up. "Fire upon water. So the two stones reacted and—"

"Blooey! There was a nasty explosion of energy as they canceled each other out of existence. I'll bet the vault is in shambles, and the other regalia a mess from the flames and steam that followed! The grandee's plans are blown away as clouds before wind."

"So it is true about the incompatibility of such jewels.... But where did you get that elemental fire one?"

Ferret tugged the reins to keep the old dray horse he led moving, for it was trying to graze. "Neva's own, old man, Neva's own! It was a nasty thing she used in her sorcerous work, her intercourse with demonkind. Likely the empyrium was what she employed to fry away poor Chasal Mer-al, the goldsmith. I thought I saw tormented souls trapped in the heart of the jewel, but I couldn't bring myself to examine it closely. Be glad you didn't get a look into it, Rake. It was awful. Have to hand it to her, though. A gem of elemental earth or one of air wouldn't have done a thing to the empyrium, although terrionds and asylphars do react against each other. She definately had it as a counter to the Lord of the Penumbratos's magickal powers. If the grandee got out of line, I'll bet little Neva had some ready tricks up her sleeve."

"You say it was Neva's gem, how did you manage..."

"While you pinned Lupe 'neath that basket, I contrived to extract it from dear little Neva's jewel casket. Was she surprised when the Ægyptain's talisman of disarming worked so nicely! Remind me to send a note of thanks sometime."

Raker shook his head. "Not likely to be welcomed, considering his line of work. Let's steer clear of him and his—"

"Haul ass!"

That exclamation made the gray-eyed adventurer stop his rambling and look along their back trail. Sure enough, far in the distance were a handful of black specks. Even as Raker stared the handful became a swarm. "Looks like they've found our tracks. Don't mount up—they might not have seen us!" he commanded as Ferret placed his foot in a stirrup. "There's a nice bit of rock there, see? We'll be out of line of sight. Head along it into that cut, and we should come out still going the right direction, but a ridge away from those chasing us."

Ferret was already bent low, tugging his horse along as he tried to lope to the bare stone patch his comrade had indicated. Raker followed, and in a brief time they were wandering through a maze of dry washes and little valleys. The terrain was harsh, hot, and virtually devoid of life aside from scrub, cactus, and small animals typical of arid regions. They alternately rode the tired horses, then walked them, never stopping save when their mounts seemed about to collapse if they didn't halt.

"We can't tell if pursuit is near in this mess," Raker growled. "Any tricks, Ferret?"

His comrade couldn't help. "Used up about everything in me, and there's been no time to regain strength. 'Fraid we'll have to rely on your ability now, chum."

"No fear necessary, Ferret. I'll lose 'em. Follow me." He went along a little depression, then began to work his way up its bank, keeping to the rock shelves. This sort of travel was demanding, and it was their only hope of escaping. It was full dark when the blond man finally called a halt. Horses and men were sweat-stained, panting, but they had managed to cover several miles of incredibly rough terrain since spotting those chasing them. "The moon will rise around midnight, and then we'll move on again. Too risky to try now, and we all need a rest. I think we've given them the slip, and they won't be able to track us until daylight. How close will they come to Dertosal?"

"I doubt the grandee will want his men to violate the city's territory, Rake. There's enmity between the two, you know."

"Know? I suppose the colonel's going to be angry about one of Lord Armando's agents committing a crime in Dertosal. That's hardly undying opposition."

Ferret sat down, eased back to find a comfortable spot, his feet propped up on his saddle. "Say, Raker, I thought you had a bit of a soft spot for Neva."

"Hmmm. Maybe a little—at times."

"Then relax and listen. She was telling us some of the truth."

Raker sat, tried to see his friend's face in the darkness. "Yeah, about a tenth of the time, when it didn't count."

"Close. She wasn't lying, though, when she said she hadn't set us up for the business with the goldsmith."

"No? Then…"

His friend shifted position, sitting up and leaning closer to where Raker sat. "The set-up was managed by the colonel and his pious pal, Intensity Elfuego. They knew damned well we hadn't a thing to do with Mer-al, because those two were aware of at least most of what was going on!"

"So we were supposed to go mess things up in Torenegro, then haul Neva and the regalia back for Colonel de la Cabarro and his clerical crony."

Ferret slapped his leg in frustration. "Shit. You have a way of putting things that destroys my theories like waves do sand castles. Maybe I'm wrong…."

"Me? All I said was that we were supposed to do what we did. Wrong how?"

"What did we do, Raker? Do we have Neva? The jewels?"

"Of course not. We discredited her, though, and you blew the regalia to bits. I still don't understand all the rigmarole about the crown and scepter and all the other stuff, though. Successful challenges to kings have been made in the past without all that bullshit in tow."

That assertion was clearly erroneous. "Maybe not in the form the grandee desired," Ferret responded, "but every political entity on Ærth that's worth considering has its magickal devices, Raker. Hells, man, that goes all the way down to battle standards and banners, too. Sometimes the power rests more in people than in things, but once established, the head of state goes for objects which he can keep nice and safe—and in his grasp."

"Maybe so, but your casting ended up in Neva being made to look like a fool, and the ensorceled regalia in the dumper. And another thing," Raker added with sudden excitement, "you are wrong too about something really important!"

"I am, am I?" Ferret spoke with great skepticism evident in his voice.

"You bet your sweet ass, old son. You said we didn't have Neva as prisoner or the jewels either."

"You say we do?"

It was Raker's turn to laugh sardonically. "I say we don't, but only because you chose to leave her behind and used the opposing elemental gems to muck up the grandee's scheme for glory. We could have Neva and the whole array with us now."

"We'd have had a tough time getting away so laden. . . ."

"Now you're rationalizing, Ferret. Hells, with a little more planning, we could have had good horses waiting and been miles ahead of pursuit. Lupe would have been willing to assist, I'll bet, waited by the postern with three mounts. It was possible, but we didn't do it."

Ferret frowned. "I hate planning such things. Too many unknowns, and once I start operating by hunch and instinct, it's hard for me to switch to a more orderly path, you know."

His comrade said, "I know," and there was no rancor in his voice. "I'm not criticizing, I'm just telling you that you underestimated what you and I could do. Now think! The colonel or Intensity Elfuego had those dossiers on us. They must have quite an intelligence operation at their command—or access to one of top quality. *They* knew we could do it."

"Now that annoys the shit out of me. Did they think we'd be so godsdamned stupid as to hand them all that on a platter?"

"Not at all, old boy, not at all. But you were quick to point out how dangerous it would be to tote the regalia around, how difficult to dispose of. My guess is that they thought our natural larceny would move us to take jewels then and there, consider the consequences later."

"So we would hide it, come to them to collect reward money for Neva, and then try to get something extra for the regalia, knowing that it was doom to possess it personally."

"Do you think they would have given us much for the stuff, Ferret?"

The lean man spat. "The hot end of an iron, likely. Those machinating bastards would have known where we hid it easily enough. Then your head and mine on a platter for somebody... who?"

"You figure that part, Ferret. I'm going to catch a few winks."

"Do me a favor, Rake. Let me do the resting—an hour should suffice. Then I'll let you sleep until the moon's high enough for us to see the trail, agreed?"

Grumbling a bit for show, the blond swordsman allowed he could remain alert for an hour. He watched his comrade assume a seated position with legs crossed and folded before him, knew it was something to do with meditation and trance which Ferret had learned while in the east. Raker had tried it a couple of times, but to him the contortions and concentration were more torture than benefit. In a minute the slow, deep breathing sound coming from Ferret told him that his friend was indeed locked within himself. Raker got up and began to walk silently around their resting place, observing not only their back trail, but all other places where followers might come creeping up to surprise them.

The exercise brought him quickly out of his drowsy state. The cool night air was refreshing. Raker actually enjoyed such a wild and barren place, and after sundown there was a fair amount of activity as animal inhabitants came out of hiding from the heat and began their routines of staying alive. When winter came the cycle would be different, but now almost everything took place at night. Owls and rodents aplenty, a distant wolf howl, various other sights and sounds too, but no trace of a human ambusher. Raker wondered if the howl had been Lupe's. Perhaps she was stalking the men who followed. That made him shudder. Nasty things, weretherios, maneaters! But Lupe had been acceptable—after the bitch had decided that Neva was treacherous and not to be served.

Raker completed another circuit, wondering amongst other things just how the devious woman had become a sorceress and managed to enlist the services of three of those shape-shifting devils. Before he knew it an hour had passed—a bit more than that, from what he could estimate from the position of the stars. He crept back into camp, found his comrade standing there awaiting his return.

"All quiet out there?"

"Nobody around at all. You should keep checking though, just in case."

Ferret directed his friend to a bit of rest. "Will do that, Rake. There's a couple of hours left before we have to move on, so take it easy."

It was around two-thirty in the pre-morning darkness. A near-full moon gave the two men sufficient light to guide their horses, and those animals, refreshed from rest and a little grazing on scrub, carried Ferret and Raker along a descending slope toward what they thought was a road they could vaguely see in the distance. If indeed it was a track, then they knew that their escape would be assured, for the direction it ran angled eastward toward where Dertosal lay over the last bit of worn mountains.

"I think I have a handle on this business now, Rake," Ferret said as they progressed. "I figured it out while I was in that trance."

"You and your trances. Well, tell me. Maybe you'll convince me to take up that yodee stuff yet."

"Stop with the yodee, its *yo-ga*. Anyway, I thought I recognized the design, or the one which inspired it, I should say. The regalia was fashioned after the ancient imperial jewels of Atlantal."

Raker wasn't impressed by that revelation. "So what? Lots of art and jewelry is inspired by old masterworks—Atlantlan, Ægyptain, Grecian, Roman."

"I taught you that."

"Did not. I learned about it when I was a child."

Ferret dropped that part of the discussion. "The 'so what' is that the pieces' main gems were all blues and greens, and four had mahydrols. That's just as the Imperial Atlantlan original."

"Mer-al was a copycat!"

"Don't make fun of me! Mer-al was working from specifications, but he was an artisan, a true master of his art. He surpassed the ancient work."

Raker was still unimpressed. "What I get from that is that we really blew a fortune."

"That we did," Ferret concurred. "But the important part is the tie to Atlantal. If we dug into the grandee's background, I'll stake my life on his being related to the ancient talrañs of that island. His lineage must go back to the emperors who ruled half the known world from Atlantis."

"What makes you so certain?"

"The regalia was enchanted for power from and over water, the same as the Atlantlan original. Armando del Vargos wasn't planning on ruling Iberia, his scheme was to reconstruct the Atlantlan Empire!"

"Jupiter and Juno! And we messed it up? Brother, is the grandee going to be mad at us!"

Ferret coughed. "Going to be angry? He's probably sent out every man he can find. If we're caught, he'll use every torture known to man to make us regret our interference with his scheme! Our asses are nearly cooked, chum."

"No sweat. We'll make Dertosal before those troops of his catch up with us."

"I hate to say it, Raker, but we can't just march into that city and expect to be greeted warmly. In fact, what we can expect if the colonel gets ahold of us is a fast death and secret burial."

That took the blond swordsman aback. "What? We just saved Dertosal from tyranny… sort of."

"Oh yes. Those two there were playing their own game. They had plans of their own for those special jewels. The grandee's fury will blow this whole thing wide open. The king of Aragon, every sovereign lord in Iberia and its neighboring states, too, will know all about the plot soon. De la Cabarro and Elfuego won't want anyone connecting them to it, even laterally with an opposing plot—which you know they were hatching. We know something which they don't want bandied about. If they get their hands on us, we're dead!"

Raker reined in his plodding mount, and when Ferret did the same, the gray-eyed man stared at his companion, then growled, "What a fine fix you've managed to put us in now. The grandee's hammer is about to flatten us, and ahead is destruction. I told you we shouldn't go to Dertosal, godsdamnit!"

Because he couldn't refute any of that, Ferret said nothing as he kicked his weary jade into motion toward the road nearby. His path angled in the direction of the city that had brought their undoing.

Chapter Twenty-Two

"BACCHUS'S BUTT, MAN! Where are you going? We've got to take off for the wildest part of these damned mountains, hide out in the hills until this blows over!"

Ferret slowed his horse and turned in the saddle to look at his comrade. "Not a chance, Rake. They'd catch us in a day, two at the outside. We have only one hope, and I'm going to take that gamble." He then faced away and kept riding.

Raker, being who and what he was, didn't try arguing. He followed Ferret. The lanky adventurer was his only friend and sworn comrade. Ferret being that sure, Raker was satisfied. Slim chance or none, he'd stay with his comrade to the end. "At least tell me what we're doing," the gray-eyed swordsman said as he finally managed to get his slow steed up to where Ferret's slightly faster plug was trotting along.

"Getting the most mileage out of these nags before abandoning them," Ferret responded as he slapped his horse to keep it moving at the pace the animal thought far too brisk. "We'll keep riding until just before first light, then go on afoot."

"I'd say you had gone completely crazed from the strain, only I know you too well. Without mounts we have two possible recourses, the river or the city. Is it to be the Ebro or Dertosal?"

Ferret laughed. "Very good, Rake! Both. We lose the grandee's men at the river, then sneak into the city unbeknownst to our 'friends' there."

"Now there's a positive attitude," Raker rejoined in the same light bantering manner as Ferret affected. "Shaking the grandee's trackers is an easy matter. The rest is soft cheese to eat."

"Most likely," his friend agreed. "By the time that they find our trail, the sun will be up, and when they get this far, the whole group will start to get nervous, move cautiously."

After considering that statement for a few minutes, Raker said, "The proximity of Dertosal."

"That and the possibility that we are agents of its Lord Mayor—ostensibly a loyal vassal of the Count of Tarragona, he again a leigeman of the King of Aragon, against whom the Marquis Penumbratos plots most treasonously."

"Most," the gray-eyed man echoed drily. "When do you think to send these nags galloping off to make a false trail?"

At that query Ferret smiled. "As close to our river destination as possible, considering daylight and terrain. I leave that matter in your knowledgeable hands."

After that brief exchange the two were silent as they rode. The way was difficult, with many ups and downs, and well before dawn their sorry steeds were moving slowly and breathing in a labored manner. Feeling guilty, they kept using boot heel and slapping reins to get the worn animals to exert all they had. This allowed them to progress at a pace alternating between a walk and a slow trot.

"First light," Raker observed. "Come on, lazy, and let's show these so-called horses what a man afoot can do. With that he slid easily from the saddle, and in a second was jogging ahead. His mount seemed inspired by its unburdened state and Raker's example, and it came along after at a fair pace without more urging that the slight tugging of its reins now and then.

Following his comrade's example, Ferret did likewise, and so the two men and their animals went ahead for the half hour until the top edge of the sun showed its vermillion curve on the horizon. With full light, Raker saw a vantage point not far away, and he headed off up the long slope toward the crest of the ridge ahead. When they attained that summit the whole of the sun was visible in the sky, with a hand's breadth of space between it and the land.

"How in the name of the dozen deceiving devils did we manage it?!" Ferret was certainly surprised and happy.

Raker hated to dampen his excitement, but he knew something his companion obviously didn't. "That *is* the Ebro, old man, but don't get too confident. We were traveling north and east, so we're a long way from the city."

After some discussion they rode along the ridge for a way, heading upstream. Raker was looking for a likely place for them to dismount. When a few minutes later he spotted a ravine which continued on in their direction, cutting its way down in a gradual fashion toward the river valley below, he headed toward it. At a boulder the blond adventurer dismounted, and then Ferret clambered out of his saddle to stand beside him. Raker used his scabbarded sword to slap the horses' rumps, and both mounts trotted off, heading along the ravine, slowing quickly to a walk as they grabbed mouthfuls of this or that brush.

"Not so good," Ferret murmured as he watched the animals. "Pretty soon the'll just stop there."

"I don't think so. They're as thirsty as we are, so they'll move at their own pace but keep on until they get to the river."

Ferret watched another minute. "Looks like you're right. Time for us to get moving, too. What say we work our way down a bit, then angle southeast to hit the water a couple of miles or so downstream from where the horses end up?"

"My thoughts exactly." Being an experienced climber and much used to outdoor activities such as this, Raker set off immediately after saying that. He kept to hard ground but moved as rapidly as possible. Their foes could come up at any time, and he wanted to be well down the barren ridge and into the cover afforded by the trees in the valley below.

The pace was demanding, but it didn't actually strain the lean man as he followed his friend, for Ferret was both in excellent physical shape and a fair outdoorsman himself, having had to survive a number of adventurers in various sorts of wild places. Well below the place they had left their horses, they abandoned caution. Their progress was more rapid still, for they no longer worried about leaving signs of their passage. A good tracker, dogs, or some magickal means would discover a trail no matter what precautions were taken. Their objective was to make it difficult and time consuming for those who were searching for them. In fact, without bloodhounds or some use of castings, their pursuers might never discover just where they abandoned riding in favor of going on foot.

"Made it nicely," Ferret said as he caught his breath amongst the boles of a small stand of wild olive trees. "See anything back up there?"

Raker's gray eyes were searching the ridge above the valley. "I thought there might have been something moving just below the crest, but I don't see anything now. Let's stay under cover as much as possible, just in case. You move on through here, past the bushes, and head for the big willow over there. I'll follow in five minutes."

Because he was allowing so much time, Ferret didn't have to ask about how careful he should be. The lanky adventurer slipped off, staying low and using the trees, pausing frequently before moving on to another place of concealment. He crawled from the copse to the bushes. Screened behind that thick foliage, Ferret bent and ran, then crawled once again until he came to a gully. Sliding over its brink, he could then stand and walk without fear of anyone seeing him from the valley's rim, for the depression was fringed with tall grasses and plants. As he progressed, the channel grew broader and deepened. A brook flowed along it to feed the Ebro just a few furlongs distant. He stopped and drank his fill with cupped hands. In a little while he could just see the top of the great old willow near the river bank and a hundred yards to his left. Ferret used it as a guide as he jogged on. Just before the stream met the bigger waterway, he abandoned its sunken channel, clambered up the eroded side to cautiously peer over the top. Ferret looked back and saw that it was just about impossible for any observer to pick him out. He slithered from the gulley, wormed his way to where there was a large bush of some sort with outflun leafy stalks which afforded all the cover he needed. By keeping it between him and the crest of the ridge, he was sheltered from view again, and in no time was safely reclining against the willow's thick trunk, eyeing the river a stone's throw distant.

"Sleeping?"

Ferret opened one eye to look as Raker. "Nope, just taking a five minute rest. By the way, I heard you coming about a minute ago—you stepped on a dry branch back there by that bushy shrub."

"You left a trail a child could follow."

"Hope it helped you get here."

Raker plopped down beside him. "Okay, smart ass, what do we do now? Or do you want me to remain in charge of this expedition?"

"Did you see anything back there?"

"No, but..."

The lanky man smiled at his friend. "You should have checked the river."

"What?"

"Don't bother now, chum. I think, though, that pretty soon we'll have company. There are a couple of boys in an old skiff coming downstream who will be tying up here soon."

Unbelieving, Raker sat up, started to stand. "You're having delusions."

"Stop that! Sit down. You'll scare them away. Just wait. I know what I'm talking about."

Sure enough, about five minutes later there came floating to them the sound of excited young voices soon followed by the crunch of gravel as the skiff's bottom was sent to beach on the shore just a little way from the willow. They didn't see either of the men where they rested unmoving in the screening leaves and shadow of the tree.

"How did you know?" hissed the gray-eyed swordsman.

Ferret pointed. "That little strand of gravel and the deep pool here—also sign of past visits. A great place for fishing, swimming, and a lazy afternoon siesta, no?"

"Yah. I wish I was a kid again."

"Me too, but... Look out! Here they come. Let me do the talking."

Rods in hand, carrying a wooden pail and a a small sack, two boys of about twelve or thirteen years age came laughing and chattering happily into the shade. Both stopped abruptly as they saw Ferret and Raker reclining in their special place, then started to turn, poised for flight back to their boat.

"*Buenos dias, amigos!* Will a plata buy me all the fish you catch in the next hour?"

That was an opening gambit which made the lads pause. "You are joking, señor!" said the smaller of the pair. "Let's see the coin," the other called, still ready to run.

Ferret nudged his friend, and with hardly a protest Raker found a silver piece and sent it spinning through the air toward the boys.

Both dropped their fishing poles and went for the plata. The taller caught it, started to tuck it away as the other one interjected and began to struggle with him for possession of the coin.

"Hey! Don't quarrel! Here's another," and as he called out those words Ferret flipped the promised plata so that it struck the ground just before the lads' feet.

"You are wealthy men, señors?"

The adventurers laughed in unison. It was a friendly enough sound, and their evident friendliness made the boys approach with hesitant steps. "Not *really* rich, but we sure have plenty of that kind of money, lads," Ferret said with a jovial smile and a wink. Then he pointed back to where they had drawn their craft up on the gravel bar. "Is that your skiff? Or is it your parents?"

"It is ours, senor. We found it with its bottom stove in, repaired it ourselves. Now it is a fine boat again!"

"I'll bet you use it every day."

The older of the two grinned. He shared a confidence. "*Si!* And the fish we often catch make it easy for us to be gone—everybody at home likes a nice fish dinner!"

"And that means we don't have to be around and do chores all the time," the smaller boy chimed in, not wanting the men to suppose that he wasn't as clever as his companion.

"Is it a long way back home?"

"Just a couple of miles—why do you ask that?" The bigger lad was suspicious again.

Ferret sat back, relaxed so as to put the boys at ease again. "Oh, I was just wondering, because if it were far I wouldn't make you rich."

"It isn't far at all," the small one said urgently.

The older was still uncertain. "You said you weren't very rich, so how can you make us rich? Are you bandits? You don't look like Iberians." When he said that he began to edge away.

"So long then, sonny. I suppose you have plenty of gold at home, eh?"

Raker hissed under his breath, "Oh no you don't, weasel. I'm not going to fork over any doubloons!"

The boys were close enough to hear the word "doubloons," and it was as if they had been enchanted by some mighty magick casting. "Are you robbers?" asked the smaller lad. The bigger scoffed, "No, stupid, look at them again. They are pirates!" His mate stared, then demanded, "Is that so? Then where's their ship, dummy?!"

"Whoa there!" Raker said as the two started to square off. He was beginning to enjoy Ferret's game. "Have you guys considered that maybe we're secret agents of the king?"

Both boys stopped and stared again, mouths open. "Are you?" they chimed.

"If so, we couldn't tell you—at least not in so many words. I can say, though that we are on a very, very important mission."

"He's telling you the truth, lads," Ferret interjected, "But he left out the part about the bad men chasing us."

The two youngsters looked around. "We see nobody...." the older said with a glance at his friend.

"Maybe you won't ever. We are going to leave now, and I think you lads should head straight home. Will two doubloons be enough for your skiff?"

The boys gaped at Ferret, then looked at each other. A fortune indeed! It was enough to buy a big, new rowboat. They nodded to each other. "It is our most cherished possession," the younger one said.

"I don't want to part with it at any price," his friend agreed.

Raker sighed. "This is worse than bargaining with a Phonecian horse trader." He stood up, held out his hand. Ferret placed a pair of doubloons in it. Then the blond swordsman held the coins out for the boys to see, meanwhile adding a third one. It was his last gold piece, but he found several silver coins to add to the sum. "There you are, our final offer, three thousand one hundred and twenty-five reals. Deal?"

"The boat is yours, señors," the lads agreed, snatching the coins.

"Be sure not to tell anyone besides your parents about this," Raker called as the two started to dash off.

They stopped and stared. "We aren't stupid, señors! As far as we're concerned the rotten old thing sprang a leak and sank!" Then they ran off as quick as jackrabbits, heading along the bank in the direction of their home somewhere upriver.

Raker looked at Ferret. "You know, old boy, their words might just be portentous.... "

The lanky adventurer sprang up and hurried to where the skiff lay. "If those wretches sold us a waterlogged and leaky hulk, I'll... I'll... "

"*We'll* end up swimming," Raker supplied with a humorless laugh as he too went to inspect their purchase.

Chapter Twenty-Three

ALL THINGS CONSIDERED, the old skiff was suitable. It did leak a bit, but there were a couple of gourds lying in its bottom, so bailing by either occupant, or both if demanded by conditions, was easy. It took no more water than an inch or two an hour. The main drawback was propulsion. Having only one real oar, the boys had used their native talent to create a second. It was a bit too short and heavy, its blade narrower than it should have been. Raker rowed, so he used the defective oar in his right hand, and by dint of strength from that arm made the boat follow a straight course.

He was perspiring freely despite the fact that his armor was stripped off and getting soggy where it was bundled in the bow. A bandana of Ferret's was tied around his head to serve as protection from the hot Iberian sun and as a disguise. "Are you sure this is necessary?" the blond swordsman asked as he labored to keep the skiff in midstream and moving at a rate faster than the strong current's flow.

"We've been over this before," Ferret said firmly. "Keep rowing, and put a little more muscle into it, can't you? We don't want to be caught out here by the grandee's riders guided by some hedge-magician's puny divinations. Speed and my cloaking castings are our best defenses. Keep quiet now and let me concentrate on these difficult spells and formulas I have to manage."

Raker glanced over his shoulder for a second but said nothing in response. His comrade was, like himself, stripped of armor, leaning back comfortably against the bundle of their outer garments, his sash wound to make a hat of sorts with one end hanging behind to shade the lean man's neck. With his linen blouse's sleeves rolled partway up, feet propped up on the skiff's second seat, he could possibly pass for an Iberian fisherman taking his ease as his companion rowed. Sticking boldly skyward were a pair of straight branches that from a distance would be taken for fishing poles. They had cut them just before shoving off.

"Damned loafer," Raker muttered, turning back to watch the land as it seemed to flow slowly past to either hand, bending forward and straightening his back in regular rhythm. The work actually made him feel good, and it wasn't the effort of back, arms, and legs that galled him. He knew that it was touch and go for them. No question that the Marquis Armando would have hekabenders busily trying to use castings to locate their whereabouts. Of course, being what they were, both men had charms and amulets serving to mask their whereabouts, hide their thoughts, and cloak their aural radiations so as to make them seem commonplace and thus invisible.

He recalled how Neva had traced their flight in the castle complex, and how in the underground sewer she had laughed at them while the grille had crashed down to seemingly seal them into the subterranean maze. Once quarry was known, and certainly if near, a potent practitioner could tear the veils of protective dweomers aside. All he and Ferret could hope for was that the best ones were still back in Torenegro, while the lessers searched in the field. There was another consideration as well. If ordinary soldiers came close enough they would have no need for magick or like practice. Their own eyes would tell them what they needed to know, and with arrows and spears put paid to their fugitive prey. No, there was no question about it. The center of the River Ebro was their safest refuge, and adding oars' propulsion speed to the swift current was likewise a sound tactic. Horsed pursuit could keep pace along the relatively level valley to either hand, but only if they moved at a fast canter. In fact, as no foemen were yet in sight, the skiff was probably putting considerable distance between them and their pursuers each hour, for back in the hills and bluffs, the terrain slowed average movement to the pace of a fast walk.

No, what he was irritated about was not the plan. Raker suspected that Ferret was quite able to add whatever protective castings he could activate to assist them in their flight in a brief time. Having done that already, the lanky adventurer was now merely feigning such effort as he took his ease. That rankled.

Raker glanced over his shoulder again as he rested with oars horizontal, silvery droplets gleaming as they ran from them and returned to their parent stream. "A dog lying in the sun!"

"Tut! How can you say such a thing, let alone think what you've been thinking. For shame, sir knight! Besides my dweomers, I must keep a close eye on the water shipped in this craft. You row, I protect and bail."

"A Savoyard chevalier is not the fool. Honor does not demand bovine acceptance of injustice—to the contrary."

Ferret made an upward gesture with the fingers of his right hand, a sort of shooing motion. "Turn and face the stern. Ply those oars. Seeing as how you have canines in mind, what if the grandee's hounds have taken the road to Dertosal?"

Raker wasn't convinced. "What if they have?"

"Then, fool, they will reach Roqueta before we can pass it. Think of the boats there, man! We'll be caught easily, overcome by dozens of adversaries as they surround us in larger craft. Unless we travel at best speed, that risk is strong."

"Then you should be working one of these oars."

All Ferret said to that was, "Bah! You can manage it better alone. I must needs keep up our magickal defense and ply these gourds now and again, as I said."

"But you are by far the better boatman...."

"Always you 'but' me. Are you a goat? Or is it that you think to make *me* the goat, the butt of your cruel jests? I think it must be the latter, you being a haughty noble and I but a poor fellow of peasant stock. Keen mind and sagacious knowledge are no substitute for brute strength at such a time as this, Rake. Save your wind for work and row!"

Not bothering with any further protest, Raker bent his back and worked the unwieldy oars. The Ebro was fairly swift and straight, but as all rivers it had bends and loops. He was soon negotiating just such a turn, one which made the course kink north and then come back south to run again nearly due east. After the first alteration in direction occurred, as they were beginning to negotiate the upper portion of the loop, Raker called urgently: "There, Ferret! Did you see them?!"

Starting up from other concerns, staring behind, the lean man shot back, "What? What's that?"

"I think it was horsemen, a dozen of 'em, Ferret, but they're screened now by the point of land to the right."

"Starboard?"

"Whatever you call it—my left, the right bank of the river."

"Shit," Ferret said with great urgency as he scrambled back to where his comrade sat. "Move over and give me the right oar. We don't want them to be able to cut across land and catch us."

Raker shipped the right oar and slid sideways, giving room to the lanky adventurer as Ferret stepped over the board, seated himself. "Do we make an all-out effort?"

"Damned right. Pull!" Ferret had the homemade device out and poised above the water by then and was set.

With his own oar likewise set Raker called, "Stroke," and dipped the blade into the river. After a couple of more calls, the two were pretty well synchronized, so the broad-shouldered swordsman saved his breath for the heavy work of rowing at top speed. The little skiff fairly flew along, and in minutes they were negotiating the southward part of the bend and could see the change toward eastward flow in the watercourse as they both cast occasional glances toward the bow. "We're moving toward the right, Ferret," Raker said as he raised his oar for yet another stroke. "Can you pull harder?"

"Never mind," Ferret puffed. "We want... to put as... much distance... as we can... be*tween* us and the... other *bank*... without—uff!—*losing* the... main cur*rent!* "

With a sideways glance and expressionless face, Raker asked, "Could you say that again, old fellow? I couldn't get the sense of it between all the sounds of labor you kept interjecting."

The little vessel was turning as the flow carried it once again to the eastward course that would eventually empty the Ebro into the sea. Ferret detected not the slightest sign of any foe along either bank of the river. With a last great heave, he sent the bow a bit toward Raker's side of the boat, then upped the oar and dumped inboard. "On second thought, chum," he wheezed, "you do this better alone. I'm going to—"

Raker's laughter cut him short. "Ahh, ha, ha, ha! You're getting soft, weasel."

"Soft in the head for believing you. In a time like this you shouldn't play stupid tricks!"

"That's even funnier," Raker said and laughed more as he elbowed his comrade off the bench and took up the other oar. "Who started shabbing who first?"

Ferret, unseated so rudely, hauled himself up to a crouch in the wet bottom of the skiff, eyeing the water lapping round his feet, then after checking ahead, he swatted Raker's head. The blow had no force, and Raker ignored it. "So who's the bigger dolt, eh?"

"Who's laughing now, and who has been cozened last?"

Chuckling then as if to indict himself, Ferret cried, "Alright. What can I say?" He patter the rowing man's shoulder. "Take a rest. Let's call it even, Rake. Come on and switch places. I'll row now and you watch ahead."

"A double pleasure!" Raker beamed as he changed places, starting for the comfortable berth Ferret had been in before he had duped the lean man into rowing. Only when he had sat his bottom down where his companion's own had been did he notice something. "Damn! This bloody boat's got over an inch of water in it!"

Ferret didn't turn as he suggested, "The strain of our pulling this tub along so fast probably did it. Do as I had to—use the gourd and bail, *old man*. I'm busy rowing."

So passed the late morning, noon, and the afternoon eventually. Though there was no food, neither man was suffering unduly, for despite heat and effort, there was water aplenty to drink and with which to cool themselves. At a little past the sun's zenith rowing ceased by mutual agreement. Drifting, one watching, the other immersed himself in the Ebro, then shed all clothing to swim a little beside the drifting skiff. The boat was soon covered with drying linen as Raker and Ferret sat naked save for head covering, pretending to fish in case a curious onlooker from shore or a passing watercraft should espy them. In fact, they had seen others there on the river, but even those using sails to aid their passage upstream had been off to the side, Nothing other than shallow-draft vessels could navigate the Ebro much above Dertosal, so progress was easier if such boats stayed free of the strong central channel's force.

Because he had gone in first, Raker was already back in his somewhat damp underclothing as Ferret began to don his own in the late afternoon. "Dertosal or Roqueta?" he asked.

Understanding what was unsaid, Ferret shook his head. "Neither. I think it will be sometime after sunset when we arrive. I propose we go right on past both places. There'll be ships in the moorings below the city. With luck we'll come just after dark. We'll board one of the vessels there."

"Are we going to capture or buy it?" Raker asked sarcastically.

"My plan was less ambitious—to steal some garments to cover these too-well-known ones of our own, then take a small boat and head back upstream to Roqueta. How about it? Sometime tomorrow we can get into Dertosal—at night the guards will be more careful."

The gray-eyed swordsman ran his hand across his cheek, tugged at his moustache. The latter was a sure sign of his pondering a problem. "I could do with a shave and a bed—not to mention a hot dinner. Still, aren't we taking too much of a risk, especially when it comes to a ship's boat? That'll be missed for sure!"

"Leave it to me, Rake, I've got a little plan all figured out. Now here's what we do..."

Raker listened to his comrade, then grinned. "Still risky, but what the hells, old boy, it's in character. I'm with you."

"Never thought otherwise," Ferret told him as he began to see to drying out his leathers. "Better do the same, my friend. Not much more than an hour until the shadows will be spreading across the river."

Not knowing for certain how close their destination was, they steered but didn't row, so that the skiff went along at the speed of the main current of the Ebro. The sun sank, and there was no sign ahead of Dertosal. In the gathering dusk, they hastened to don their armor, Raker even putting on the heavier portions of his more elaborate suit. Not much past full dark they saw glimmering lights ahead. They passed by the city and its suburban cross-river village a little thereafter. A mile below Dertosal the skiff bobbed into the wide portion of the river that was the mooring basin of the community, and without speaking Raker began to work the oars once more, heading for a smallish, two-masted caique which showed only a bow and stern lantern as lights.

As they came to its hull Ferret fended off so the skiff made only a slight noise instead of a solid thump as it came parallel to the ship. His comrade had stowed the boat's oars; as the skiff slipped along the caique's timbers, Raker stood, seized a dangling rope, and held the little boat fast there, feet spread so that the stern didn't counter by moving out from the other craft.

Even as he secured them thus, Ferret was upright also and with a silent spring reached up and seized the gunwale. He disappeared from Raker's view in a flash, moving as sinuously as his namesake to clear the rail and slide onto the deck above. As Ferret vanished, the blond man drew his sword, holding on to the rope with his left hand. Silently Raker began to keep track of time.

About two minutes time had passed when there was a scraping sound, and then Ferret's whisper, "Prepare to receive cargo."

Raker braced himself, called back softly, "Ready." The limp feet and legs which came dangling down nearly struck him on the head, but Raker pushed them aside, and the body dropped the few feet to the boat's bottom with a thud. It groaned softly but didn't move thereafter.

"One down," came from the darkness of the caique's deck.

The third time this was repeated, Raker put away his blade, grabbed the rope with both hands again, and shoved backward with his feet as he swarmed up the line. The skiff shot sideways away from the bigger vessel, drifted, and was nothing more than a dark shape at a couple of rods' distance as the Ebro carried it off downstream. "How many left aboard?" queried Raker in a hushed voice as he clambered on deck.

"That last was the whole of the watch," Ferret informed his comrade. "Just as I had hoped. They'll end up aground somewhere below here or maybe drift out to sea. Either way it'll be hours or days before they can tell their tale. Meanwhile, when it's discovered they're missing from here, the stolen boat will be explained. Crew deserted their posts to have fun ashore."

Raker grinned, his smile barely visible in the dim light of the fore lantern. "The watch will be looking for three sailors of a certain description, likely to forget that of two others given to them days ago. Should work, sly weasel!"

"Yes," Ferret said, "but we can't waste time here. Help me find some gear below for our disguises."

They went below and soon located a couple of burlap seabags. Into one went another like bag and various odds and ends of clothing they grabbed. The second was then filled with officer's garments from the little cabins at the stern. There was a boat not much bigger than a dingy nearby, and they tossed their loot into it, lowered the vessel over the side, and were themselves aboard it in seconds after it splashed into the river. Each pulled an oar, cutting across the main current, then rowing partway back upstream to beach the small boat a bowshot below Roqueta. Ferret sent the boat back into the river as Raker carried the seabags away.

"Hide those where nobody is likely to locate them for at least three or four days, chum," Ferret admonished as he adjusted the Berber robe which he had selected to conceal the dark leather he wore beneath. He had a few odd things stuffed into a sling carrier suited to his garb. Nobody would think him other than some sailor whose vessel was in port here.

Raker spat. "It's be more like a week before this stuff is turned up, never fear. When I stash stuff it is *hidden.* Where do we meet?"

"Let's make it the second place you come to on the left, first street in from the one parallel to the river. I'll get a private room there, and you do the same. We'll have to stay separated—strangers alone as far as anyone knows."

"Makes sense. Give me some coin." The blond man was now wearing a seaman's cloak and a hat atop the bandana. He would retain one of the stolen seabags as a part of this new persona he had created thus. He looked every inch a rascal, but not a particularly notable one.

Ferret squinted suspiciously. "Use your own. This is a—"

"Partnership," Raker interjected, "and you made me give up my last funds to buy that old skiff from those boys at a ridiculously high price. Hand over some operating cash, partner!"

Grumbling in disgust, the lean adventurer grudgingly gave his comrade a few coins, additional silver ones upon Raker's insistant urgings. "Two hundred is a ridiculous amount for expenses one night in this hole," Ferret could be heard saying as he stumped off towards the noisy collection of ramshackle structures called Roqueta.

"I'll drink a well-earned toast to you, old boy—and thanks!" Raker called after him as he went in the opposite direction with the two unwanted purloined bags and their superfluous contents. In fifteen minutes he was back, unburdened by anything other than his own gear, and striding along the route his comrade had taken. Raker rattled the coins in his purse and burst into song. The strains of, "There you'll find burning brandy to dizzy your head, and wenches hotter still to fire your bed," preceded his entry into the village.

Chapter Twenty-Four

THEY WERE AWAKENED by the clanging of a bell and loud voices in the streets below. Raker had managed to get an adjoining room to Ferret's, so in no time the two met in the hall, fully dressed and armed.

"Bacchus's balls, my poor head," groaned the gray-eyed man as he attempted to close his door so as to not make a bang. "Can't they stop that damned racket outside?"

Ferret had a self-righteous expression as he admonished, "I tried to keep you from such folly. *I* have no hangover, and who said 'no more wine'?"

"Oh do shut up. That had nothing to do with concern, you didn't want me to spend the coins you gave me."

"Gave? In no sense did I—"

"Let's go see what the locals are all het up about." Raker's tone was firm, voice clipped as he broke into Ferret's denial. Without waiting to see the result, he walked gingerly to the stairs and went down to the public room. "Oi, landlord!" He had to call more loudly than he wished, held his head as he continued, "Wine, for the love of Liber, or I shall expire on your floor."

The sour face of the owner peered forth from the kitchen. "None of your Roman gods here, fellow. If you want something, you have to wait until I have finished seeing to the work of cleaning up...."

He stopped when he saw Ferret flipping a silver coin into the air and catching it. The lanky adventurer had taken pity on his suffering friend and interceded thus: "Ah, dear landlord," he smiled. "I detect that you are indeed attentive to your customers. Excellent. A plata, then, for two cups of watered wine and a little bread. Then we shall be on our way and trouble you no more."

The wrinkled visage showed no sign of joy when it disappeared back into the kitchen. However, it and its owner reappeared almost immediately thereafter. In the proprietor's hand was a quarter of a round loaf. He dropped it on the board, set a pair of cups by the bread. Pouring the wine he said, "Water's in the pitcher there." Finished giving a scant measure in each vessel, he pointed to the clay beaker in which water was kept. "The plata, señor!" His hands hovered near the cups as if to draw them back unless paid immediately.

Ferret, still smiling in a superior manner, dropped the silver coin on the wood. "Gladly, good fellow, gladly.

"I'll have mine without water," Raker mumbled with the rim of the cup already at his lips. "Ahh, better. I can feel the headache subsiding already, and my stomach quiets its churning." He set the crockery vessel down carefully, tore off a small piece of the bread, sopped up the last dregs of wine in the cup, and ate the purplish mess in a gulp.

Ferret watched, advised, "Now some of the water to flush the poisons from your system and restore your humors to proper balance."

Seeing that the landlord had gone back to his inner sanctum and there was little prospect of a second draught of wine, Raker followed his companion's suggestions, even eating another few bits of bread as he slowly quaffed the water. "Thanks, I was actually quite parched."

"Welcome," Ferret said as he devoured the last of the quarter loaf and washed it down with his carefully watered drink. "I feel splendid!"

"Gloat, you smug bastard," Raker said with greater vivacity than he had previously shown since awakening. "But I'll mark this, and next time I am providing the sauce I shall see you overindulge and then—"

Ferret held up both hands in surrender as he interjected, "The boot pinching a foot will be mine own. I am chastised. Come on then, old comrade. Let's venture forth on this bright morning and determine the cause of the rowdiness without which so rudely interrupted our deserved rest, eh? We can then cross to the city, where I'll stand a pot of ale or wine to show I know I was in the wrong."

Arm in arm the two adventurers left the shabby tavern and blinked as the bright Iberian sun struck their eyes with its dazzling force. There were people running hither and thither in the dusty street, calling excitedly to one another, gathering in knots and then dissolving as quickly. Most of the folk were heading toward the river, however, evidently assembling in the village's center for some reason. Rather than attract any attention by questioning a citizen, Ferret and Raker decided to stroll toward the place where citizens of and strangers visiting Roqueta were congregating.

The assembly point proved to be the riverside plaza which fronted the pier and quay. The square served as marketplace, of course, as well as space for the disgorging of cargoes from the few boats and barges docking at the village. This morning it was alive with another sort of activity. The village crier was standing by trying to look important next to the chief elder and his half-dozen council members. All, however, were quite in the shadow of a squad of Dertosal's guardsmen there seemingly to protect several serjeants and a pair of officers wearing uniforms of slightly different sort than either of the two had seen when they had been in the city.

"I wonder what that sort of dress betokens?" mused Ferret.

Raker cocked his head, thought a moment. "A little less elaborate, all things considered, than the watch and guards. Militia, I'll hazard."

It had been half an hour since the first ringing of the bell and attendant hubbub, and everyone in Roqueta who intended to get to the plaza to see what was going on was there. In fact, a crowd of several hundred had gathered. The serjeants had been observing the assembly, and at about the same time Raker ventured his estimate of their uniform's indication, the senior of the four non-commissioned officers spoke to the junior of the pair of officers. That worthy, in turn, turned and said something to his superior, received a nod, saluted, and stepped over to stand beside the senior serjeant. After listening to the young officer speak, the serjeant strode into the middle of the open space between the crowd and his fellow soldiers.

The village crier began pealing his bell furiously, arm working up and down as if he were a smith hammering metal on his forge. The clamor of the crowd dropped gradually to a hum under the blows of the handbell's brass. Perhaps the fellow would never have ceased his ringing, save one of the other serjeants cried, "Stop!" The crowd, too, hushed at that command's bark.

'ALL ABLE-BODIED MEN, ATTEND!" shouted the senior serjeant in a fitting basso which filled the square. "The Most Honorable Lord Mayor Don Sancho Terenchiol, speaking with the authority of Prince Alexandro of Catelonia," the soldier continued in somewhat less stentorious tone, "calls upon you to take up arms!"

There was a babble of excitement from the crowd. "War?" someone shouted the question above the lesser noise. Another spectator was even more direct. "Are we in danger?"

"SILENCE! THERE IS NO IMMEDIATE DANGER. BE STILL! A small force of mercenaries and soldiers of the Marquis of Torenegro violated the free territory of Dertosal last night, but they were repulsed. The enemy is now gathering a greater force to invade our land. Do I make myself clear?"

At that news there was an even greater stir in the crowd. People near the front began to move back, and a few of those already at the rear slunk off. Boys dashed this way and that in high excitement, many heading off to alert those heretofore uninterested in the gathering. While this was occurring the two officers marched up to stand beside the serjeant.

The senior officer held up a document. The serjeant shouted a final time to bring quiet. The officer began to read: "Male citizens of Roqueta ages sixteen to forty-five are hereby ordered to step forward now."

"STAND OVER THERE!" bellowed the serjeant, pointing to a place to his right as a few of the more eager or perhaps fearful of being disobedient started to approach hesitantly. "HURRY UP! THE MAJOR HASN'T GOT ALL DAY!" As he said that, two of his fellows motioned, and the squad of guardsmen came marching up, half going right, the other left, each portion then being directed by one of the pair of non-commissioned officers. They moved into the assembly, asking each likely looking man if he was a villager, then pushing those who said they were indeed citizens out of the throng toward the place their company was forming.

Ferret and Raker's turn came quickly enough, and both men merely shook their heads. The guardsman looked closely at them, received hard-eyed stares in return, and moved on. The process took some time, for more people were now coming into the plaza. In about a quarter-hour, there was a company of a couple of hundred souls in rough formation where the senior serjeant stood as a dog might guard sheep. In a few more minutes the regular soldiers came filtering back through the throng, driving before them or having in tow another score or so of boys and men. The number was now near three hundred, and the major must have deemed this the best that could be hoped for. He bent his head to read aloud again, this time directing his words to the new "recruits."

"You are hereby sworn into duty as Dertosal Militia for the duration of hostilities or for 30 days, whichever is the shorter period. You will obey all orders. Desertion or cowardice in the face of the enemy is punishable by death." He looked up from the paper. "Your commanding officer is Lieutenant Lucio. Serjeant Garzal is in charge of you as far as all things are concerned, including seeing that you are issued uniforms, armor, and weapons. Lieutenant Lucio, take command!"

Women were waving farewell bravely, calling, crying, shrieking.

The lieutenant cried, "Serjeant Garzal!"

"SIR!" bellowed the serjeant. He then shouted orders, and the two serjeants and company of guards formed up so that half were in front of and half were behind the militia. With more shouts and much urging from the regulars, the formation marched raggedly to the pier, where several barges awaited to transport them across the Ebro and into the walled city.

As this occurred, the remaining serjeant came to attention at a word from the major, then called loudly: "ATTENTION, ALL FOREIGN MEN AND WOMEN WHO KNOW ARMS AND WOULD HAVE EMPLOYMENT AS SOLDIERS!"

Surprisingly, the crowd, still relatively large, and certainly with many able-bodied men in its throng, became still as they heard that.

"MAJOR VARGOS WILL NOW ADDRESS YOU. THOSE INTERESTED IN SERVING FOR A HANDSOME FEE STEP FORWARD." A few bold members of the crowd came forth. "COME ON, I AM SPEAKING OF AN *ESCUTO* A DAY, WITH ARMS, ARMOR, UNIFORM, FOOD, AND QUARTERS THROWN IN! ARE YOU ALL SISSIES?" He laughed as one man tried to slide behind a clump of women. "HE IS? WHAT ABOUT YOU TWO?" The serjeant was now pointing at Ferret and Raker.

Without hesitation the lean man moved to join the dozen at the fore, and Raker was beside him. That brought more men and even a handful of brawny women forth as well. In no time there were fifty or sixty people standing there. Most weren't Iberians but hailed from some other portion of Æropa. In addition, besides Atlantlans and Berbers, there were several black Afrikans, and even a slant-eyed Azirian with a strange sword and bow. Many were obviously seafarers, the others surely experienced in hardship and combat, and in such company neither Ferret nor the gray-eyed Raker stood out.

The serjeant beamed, looked at the officer and saluted.

Major Borgosal nodded rather than returning the salute. He looked at the potential volunteers with a cold and appraising eye. "You'll do," he said in his clear, harsh voice. "As you are aware, I am Major Borgosal. Because of the hostilities I have formed a tercio of volunteers. There are already two companies in Dertosal, and you will form the third and final one in the unit. Minimum enlistment is thirty days, pay at the end of that time of three doubloons each—that's as Serjeant Emilio told you, a hundred reals a day.

"Before you all come forward to sign up, let me make one thing clear. This is *not* a second-rate unit! I want only veterans, those who know how to be soldiers and are most able to use arms." Although there had been no move toward him, when they heard that a half-dozen of the onlookers began approaching.

The officer showed a doubting expression as he glanced over these fellows. They were a motley and hard-bitten lot. "Serjeant Emilo! Check each volunteer to see that he is indeed qualified. Remember, archers will receive a bonus of an escudo a week, and we need corporals too at the same bonus."

As he finished that most of the listeners were moving toward the serjeant actually jostling and saying, "I'm an ex-serjeant!" or, "I've been a petty officer of, er, marines!" and, "Sign me up now, I use a bow," or, "Four years with the Red Pikes enough experience for you?" and so forth.

Ferret watched a couple of minutes, then nudged his friend. "Come on, chum," he hissed under his breath. "We're going to join Major Vargos's tercio."

"Got you," answered Raker. "Where in the hells is he getting so much cash?"

"Amongst some other things, that's what we're going to learn.... Let's queue up."

The officer had walked away to his own barge by then. He evidently didn't care to be too close to the ranks. It seemed that Serjeant Emilo would be overwhelmed, for the number of persons willing to join the major's unit was greater even than it had seemed. Now there were men appearing from the village and getting into line to sign on. As if conjured a couple of corporals and several soldiers sporting maroon tabards with a black emblem of a two-headed snake on them were there to assist. The corporals began taking names, as the soldiers got the volunteers into three lines. Soon it was the turn of Ferret and Raker.

"Name?"

"Damion," Ferret supplied "and this here's Pythias. We're inseparable."

The corporal asked him to spell both names, wrote slowly, then looked them over. "Pals, huh? Youse Grecians?"

"Sort of," the lean man responded.

"Thought so," the fellow said with a smirk. The expression changed when he saw the looks in Ferret's and Raker's eyes. "Hey, I aint got nuttin' against—ah. Hey, youse are vets, right?"

Raker was still flushed with outrage. "I'll show you just how experienced I am. Draw your blade!"

The serjeant overheard and barked, "Cut the crap." He looked at the pair the corporal had enlisted, nodded to them, and said matter-of-factly. "You'll get a chance to show your skill when we get to the barracks. The corporal will test you then."

"Hey, wait Sarge!"

"Next man," the non-commissioned officer growled, and the glum-faced man went back to work after motioning Ferret and Raker toward the river.

Chapter Twenty-Five

More than two-score other recruits were already standing and waiting for transportation across the Ebro. Two of the barges which had carried the Roqueta militia contingent to Dertosal were slowly approaching the village pier. Each would accommodate fifty men, so Ferret and Raker would be in the first lot to cross to the walled city. Major Borgosal had hit the jackpot in Roqueta, for almost two hundred mercenaries stood ready to join or had already.

"Some ships will be short hands tomorrow," Ferret said as he surveyed his fellow volunteers.

Raker shrugged. "Merchant ships are made happy places when pirates forsake the sea. I wonder if they'll quarter us in the citadel."

"Won't make much difference—a tower or a vacant stable. Hard beds wherever and full of vermin too."

"But the pay is good."

"As if we are going to be ar—" Ferret cut himself off. There were too many others around to talk in such vein. Instead he chose a likely looking rogue, an Iberian from her appearance, and one who had seen such service as this before. She was taller than he, twice as heavy, and her face was leathery, scarred, and ugly. "Pardon, señorita," Ferret said tapping her massive arm. "Who is this rich major to pay us so well, do you know?"

The beefy woman snorted, staring Ferret up and down before answering. "Señorita your ass! Speakin' o' which, you could do with some meat on those bones. I'd break your back in bed, beanpole." She gave a guffaw, and a man who evidentially knew her joined in the mirth.

"That you would, Lorrita, I—"

Whack! The big fist she held in front of his face silenced the man more surely than had the open-handed slap it had just delivered. Her beady eyes seemed to aim along the blob that was her nose, using the wart on it as a sight, perhaps. "Shaddup!"

The hard-bitten man looked away from that stare, moved off surreptitiously as her attention left him.

"So who's the major?" Raker looked levelly at the woman as he asked the question which she had ignored when his comrade had posed it to her. His gray eyes were like granite, daring her to try assailing him as she had the rough-looking mercenary she had just sent packing.

Lorrita moved as if to accept the challenge, but as she noticed his looks her hostile expression slid away. "Say there, cutie, you're more to my likin'!" Her smile showed a missing tooth as well as one of gold in the snaggle so displayed by the gaping of her thick-lipped, great mouth. "Whazzat you asked? Gimme a kiss, boy, an' I'll tell you anything."

Raker flinched as he never would before a man. "The major—never mind."

"Ah, it's shy you are? Well, come and I'll—" Just then there was a shouting and commotion as the corporals began to form up the amorphous mass into some semblance of order so as to make boarding of the barges possible. The horrible woman turned and thrust her way to the fore to make sure she got a comfortable berth, forgetting all about Raker and Ferret's question.

"Gods, Ferret! Next time question one like her," he said in relief as he nodded toward a good-looking, if powerfully muscular, amazon nearby. "Don't choose some bag that would put the Witch Louhi to shame!"

Unable to keep from chuckling, Ferret slapped his friend on the back. "That was a poor choice, Rake, I admit. Fortunately, she found you, not me, to her liking." When Ferret looked threateningly as him, Ferret put on his most innocent expression as he added, "Say, do you suppose we'll be in the same barracks room as Lorrita . . . ?"

At this juncture the corporals intervened again, shouting at them to get aboard the second of the barges. That Lorrita was in the first of the two vessels gladdened both men as they got into their conveyance. Soon it was away, managed by a a dozen oarsmen pulling great sweeps. Neither Ferret nor Raker spoke during the brief passage, for they were surrounded by strangers, most of whom were likewise silent.

The enlistees were formed up and actually marched in good order through Dertosal's river gate and through the streets. They then were headed up the slope of the ridge, not toward the city's fortress but instead to a walled temple complex adjoining that place. Inside of it, they were halted, and the corporal in charge said: "Inside that barracks now, you lot. You know the routine. Stay put until someone orders you to do otherwise. This here's home fer awhile, 'cause Major Borgosal is a loyal member of the Temple of Keganul. It's a better billet than most, let me tell you! In case yer ignorant, Keganul is chief god of this here city, see? Better still, Keganul is the Atlantlan lord of fire and warfare. Services every mornin' and evenin' at six. You can do worse than joinin', if you get my drift."

Nobody replied as the group of fifty filed inside the long room that was theirs. It contained three score narrow bunks and nothing else save for a couple of rough tables with benches on either side. Ferret and Raker managed to get a bunk by the second door to the place, figuring that even if it was now closed, it could be opened, unlocked or otherwise, when they needed to leave. Because the group was comprised of little bands of associates and many lone volunteers, there was no attention directed toward the pair. They sat on the lower pallet, conversing in low tones. In a few minutes a handful of regulars came in, calling derisively, "Here you go, troops! Uniforms. Soon the fun begins!" Tossing their bundles down near the door, the soldiers departed without further enlightenment despite calls for just that from those new recruits nearby.

Everybody hastened over. The bundles were tabards of maroon with the black two-headed snake emblem on front and back. There were only two sizes, large and larger. Raker grabbed a couple of the smaller ones before anyone else could get them, tossed one to Ferret. They donned them, tied the lacings to either side, and looked at each other.

"Helmets," Raker said laconically.

"Probably not for a bit," Ferret answered just as enigmatically.

It was noon before anything else happened. They were then taken out, formed up, counted off against names on the serjeant's roster, and marched to the temple kitchens. There, with wooden bowl and cup, they were doled out food. "Straggle back to yer quarters soon as yer grubb's given yer," a corporal ordered. They did. By the time Ferret and Raker re-entered the barracks room the tables were filled, so they again sat on the bunk.

"So," Ferret said as he ate listlessly, "we managed getting back into the city nicely. Now for the dear colonel..."

Raker agreed, "Exactly, old man, and don't forget the priest!"

Neither was vindictive. It was a matter of survival. If they could be manipulated by such minor figures as Colonel de la Cabarro and Intensity Elfuego, then not only was their reputation in ruins, but both would soon be dead. That so much information regarding them was in the hands of a small city guard commander and a petty priest was disturbing. So was how it got there, now that they knew Neva wasn't responsible. There was certainly a score to settle as well as information to be gained and records to be destroyed.

When the afternoon siesta was past, the whole of the new company was assembled in the side temple courtyard. New recruits were questioned about what experience they had, the arms with which they were proficient, if they had naval training, and how well they could ride a horse. Raker denied archery skill, although he was a deadly bowman, and both men indicated only marginal seamanship and ability as horsemen. "Archers front and left, able marine-trained troops front and center, and cavalry front and right!" bawled the serjeant. "All the rest of you follow the corporal."

The regular troops were led off again, this time to get boots, jacks, and helmets and then receive their standard arms—shield, short sword, and long spear. It took all afternoon. Another meal was served up, and then they were locked into their barracks by the corporal, who told them as he left, "Tomorrow the major'll talk some, and then we'll see how well ya can do with weapons.

Yer a sorry lot, but likely one or two of ya'll make corporal." He shook his head and spat when he finished that sentence. "Five days to get ya inta shape's all we got. Get yer beauty sleep, 'cause tomorra I roust ya at dawn! Anyone caught outside will be cut down, by the way, so's ya better stay put!"

There were only a couple of lanterns illuminating the big room. With their wicks lowered, the place was gloomy, soon filled with snores and the other sounds of sleep. It was near the third hour after midnight before Ferret slipped out of the upper bunk, touched Raker. "Be ready," he whispered.

Raker signaled he was, watched as his comrade went to the nearby door, crouched. There was a soft sound of metal snicking on metal, and a tiny creaking as the door was eased open an inch or two. The blond swordsman crept to the exit, slipped through. He flattened himself against the wall in the deep shadows there. Like his companion, they had the tabards and helmets for possible disguise purposes but left behind all the other gear they had been issued.

When Ferret was likewise outside and the door shut and relocked, the two went along the building's face to a spot they had seen earlier, then began climbing upward. "Not likely the good Intensity will be any place other than with Cabarro," Ferret had observed earlier, so their destination was the main citadel of Dertosal. It was an easy climb to the compound wall's ramparts, just as simple to descend. Similarly, as nobody thought it likely that someone would be interested in scaling the fortress's inner wall, they managed to get up and inside that place without being spotted.

"Maybe this is too easy," Raker hissed nervously as they headed for the building that they had been brought to not many days earlier.

Ferret scanned the area. "Now we know why hatchet-face Elfuego said that the fortress was the unsleeping heart of the city. There's more than the threat of invasion from Torenegro keeping this place hopping. Let's go. Walk as if we belong here." The caution was unnecessary, but the lanky adventurer was jittery.

They marched purposefully, covering the last bit of distance between one outbuilding and another nearly abutting the main structure. Of course the main bailey and front entrance were far too well watched and busy to attempt entry of the colonel's headquarters there. This place provided a much better opportunity; there was an outer stair… and a guard.

"Halt! Who goes there?" It was a big, alert guardsman.

The two came to a halt in good military fashion. Raker answered loudly, "Message for Colonel de la Cabarro from Major Borgosal."

"Screwed up mercs! Newcomers, ain'tcha? This ain't the way to headquarters. I'll call the corporal of the gu—"

At that moment there was a jingling, and several coins bounced and rolled on the pavement between Ferret and Raker and the guard. "Shit! exclaimed Raker as he slapped his tabard. More coins came spilling forth. "My godsdamned purse's busted!" he groaned as he dropped down and began grabbing at the welter of bronze, copper, and even silver discs.

"I'll help," the guard said with an avaricious gleam in his eye. He set his pole arm aside hastily, began clutching at the brighter silver coins.

Ferret yanked off the man's helmet, delivered a thumping blow which sent the man down on his face with a groan. He added a second for good measure.

"They always fall for that one, don't they? Come on, Rake! Help me prop up this dunce."

"I'm getting my money."

"Screw that change. Come on!"

Grumbling, the blond swordsman grabbed up a last couple of coins and stuffed them inside his waistband as he used his other hand to hoist up the unconscious guardsman. They propped the fellow up against stairs and wall, using his voulge as a brace. "That'll do as far as anyone glancing from a distance."

Ferret was in agreement, feet already set on the steps. "Onward, chum. From now on we'll have to take out anyone we run into."

At the top of the stairway was a door. Ferret tried it, found it locked. It surprised neither man. Ferret began climbing, and as soon as he was at a point higher than his comrade's head, Raker followed suit. There was a window above, fairly narrow, with a single bar. As soon as Ferret was next to it, he knew all was well. Wedging his helmet into the far side of the aperture, he thrust an arm through the near side, slid sideways with that arm and then his other, pulling himself through.

Ferret found himself in a dark room, but he heard heavy breathing and his eyesight enabled him to see a sleeping man sprawled in a bed.

At that moment Raker's shadow cut off some of the light. He had hauled himself up and was peering into the place. "Psst! Ferret! Help me get through," he called softly.

The sleeper stirred, began to sit up. Ferret sprang and delivered a pummeling blow like that he had used to silence the sentry. The fellow flopped back onto the mattress in an altogether different form of slumber.

"Hey! Ferret!"

"Be quiet. I'm here," Ferret hissed in response as he pulled his helmet inside the room, set it on the floor. Raker now held on with one arm, passed his own headgear and then his sword inside. "My armor's too bulky for me to get through," he said after one attempt.

"Stay put. I'll be right back." Ferret went to the door, cracked it and looked out. A corridor running off to the right and a spiral stairway up and down. He shut the door, went to the window again. "Back down as quick as you can. I'll open the door below in thirty seconds or less." He did so, and Raker dropped in front of it from a couple of feet up the wall. He came inside, Ferret locked the door again, and then the two intruders stole upstairs and back into the room whose window Ferret had entered initially. "Let's have some light."

The dweomered garnet still shed the harsh white rays Ferret had evoked from it when they were in the subterranean sewer. Raker just cracked the wooden case, so a plane of illumination shot forth. "You didn't kill him," he whispered as the man on the bed was revealed.

"Naw," Ferret said half-apologetically. Then he saw the face. "I'm glad, too. Look, chum, its Serjeant Mendez—the one who was okay."

"Better tie and gag him," Raker said in matter of fact voice. "Otherwise he'd blow it for us if he woke up." His friend nodded, went to work with strips from the thin blanket. Raker set the box down so that the light was steady, then stripped off his tunic. "I'm going to be a guard serjeant, old man. You'll be a mercenary I'm escorting."

Ferret had completed his task. "Good idea, Rake. Let's move!"

Although they were a story above the one that contained the commandant's office, the two went out and along the passage there rather than descending. In their scouting of the place they had seen a flying bridge connecting this building to the main one, and it was on the second floor. Knowing it had to be to their left, they began checking each door they found in that direction. Ferret did the work, for his keen senses gave him an advantage. The first revealed nothing save an empty sleeping room. The second had a snoring tenant but no other exit. The lean man closed the door without disturbing the sleeping occupant, and on they went quickly, with Raker alert for anyone coming.

"Got to be it," Ferret snarled as he saw the heavy door which was next along the way. "I knew I should have checked by sight before—"

"Can it," Raker smirked as he opened it and peered in. "It's the bridge all right. Door at the end's open."

Ferret followed. Raker was already looking out through the narrow corridor's outer exit. Its door was open wide. The one opposite leading into the main building was not. "Anybody above?" queried Ferret.

Raker looker up and around to all sides, gradually moving onto the span. "Come ahead."

Moving at a walk, Ferret crossed the bridge, then crouched, tried the heavy closure. It swung inward, and he darted through.

After making sure there was nobody there to object to his presence, Ferret opened it wider as a signal to his friend. With his back to the entrance, the lean man began to advance slowly down the dimly illuminated passage. He could hear noise just up ahead, thumps and the voices of men talking in some room or turning not far off.

"Where next?"

Ferret pointed to his ear, then down the corridor and motioned right, then drew his left-hand dagger. Raker said nothing, but he freed his rapier from its scabbard. The two tiptoed along about thirty paces. Raker motioned a halt as he peeped into a bright room. Two soldiers were playing dominoes as a third watched. At that moment the observer turned by chance and spotted Ferret.

There was no time for anything else. Ferret hurled his dag, drew and sent the second after it in a second flat, leaping into the room after it. The guard managed only a croak as the first blade struck his throat, made a further weird noise as the second sank just below the first. He clutched at them, half turning, and trying to give vent to a warning.

"Don't kibitz," the soldier with his back to the entrance muttered. His opponent had his eyes fixed on the table, either looking for a play or fearful that there would be cheating if he looked away.

When Raker came dashing in he shut the door without regard to the noise, and at the same moment the soldier struck by Ferret's daggers fell to the floor with a thud. Then the two players discovered what was happening, tried to get up. Raker went for the one facing him across the table, lunging with his rapier to strike the armored man through the opening where the cuirasse gaped as he bent forward and shoved back his chair. The one with his back to them had thrown himself sideways to the left, trying to draw his short sword as he did so.

Raker's thrust went home truly. The guard shrieked, doubled over, collapsed to the floor.

Ferret had only a pair of short throwing knives left with which to fight, but his quickness and dexterity enabled him to get them in hand and attack even as his foe was rolling from his left shoulder to come up on his right knee with sword ready. Struck a half-dozen times before he knew it, that guardsman too simply groaned and dropped back down to add his blood to that already staining the floor.

"You're getting sloppy," Raker snapped. "Too much noise from them!"

"Look to your own work, chum," Ferret countered. "Get my daggers for me. I'll check to see if the commotion roused anyone's curiosity." With that, he went to the door.

Raker had the twin poinards wiped clean and ready for his comrade in no time. He looked, saw Ferret with door ajar, looking out. "Well?"

"Nothing. Must be used to disagreements here—upper duty room for guards?"

"Likely. Let's get out of here."

Ferret opened the door, Raker closed it gently as he came after. "There's got to be a way down just around that corner," the lanky adventurer said in a hushed voice as he stole ahead. "I remember seeing steps going up when we were brought into the main hall down there and marched in for our little chat with the colonel.

"Gods, Ferret. That place is full of guards!"

"Just two with spontoons outside Cabarro's office."

Raker scoffed. "Pah! There are a dozen in that big passage." But Ferret was already going around the corner, though, so he had no choice but to hurry after. Sure enough, the stairs were there, and his comrade was starting down. "Hold on, merc! I'm the guard serjeant here!"

At his friend's insistent whisper, Ferret paused, allowed Raker to pass one step ahead, then continued down. "We get the guards to usher us inside the colonel's room, then we take 'em out. After that we deal with Cabarro, but don't kill him, whatever you do. We might need a hostage."

"Great," muttered Raker sourly. "Just fuckin' splendid!"

Chapter Twenty-Six

"SERJEANT RENALDO ESCORTING Corporal er—Stoat of Major Borgosal's Tercio to answer the colonel's inquiry," Raker managed to get out without appearing nervous.

If the guard he spoke to noticed his hesitation in naming Ferret, he passed it off as simple unfamiliarity with the man Raker had with him. Likewise, if the corporal's name sounded odd, he probably chalked it up to the fact that the new unit was comprised of many foreign mercenaries. Neither soldier specially noted the direction from which the two had come, nor did they question their authenticity or being where they were. "I'll can see if colonel will see you—but I doubt it, compadre. Both Intensity Elfuego and Don Filberto are inside."

Raker shrugged. "You're calling the shots. Major Borgosal was pretty hot about this though..."

The guard glanced at the other sentinel, who looked blank. "If I get my ass chewed for this I'll blame you," the man said as he reached for the latch. "Your pardon, sir," he said loudly as he opened the door and stepped part way into the cluttered office of de la Cabarro, "A serjeant Renaldo is reporting with a corporal from Major Borgosal's Tercio. He claims its something about an inquiry, sir."

"Not now, I'm busy." The voice was distracted, and its tone such that it brooked no further interruption. Just as the sentry was about to say "Yessir" and withdraw in haste, the colonel said sharply, "What's that? Borgosal sent who here?"

As the first guardsman had opened the door, Ferret had moved sideways and assailed the other sentry. The daggers appeared as if from thin air, struck, and then the lean man was holding up a corpse, turning and moving it toward the entrance to the commandant's office. At the same moment he did so, Raker planted his boot sole squarely in the back of the soldier standing partway inside the door. Colonel de la Cabarro's last words were hardly out when Raker's kick propelled the guard inside, sent him flying across the intervening space to crash headlong into Intensity Elfuego's chair and then the commandant's desk. *Crash! Whump!*

"By the—"

"Who—"

"I'll—"

As that chorus came from the three men inside, Raker entered with naked rapier in hand, stepping aside for those to follow. Three jaws dropped as the body of the second guardsman was hurled in, sent sprawling with gory trail behind, and after that spectacle came the lean Ferret with twin daggers dripping crimson. Immediately upon gaining access, Ferret shut and bolted the door. "We've returned," he announced with a grim smile.

"And we're pretty pissed off," Raker added with a wicked look in his eye.

The big commandant managed to gather his composure immediately. "Welcome then, my friends—but you shouldn't be so hard on my soldiers!" He started to arise. "Here, I'll—"

"Shut up and sit down!" Raker moved to one side of the desk, keeping all three of the seated men in his sight, but with the point of his sword aimed at the colonel.

"Better listen, chum," Ferret advised flatly as he moved to a point behind the priest of Keganul. Intensity Elfuego had been rudely jostled, knocked half out of his chair by the impact of the guard as he was sent in so unexpectedly by Raker's tremendous blow. "And never mind any crap with castings, either. I'll ram these blades right into your eardrums if you try to use heka."

"You stinking dogs!" Don Filberto spat, one hand on his sword but not actually drawing the weapon nor even arising from where he sat.

"What makes you think I haven't already?" Elfuego replied smoothly, ignoring the aristocratic don's insult as if it hadn't interposed. "I assure you, you can't harm me with those knives."

The man's hatchet face was untroubled, his eyes steady, voice calm. Ferret didn't flinch. "Maybe so, maybe not. Care to try? Even if that's so, priest, I don't think your pal the colonel will escape a couple of feet of steel in his paunch."

"No problem about that, old boy," Raker said heartily as he advanced with rapid little steps as if ready to run the commandant through.

"Please, please!" de la Cabarro cried. "No more killing, especially me! I guarantee that neither Intensity Elfuego or the good Don Filberto will molest you. Stop threatening, my friends, and tell me, what made you return?"

Neither man relaxed their guard, but both withdrew slightly to indicate they would not instantly strike. "Stick that 'friends' stuff up your ass," Ferret shot to the colonel. "We know godsdamned well who really set us up. We're here to ask why—and to find out how you came by so much information on us."

"You are dead men," the fancy little Don Filberto sneered.

Colonel de la Cabarro smiled at the lieutenant, then up at Ferret and Raker. "Don't be too hasty, Don Filberto. After all, these two men did foil a treasonous plot being hatched by Penumbratos."

"The marquis?! That fool would never have lived to use the power we—"

"That is enough, Filberto!" the sharp-visaged priest spat.

The small fellow clamped his mouth shut, glaring at Raker, then over his shoulder at Ferret. His face was now absolutely white save where two spots of rage mottled his cheeks.

Raker stared back, laughter plain on his face, and he made a puckering with his lips as he did so, implying something the aristocrat didn't like at all. Don Filberto's eyes were nearly popping from his head as he sat in silent fury.

"Don't worry, Elfuego. We know all about those stones and what they were really meant for. Why do you think I screwed up the regalia?"

"You did that on purpose?!" For the first time the priest showed real emotion. It was a deep anger more fierce than anything Don Filberto could manage.

The commandant intervened. "A moment, honored Intensity, if you please. I would hear more of what our friends—these two have to say." Colonel de la Cabarro sat back, and he was now obviously at ease.

Raker shot a glance at Ferret, for the big man's attitude worried him. Ferret seemed as cool and confident as ever, so Raker didn't say anything.

"Here's what I have to say," Ferret said after looking at the colonel for the space of a few heartbeats. "Who gave you those dossiers on us?"

"Tut! That's a secret I can't tell you," de la Cabarro said with an easy manner. "Instead, you tell us about Grandee Armando del Vargos, Marquis of the Penumbratos, Lord of Torenegro and his jewels, eh?"

Ferret smirked back at the gently smiling commandant. "How's this then, chum? The big uproar about Vargos attacking isn't because he thinks we're here. Son of a bitch! He wasn't even chasing us. The marquis was coming straight for you!" The broad face registered surprise as Ferret said that.

"Is that so?"

"You bet your big butt it's so," Ferret snarled. "You were part of the scheme—probably promised Dertosal's support, didn't you?" Without waiting for a response, Ferret went on. "But all the time you wanted to get those jewels for yourself... or maybe somebody else with a claim and who promised you more. Sure. We were pawns you sent chasing off after Neva. You knew we'd have a chance of getting the stuff. If we failed, well, there are other dupes! You rotten bastard!"

The colonel wasn't moved. "You haven't a shred of proof. This is a wild fabrication."

"If we did get to the regalia odds were that we'd know enough not to steal it and then try to dump it anywhere—except in your lap. Too dangerous and deadly. But you'd been helpful, supplied us with that blade Rake's got aimed at your heart now, and promised us a good bit of gold for bringing back the make-believe culprit who did in the goldsmith. Now where else to show off our skill at liberating jewels than to bring the booty straight back to you? Of course we would expect a big bonus for that, and you'd have delivered. We'd die quickly."

The big man cocked an eyebrow. "Not bad for a children's tale. Again, there is no proof at all. Why, I haven't a reason to *want* the regalia!"

"You know, old man," Raker said before his comrade could respond, "you're right! That's just what I wanted to know when we got into the grandee's vault and realized we couldn't fence that stuff. What reason does the colonel have for wanting to get the regalia away from Torenegro and have it here—unless it's to turn it over to the king?"

"Just what I'd do," said de la Cabarro with a nod.

"Horseshit," Ferret replied. "You were absolutely furious when you learned that I'd messed up that stuff, blown the mahydrols to smithereens. You wanted the regalia all right, colonel. It was for… whomever it was that supplied you with the details about us!"

"Arawan's ass, Ferret!" Raker was so excited he nearly forgot to keep his blade pointing at the big man behind the desk. "The bastard's in league with the Duke of Mago! How else could he have known about the trouble we had in Puertal Mago just a few weeks back?!"

Ferret was startled to hear that, but he caught something in the colonel's face which alerted him, spurred his memory. "And there we have it. The duke's father was a Phonecian, but his mother an Atlantal, of high birth—royal blood, in fact. He's the one you wanted to have the regalia, Cabarro. Of course! A sea-based empire bigger than anything ever heard of, not just Iberia. With Atlantlan *and* Phonecian backing the duke's scheme might actually have gotten someplace."

"That's enough. Elfuego!"

Something in the commandant's voice triggered Raker to act. It was instinctive self-preservation. De la Cabarro meant to kill them. The gray eyes were hard, fixed on his target as he struck.

The colonel was moving, surprisingly fast for so big a man.

Ferret, too, sent his two blades towards the priest, but some invisible aura surrounding Intensity Elfuego turned them aside harmlessly.

With yet another oath, Don Filberto was scrambling from his chair so as to be able to draw his sword.

Even the half-conscious guard crumpled on the floor at the front of the desk was stirring.

Raker was quick, faster than Colonel de la Cabarro. His point took the commandant, but in the left arm, not the heart.

Even as Ferret's daggers were futily threatening him, the priest of Keganal had withdrawn something from his robe, and with that instrument he activated a casting just as the tip of the rapier sunk into the colonel's flesh. There was a bright flash and sharp crack of an electrical discharge. Both Raker and de la Cabarro uttered cries of agony, were thrown back and sent down by the energy which had suddenly emanated from the sword. Only the fact that Raker had touched the colonel at that instant saved his life. The deadly charm had been meant to slay the one holding the sword. With two recipients, the force was more than halved. Both Raker and de la Cabarro were stunned, injured but not mortally so, by any means. The enchanted rapier clattered to the floor, came to rest between the two who had been its victims.

It was plain to Ferret that his blades would not affect Elfuego, so he did the only other thing he could. Discarding the useless daggers, Ferret used his hands. As the priest completed his triggering of his cleverly prepared trap and was attempting to turn to deal with his other adversary, the lean adventurer seized the cleric's shoulders, yanked back. The priest's feet flew over his head as the chair went crashing down. Ferret grabbed the flowing robes, pulled them over Elfuego's head, and then pounced upon him.

All of that happened very quickly. Don Filberto was not deterred by any of the confusion. He was single-minded in his purpose. The little man caught the attack action and the seemingly instantaneous electrical discharge following it from the corner of his eye, then fixed his attention on Ferret's assault of Intensity Elfuego. The blond man was now weaponless and no longer threatened. The dark one was actively attacking. Don Filberto had his sword free now, and he would sink it into the vile man who had affronted him once before, again this very night! None who crossed him thus lived long.

Don Filberto was small and very agile. With his weapon poised, he moved to strike. Unfortunately for the guard, he managed to recover sufficiently to come to hands and knees at the moment Don Filberto was acting. The aristocrat stumbled over the groaning soldier, his attack spoiled.

"Devils take you, clod!" he screamed at the guard, then plied his blade on the helpless man in fury. "Never! Interfere! With! Me!" he cried, each word an exclamation accompanying a thrust. Four deep thrusts. The soldier dropped back to where he had lain, twitching and convulsing in his death throes. Don Filberto watched only a second. Satisfied, he again turned his eyes toward Ferret.

The delay had been sufficient for the lean man to deal severely with his opponent. Ferret was an accomplished street fighter, knew bits and pieces of more disciplined kinds of fighting as well. Knowing that the priest was undoubtedly shielded from most if not all physical harm of this sort, Ferret simply struck at nerves, then throttled his foe. If he could not kill him, then he would see to it that Intensity Elfuego was *hors de combat* for as long as possible. The cursing from Don Filberto distracted him from that process and saved his life. Seeing what the aristocrat meant to do, Ferret hastily loosed his hold on the priest and scrambled for his daggers.

A tortured gasp and muffled wheezing indicated that Intensity Elfuego had indeed weathered Ferret's attempts to slay him, but Ferret was too busy to worry about that now. He could feel Don Filberto closing even as he managed to get his second dagger in his grasp. Ferret rolled, and the don's sword struck the floor where he had been an instant earlier. With a kick of feet and arch of back Ferret was up and clear before the sword could strike again.

"Quick as a weasel, but you'll die like the pig you are!" Don Filberto snarled when he saw what had happened and gathered himself for a more careful attack. He saw the twin daggers, feinted with his sword, then stepped back and quickly drew his own to use as a main gauche. Now the match was highly weighted in his favor again, more to his liking. Not that he was a mediocre swordsman. On the contrary, the small Iberian aristocrat was indeed a master of the art. It was a matter of enjoyment. Don Filberto took great pleasure in seeing his opponent die slowly. With a sword against two daggers he would have had to be cautious, strike to kill or else risk being slain himself. Now with a pair of weapons himself, he could play the game he loved. "Come on then, you stinking pig! Let's see what you are made of."

Ferret wasn't goaded by anything his foe said. He knew all too well that his chances were slim when facing a swordsman at a distance. He needed to get in close, but Don Filberto's main gauche made that near impossible now. If he managed to get past the threat defense of the long blade, then the left-hand one would be there to attack. Then again, he had seen the little man move. Don Filberto was graceful and fast. He could dance back, keep Ferret where he wanted him before his sword point.

The priest could recover at any moment—or Colonel de la Cabarro for that matter. Guardsmen might come in. Time was his worst foe, and Ferret knew that all too well. He could not fence with Don Filberto, hope that some obstacle in the cluttered office would throw the man of balance and expose him to attack thus. Ferret had to attack. "You *are* a nasty little mannikin, aren't you?" he said with derision. "You must have been the runt of the litter your bitch mother whelped!"

The words made Don Filberto seethe with fury. He was most sensitive of his barely-over-five-foot height, and any insult to his mother spelled death to the one speaking. The rage didn't make him inept, though, but actually gave him a deadly calmness now. It had been used against him before, and Don Filberto was a veteran who had been schooled well. He made no reply, and attacked.

Ferret was caught in the act of attacking at the same moment his foe went into action, gauging that his insults had had effect. That was a reasonable guess based on the aristocrat's expression. Reasonable, but wrong. His armor saved him from a serious wound, but Ferret had to dance away, using his daggers madly to defend against the lightning-like series of attacks from Don Filberto's darting sword. In hardly more than a minute the lean adventurer was clad in what appeared to be leather ribbons, a half-dozen little stab wounds and slashes decorating him with scarlet.

"See now how you bleed, you pig!" The little man laughed mirthlessly, but with eyes shining with unspeakable excitement. "Soon I'll make you a shoat, listen to your dying squeals!" As he finished the last Don Filberto attacked, but in the exchange he himself finally took a wound even as he again scored on his opponent.

Ferret managed to slip past the don's sword, accepted a slash from the man's main gauche, and in the process of so closing and then moving to his right drove his own left-hand dagger deep into the thigh of the frenzied aristocrat's outthrust limb. As Don Filberto shrieked, more in outrage at being struck by an opponent he considered unworthy than from the considerable pain of the stab, Ferret retreated quickly from him, for the fellow was as deadly at infighting as he was at long range. "If you managed to to that to me," Ferret taunted, "you'd but make us even, bandy capon!" The lanky adventurer was brave in words but cautious in his actions now, for he knew that his only hope was to defend and hope his blow would take a toll on Filberto's speed. He was overmatched, and realized it.

The ringing of steel on steel, the stamping and panting, the shouted words of the fencers stimulated Raker's mind. He came from semi-consciousness to full alertness in seconds. As he propped himself up, Raker saw that the colonel was still inert, that the rapier lay nearby. "What the hells," he muttered as the sounds of the unequal contest between his comrade and the little Iberian aristocrat filled his ears. "All it can do is kill me." Gritting his teeth, he grabbed the hilt. The weight came into his hand easily. Nothing happened as he squeezed, raised the blade.

Raker expelled his breath in a whoosh of relief, scrambled upright. One glance told him his mental vision of what was occurring had been correct. Ferret was in desperate straits.

In fact his comrade was nearly finished. Don Filberto had managed to turn him, was now forcing him backwards. In a moment Ferret would stumble over the prostrate priest, and then he would be at the mercy of the man with the sword. Raker leaped atop the desk. "En garde, you popinjay!" He shouted those words barely in time.

Don Filberto had accomplished his purpose, saw his opponent's heel catch in the robes of Intensity Elfuego, watched as he lost balance and fell backward. Just as he prepared to make good on his threat to unman Ferret, Raker's warning challenge rang in his ears. Don Filberto spun, went into a guard position, and fended off the thrust from above, backed. Then he laughed, moved his weapons inviting the blonde man to come ahead. "Your friend spoke boldly too, dog. I'll enjoy making it both of you I kill this night."

Raker jumped down, attacked. Their blades crossed and recrossed with a harsh plangency. Neither spoke as they fought, each judging the other. Raker had been badly used by the jolt of the priest's hidden casting he had triggered to deliver death to the one touching the enchanted sword that had been his "gift." Don Filberto had fought hard against Ferret, now bled freely from the deep puncture in his thigh. Broad-shouldered adventurer and slim little Iberian aristocrat danced and stamped, panted and fought. It was an even match. A bout whose duration had been less than a minute, but during which time a dozen exchanges, some faster than the untrained eye could follow, had occurred. The two were close in skill—too close. The dagger in Don Filberto's left hand gave him a critical edge.

Ferret had been momentarily stunned, was dazed still as he watched what was happening. Despite his condition, Ferret's mind was able to function well enough to note what must be done. He readied, awaiting the right moment, acted. As Don Filberto forced Raker back toward the wall, Ferret sent one of his daggers flying. He dared not try for the don, for in his current state a miss might strike his friend instead, So Ferret did the only thing he could, and cried, "Your left!" as his dirk flashed past Raker and sunk its point into the panel a foot from the blond swordsman's head.

Filberto lunged. Raker spun, avoided the thrust, then had the dagger in his hand. "Now we will have a fair fight, eh mannikin?"

During this confusion Intensity Elfuego had been active, albeit secretly so. Recovering from the assault by Ferret, the priest regained his wits, moved to get those things he required to employ his considerable powers of casting against the two intruders who had come in such foolhardy fashion into this place. Elfuego had his clerical amulet in hand, was calling forth its store of energy as he sat up.

Ferret saw the stiring, could devise only one counter. Somehow he managed to fumble free the bejeweled egg he had taken from Neva's coffer. Inside that oval box were three compartments, one of which contained two dozen small mahydrols. If the cleric was deeply dedicated to his deity, then Intensity Elfuego might rely upon the heka forces drawn from the element of fire. It was a long shot, but in his dazed state Ferret could do nothing else. With the beautiful gems in his fist, the lean man crawled so as to be in front of the priest. "Elfuego!" he croaked.

Intensity Elfuego turned, saw Ferret, and raised his amulet. He would blast this dark-eyed rogue into oblivion. The stones struck him in a glittering shower of green. They were caught up in the energy the priest had summoned. It was indeed that of the sphere of fire, and gems and heka met and neutralized each other in flash of incredible brightness. The contact of elemental gems brought a too-early and uncontained release of energy into being not a foot from the one attempting to wield the power. Elfuego was staring, so the mutually annihilating forces first blinded, then slew him in an instant.

Ferret, meanwhile, had fallen flat and rolled after hurling his seemingly pitiful handful of missiles at his foe. Not dreaming that he would obtain so great a result, the lean man was simply doing his best to make himself a difficult target for the magickal attack he thought was to come. Thus, when the priest died in a blaze of soundless destruction, Ferret was flat on the floor some six feet distant, facing away from it.

The great wash of light that flared and died in an instant made both swordsmen blink but neither distracted them nor abated their mutual determination to prevail. Don Filberto made as if to feint, then actually carried out the attack. The move almost took Raker by surprise, but perhaps the wound had slowed the little Iberian, for in his thrusting he allowed an opening. With main gauche used to turn the don's sword a fraction of an inch, Raker managed to send his own point angling upward through Don Filberto's body, withdrew it just as quickly.

The man's eye's registered shocked disbelief. "You cannot have—"

Without hesitation, Raker struck again, this time into the heart. Don Filberto stepped back as the blade left his chest, tried to curse, then crumpled. "Wrong... again, little... fop," Raker tried to drawl as he panted. "I did... do for... you!" He looked around, saw the charred heap that had been Intensity Elfuego, Ferret swaying, steadying himself against the wall with one hand holding himself to remain upright there.

"Are you wounded, Ferret?"

"A dozen times, chum," Ferret replied. "Don't worry. The little bastard didn't do me great damage—he was taking his time so as to kill me by inches."

Raker let out a sigh of relief. "Well, I wasn't so careless. He's now drilled through and through again. I hope his miserable little spirit is howling far down in the nether realms at this moment. But tell me, what's wrong with you?"

"Nothing that a couple of bandages, a swig of brandy, and a couple of minutes rest won't cure," Ferret said in half-truth. "Where the hells do you suppose the colonel keeps his liquor?"

"That reminds me," Raker grated with a glance towards the desk. "I have some unfinished business with him, too."

Chapter Twenty-Seven

"THIS IS A splendid steed," Raker said happily as he urged the courser to a canter. "Having it from de la Cabarro almost makes up for what he tried to do to us!"

Ferret wasn't so forgiving, perhaps because he wasn't the horseman his friend was. His own mount was nearly as fine as that Raker rode, it being likewise taken from the commandant's private stables. "I regret only that we couldn't find out where that bastard kept his cash before we had to get away."

The two men were riding along the coast road leading northeastward, beyond Tarragona now and heading toward Barcelona. That nobody would be searching for them they were sure. Colonel de la Cabarro was probably himself in flight, likely aboard some fast ship bound for the islands of the Duchy of Mago, where he hoped to find refuge. The king of Aragon, the prince of Catalonia, and all the rest of the nobles in the kingdom were now in arms and seeking the rebel Marquis Penumbratos and his fellow conspirators. Eventually that one would either likewise flee Iberia or be brought up by the heels to answer for his treason. Odds were that the cooperation, albeit duplicitous, of Dertosal would come to light soon as well. In that case, especially if there was any hint of Mago being involved in the plot, the colonel would be slain and his head, well enchanted against any divinatory reading, be sent to placate the outraged monarch of Aragon.

"You know, old fellow," Raker said, "I will have to get my share of the few coins you found there in the colonel's office. I haven't but a handful of reals to my name after having to spread the contents of my purse at that guardsman's feet back there."

They had made sure that Colonel de la Cabarro wouldn't trouble them in their escape from the fortress by trussing him up. Neither wanted to make his life easier by slaying him. Better to leave him alive to wallow in the mire of his own making. Ferret had taken time to search him, the corpses of his two cronies as well, for money. He and Raker needed funds in order to make good their flight from Dertosal. The yield had been small.

Then, following the same route through the citadel that commandant and priest had shown them but a few days previously, the two men had in the pre-dawn hour gotten free of the city without much difficulty. "Not as much as would equal a gold doubloon, Rake, but I'll gladly give you your half."

At that Raker rode closer to his companion, held out a hand. "Not that I doubt you, my dear comrade, but I think I'll take it now rather than later, if you please."

"Certes, old boy," Ferret responded just as warmly. "Here, this is more than half!" He placed a clutch of coins into Raker's hand, signaled, and did that again with a second batch. "That leaves me but a handful for myself. Satisfied?"

Raker glanced down at the mixture of bronze, copper, and silver Iberian coins. Something was wrong. Never was Ferret likely to give over more than an equal share. "No gold?"

"I swear it. None had anything more valuable than a plata—cheap lot!"

By swearing, Ferret allayed that suspicion, but Raker was still not satisfied. "You found nothing else of value on them? Not even the priest?"

"He and all he had were near cinders, chum," Ferret replied with a disgusted tone.

"Well, damn it, how am I to get some proper armor? This stuff I wear is unsuitable."

That made Ferret laugh. "What about this mass of tatters I sport beneath this cloak? Ribbons? At least yours can be mended."

"Mended? Well, yes if that's what I can afford, then I suppose… Say, what about Neva?"

Ferret looked very uneasy, shifted in his saddle, looked at his comrade. "Neva?"

"Yes, Neva! If she wasn't working hand-in-glove with the colonel, then how in the name of all the Atlantlan gods did he know all about what had happened in Torenegro?"

"Whatever made you think of that?"

"Mending. The word made me think of what you did to the magickal regalia the marquis had had fashioned to empower his plot. How the jewels had been blasted beyond recovery by that—what a great waste of valuable gold and gems that was."

"And that brought Neva to mind."

Raker noted his friend's unease. "Yes, Neva. Who else could have passed on information about what we'd done there in Torenegro except her?" As he spoke he kept his eyes fastened on Ferret's profile.

Turning, Ferret looked into the gray eyes. "You know, Rake, I don't have a bloody clue, but who gives a damn! We're out from under, and nobody's likely to try to again maneuver us as if we were pawns on a fidchell board—not after word gets around as to what happened to those who attempted that in Dertosal."

"It was cheering to see those dossiers providing a merry little fire," Raker added. "Yet I still—"

"Oh very *well*!" Ferret's voice held resignation as he cut his friend short. "I insisted we go to Valencia for a good reason."

Raker held his face in hard lines. "Go on."

"There we can dispose of a gem and buy passage aboard a ship bound for Rome. Don't you think it's a sound idea to stay clear of Iberia and even Phonecian and Atlantlan lands for a bit?"

"Gem?" said the blond man, ignoring the distraction.

"We'll be most unpopular with those in Mago and other Phonecian states who had an interest in the plot. And surely the Atlantlans privy to what was going on will be most upset about the destruction of the second suite of imperial regalia."

"A gem, you say?"

"Ah well, what's the use." With a resigned expression Ferret brought forth the fabulous little box of wrought gold and precious stones. "I never planned to keep this for myself."

"Of course not..."

"You wound me, Rake! I was going to show it to you as soon as we arrived in Valencia."

"Sure you were."

Ferret handed the glittering oval to his companion. "You hold it then. Maybe that will convince you."

Smiling, Raker tucked it inside his girdle. "You're right, Ferret. *Now* I'm convinced. Is there aught inside?"

"One tiny gem only remains—but it's a mahydrol. The egg will fetch us a fortune, though. We'll have enough to live in high style for a goodly time somewhere far distant from this place!"

A frown played across the fair features of Raker's handsome face. "What *used* to be inside?" he inquired sharply.

"I don't want to talk about it," Ferret told him with a tone of finality.

Raker considered, then shrugged. With a pat to reassure himself that the bejewelled little box made to resemble a big goose egg was securely tucked away, he concentrated on the way ahead. Soon they would arrive in the beautiful city of Barcelona. Then they would sail away to somewhere else, find more adventures. Eventually his comrade would tell him, and in the meantime he was satisfied to think about what he'd do with his share of money when they disposed of the golden egg.

Ferret noticed the change in his friend. "I thought you'd be pleased at seeing the wealth I managed to acquire for us. Frankly, chum, you seem deflated."

"Don't speak of francs, old man, let's talk of ducats... and hope that deflation hasn't taken the Italics!"

Both men laughed as they spurred their mounts onward, toward Valencia.

ABOUT THE AUTHOR

In 1974, Gary Gygax (1938–2008) co-created the Dungeons & Dragons roleplaying game, forever changing the face of fantasy. The hand-assembled first print run of 1000 boxed rulesets sold out in nine months, and by 1978 the game's success warranted a three-volume hardcover rules expansion called Advanced Dungeons & Dragons authored by Gygax. The release of AD&D coincided with the explosive popularity that catapulted the game into a true cultural phenomenon, introducing fantasy to a generation of new readers. D&D's literary roots drew upon the sword and sorcery work of authors like Fritz Leiber, Jack Vance, and Robert E. Howard, and by the mid-1980s D&D's publisher, TSR, began to release their own line of fantasy fiction.

Thus was born Gord the Rogue, Gygax's rakish, metropolitan thief whose daring adventures span seven novels: *Saga of Old City*, *Artifact of Evil*, *Sea of Death*, *City of Hawks*, *Night Arrant*, *Come Endless Darkness*, and *Dance of Demons*. Years later he introduced a new character, the crime-solving Ægyptian wizard-priest Magister Setne Inhetep, in a trilogy of novels: *The Anubis Murders*, *The Samarkand Solution*, and *Death in Delhi*.

Gygax has been called "a pioneer of the imagination" by the *New York Times* and "one of America's most talented writers" by *The Guardian*. His importance to American popular culture was solidified with an animated cameo alongside Al Gore, Stephen Hawking, and *Star Trek*'s Nichelle Nichols in a 2000 episode of *Futurama*.

Collect all of these exciting Planet Stories adventures!

The Anubis Murders
by Gary Gygax
introduction by Erik Mona

The father of Dungeons & Dragons follows Magister Setne Inhetep, wizard-priest and master sleuth, as he tracks a murderer from ancient Ægypt to medieval England. But what if the gods themselves are behind the crimes?

ISBN: 978-1-60125-042-1

Elak of Atlantis
by Henry Kuttner
introduction by Joe R. Lansdale

A dashing swordsman with a mysterious past battles his way across ancient Atlantis in the stories that helped found the sword and sorcery genre. Also includes two rare tales featuring Prince Raynor of Imperial Gobi!

ISBN: 978-1-60125-046-9

City of the Beast
by Michael Moorcock
introduction by Kim Mohan

Moorcock's Eternal Champion returns as Michael Kane, an American physicist and expert duelist whose strange experiments catapult him through space and time to a Mars of the distant past—and into the arms of the gorgeous princess Shizala. But can he defeat the Blue Giants of the Argzoon in time to win her hand?

ISBN: 978-1-60125-044-5

Almuric
by Robert E. Howard
introduction by Joe R. Lansdale

From the creator of Conan, Almuric is a savage planet of crumbling stone ruins and debased, near-human inhabitants. Into this world comes Esau Cairn—Earthman, swordsman, murderer. Can one man overthrow the terrible devils that enslave Almuric?

ISBN: 978-1-60125-043-8

Black God's Kiss
by C. L. Moore
introduction by Suzy McKee Charnas

The first female sword and sorcery protagonist takes up her greatsword and challenges dark gods and monsters in the ground-breaking stories that made her famous and inspired a generation of female authors, while earning high praise from Fritz Leiber and H. P. Lovecraft.

ISBN: 978-1-60125-045-2

The Samarkand Solution
by Gary Gygax
introduction by Ed Greenwood

Magister Setne Inhetep returns to track a deadly assassin through the Ægyptian city of On to stop a rebellion that could topple the empire—and an enemy even more dangerous than Set himself!

ISBN: 978-1-60125-083-4

Pick your favorites or subscribe today at paizo.com/planetstories!
